A BAFFLING SHORT STORIES COLLECTION

A BAFFLING SHORT STORIES COLLECTION

Norma Iris Pagan Morales

ISBN 978-1-957582-70-2 (paperback)
ISBN 978-1-957582-71-9 (eBook)

Copyright © 2022 by Norma Iris Pagan Morales

All rights reserved. No part of this publication may be reproduced, distributed, or transmitted in any form or by any means, including photocopying, recording, or other electronic or mechanical methods without the prior written permission of the publisher.

Printed in the United States of America

Dedication

This book is dedicated to my dear sister, Adelin M. Pagan Morales. She is not only my sister; she is also my best friend. She is the only one that is always praising my work. Thank you, sis.

Contents

My Memoir xi
Overview xiii
Introduction xv
Chapter 1:   An Abusive Relationship 1
Chapter 2:   Tough Love 8
Chapter 3:   Puppy Love 10
Chapter 4:   Pepito 12
Chapter 5:   Summer Romance 17
Chapter 6:   Six Feet Under 21
Chapter 7:   An old Buddy 24
Chapter 8:   A Tale from the Heart 28
Chapter 9:   The Accident 30
Chapter 10: A Loving Father 32
Chapter 11: The Immigrant 33
Chapter 12: A Bizarre Love Story 36
Chapter 13: Father and Son fighting for the Same Cause 38
Chapter 14: Getting Deployed 40
Chapter 15: Waiting For The Worst 42
Chapter 16: In Korea 45
Chapter 17: The Surgery 49
Chapter 18: City Life 50
Chapter 19: The City that Never Sleeps 56
Chapter 20: Loving world history 59
Chapter 21: The Punch 63
Chapter 22: Damage Control 68
Chapter 23: Let the Music Play 71
Chapter 24: Prince Charming 74
Chapter 25: Halloween 77

Chapter 26: Sixteen and Never Been Kissed 84
Chapter 27: The Complicated Teenager 93
Chapter 28: Giving Thanks 97
Chapter 29: The Bra 100
Chapter 30: Heavenly Body 105
Chapter 31: The club 109
Chapter 32: In Love 112
Chapter 33: The Ice Princess Strikes Again 114
Chapter 34: Feeling Low 116
Chapter 35: It's Christmas 118
Chapter 36: Just One Call 120
Chapter 37: The Camp Band 121
Chapter 38: Found Romance Instead 122
Chapter 39: The Cupid's Arrow 123
Chapter 40: Lost at Sea 124
Chapter 41: The Unwanted 126
Chapter 42: Missing 128
Chapter 43: Active Hormones 135
Chapter 44: The Vulnerable Girl 137
Chapter 45: Top of the World 140
Chapter 46: The Wrong Decision 143
Chapter 47: The Silence 145
Chapter 48: Remains of Dark Memories 147
Chapter 49: The Alien 149
Chapter 50: Four Eyes 150
Chapter 51: The Birth 152
Chapter 52: Do you believe in Angels? 154
Chapter 53: Imagination 156
Chapter 54: The Process of Life 165
Chapter 55: Living with Dementia 166
Chapter 56: My Sister and Best Friend 169
Chapter 57: The Retirement Home in Paradise 173
Chapter 58: The Fact of Life 176
Chapter 59: The Lonely Old Maid 178
Chapter 60: In Arms 181
Chapter 61: First Love 183

Chapter 62:	Just A Brief Romance	186
Chapter 63:	The Departure	188
Chapter 64:	Deceiving Love	190
Chapter 65:	The Rain Child	192
Chapter 66:	Nothing Matters	194
Chapter 67:	The Sacrifice	196
Chapter 68:	The Interview	198
Chapter 69:	The Wrong Number	200
Chapter 70:	The Coffee House	201
Chapter 71:	The lot	202
Chapter 72:	Dog meets Dog	203
Chapter 73:	Love	204
Chapter 74:	The Creativity	208
Chapter 75:	The Farewell Notes	210
Chapter 76:	Love letters from an Enchanted Island	212
Chapter 77:	Happy Ending	214
Chapter 78:	Simply Pure Love	216
Chapter 79:	Declaration	218
Chapter 80:	The Most Horrible News	220
Chapter 81:	Getting Dumped	225
Chapter 82:	The Jogging Partner	227
Chapter 83:	The Smooth Talker	229
Chapter 84:	My Best Friend	234
Chapter 85:	Making Friends	237
Chapter 86:	Vicente Pagan Rodriguez	240
Chapter 87:	The Parachutes	249
Chapter 88:	Liduvina Perez Echevarria	251
Chapter 89:	My kids have paws	258
Chapter 90:	My Nephews	264
Chapter 91:	The Language Center, Fort Allen Juana Diaz PR	268
The History of Short Stories		273
Glossary		275
References		279
About the Author		281

MY MEMOIR

(a bit of information about me)

Who am I?

The motto of my life is a lot of stories and not much time to write.

You are going to see that as an educator, I love giving explanations and definitions on every piece I write. Why do I do this? Well, when I was in grammar school, high school and then college, I noticed that there was a lack of explanation on everything I read. Half of the time I was lost.

I had problems with my professors because they informed me that if I wanted to be an English teacher, it would be my job to explain each poem or story to my students.

Seriously, just look at the books that I have written, and you will understand me better.

I'm a fool for romance, therefore, my stories will indicate what I mean. You will see it make an appearance, in some form, in my writings.

I want to tell all my readers that I love dogs. I have two however, I want to talk about one. Its name is Titi. She is smarter than most people I know though she doesn't look it. My dog, Titi, is a genius! When I write a new story, I would read it at loud. Titi would sit there and wag its tail. If the story is boring, I see no reaction whatsoever.

Another thing that I must tell you is that I have found true love. Its name is chocolate chip cookies!

As all authentic love, it's love and hate. My body loves it, and my self-esteem hates it. I am just joking. All this might trickle down into my stories.

Some people may say I kid a lot but believe me that this is the main reason I am so unique....

OVERVIEW

How many people can really bring back the romance of their teenage love? Can you ever forget your high school sweetheart? Can that spark come alive when you see each other after twenty or even thirty years?

Teenage love is something that packs enough innocent charm to make even the coldest hearts go warm. It is love in its most pure, immaculate and unspoiled form because it is the first time ever in life that the heart has blossomed to love.

As adults, we observe love as something more complex than it is, however, during the teenage years, it is just a simple sensation of caring for someone else.

Many may argue that teenage love is ignorant, but hey, ignorance is heaven. Am I right?

INTRODUCTION

Short stories are pieces of prose fiction that can be read in one sit. The oral storytelling traditions have been in fashion since the 17th century. They have grown to cover a body of work so varied as to challenge easy characterization.

At its most ideal, the short story features a small cast of named characters. Its intention is to focus on a self-contained incident with by suggesting a single effect to capture an audience.

By doing so, short stories make use of plot, quality, and other dynamic components to a far greater degree than is typical tale. I want to bring out that a short story is far lesser degree than a novel.

Although the short story is largely distinct from the novel, authors of both generally are lure from a common pool of literary techniques. Short stories have no set length.

In terms of word count, there is no official separation between short story, and a novel.

STORY 1

An Abusive Relationship

When I look back to the person I used to be, it makes me wonder. What happened to me? Why did I just let this man control my life?

Before I met the love of my life, the only man in my life, I was gorgeous. Always dressed to kill. My hair was always neat and very stylist. I dressed in the finest dresses, pants and accessories.

He in the other hand, always had the same shirt. He never put any perfume or even a cheap after shave lotion. My siblings used to make so much fun of him.

I saw something different. I saw my prince charming. He was tall, slim and had a very deep voice. The perfect man.

We met at his friends' house. He, right away, asked me for my phone number. I gave to him without hesitating. He called me every day and on weekends we went to a movie or just a walk in the park.

My parents were very strict. He loved that because that meant that I was always locked up at home.

When Victor came to visit me, he would bring flowers and would inform me that he had made a dinner reservation at fancy restaurant. I couldn't believe what was happening.

I wasn't to go without a chaperon. Victor said no chaperon. I did what Victor wanted. I left the house without my parents' blessings. I just wanted to pleased Victor.

One Saturday afternoon, in a hot summer day, my father confronted Victor. My dad asked him, "What are your intentions with my daughter Audrey"?

Victor looked at him and simply replied, "I just met Audrey. I have at this point, no answer to your question".

My father got very angry. My mom had a nervous breakdown and we had to rush her to the hospital.

My dad didn't talk to me for a whole week.

The following weekend, Victor showed up at the house with an engagement ring! I was the happiest person in the world.

Victor started making plans. I just stayed quiet. The first thing he did was asking me for my bank account. He wanted to start controlling my money because he saw how much I spent on clothing. Victor was also concerned about me spending too much money on my friends.

He told once, "Audrey, Why are giving birthday gifts, anniversary gifts and even baby or bridal showers to your friends"?

I said, "Look Victor, my friends are just like family to me. I will always be there for them".

Slowly I was letting Victor control me...

You know I didn't see anything wrong. He worked at a bank, and he used to brag about his investments and customers. I was just a fool in love.

I started to get the feeling that I was not good enough for him. This started to affect our relationships. The career choices I made started to slow down.

We got married a couple of months after we met....

The minute we got married things changed. I went right into a real roller coaster relationship. I was being abuse and never saw it coming. I was ashamed to tell my family or even friends.

Domestic violence is dangerous because of the shame and silence surrounding it...

At 27 years of age, I was lost. I came from a good family and finished the university, but I didn't have confidence or a sense of self-worth. All I wanted was someone to love me.

I attached myself to the first man who showed signs of commitment. It came at a cost. He wined and dined me, but slowly broke away at my already low self-esteem. He isolated me from family and friends.

"Why do you want to look pretty? Why did you leave the blinds open? Do you want men staring at you?" he asked.

I was confused, and constantly I was trying to prove to him that I wasn't a bad person. Arguments exploded.

Our relationship was volcanic, and I sense violence setting in. He never pushed me or shoved me. He never smacked or punched; however, it was worse.......

He was always verbally abusing me. He never said.... "Sorry, it won't happen again."

I wanted to have babies because I was getting too old. His answer was always the same. He wanted to wait three more years. He was gone must of the time.

Let me tell you that after our honeymoon. He started leaving the house on Monday morning and returning on Friday night. He always was away on training or something. I never questioned him. He would come and get my paycheck and disappear again. I was the bread winner. He was just a stupid clerk at a bank.

We always made love or something similar once a month. I kept telling him that I wanted a baby. He always made sure that I was drunk before going to bed. To me, it was love, to him, it was lust.

I had no idea I was being raped. He was my husband. This savage wanted anal sex and put strange things in my anal. I used to scream, but he didn't care.

Finally, I put my foot down. I told him to clean his act. He got me pregnant with two kids.

He went and got a house for us without asking me. I wasn't too happy with the idea that he was using my money and buying things without my approval.

After the birth of my first born, I never lost a pound. I got pregnant again. I double my weight. I didn't care about my appearance. I used all my energy and money on my kids. Money that I used to hide because Victor took every penny I earned.

I had to leave my good paying job because I wanted to spend all my time with the kids. I got part time jobs at the mall and did babysitting. All the money I made he took it from me. I began to look like the good year blimp.

My latest fashion was hand me downs from my neighbors. They all were feeling sorry for me. They noticed all the abuse this jerk was doing to me.

He was always calling me fat. Repeatedly he would say, "I don't like fat women". I would just answer, well my dear, you are married to one.

Verbal abuse was worse than hands tight around your throat. "Sorry, I won't say it again." He would never say...

After taking all my pension and savings, he bought a new car that I never used nor the kids.

All the verbal abuse was worse than a broken arm. I never heard "Sorry, it won't happen again." No apologies whatsoever.

He didn't kill me, but it was my spirit that he was trying to crush. I never called my family. They didn't know that I was being abuse.

You see, I was always the quiet one in the family....

My sister, Martha, was always looking out after me. She was always questioning me about my relationship with Victor. She said many times he was seen around the old neighbor.

Since my sister was divorced with no kids, Victor told me to keep away from her. Once again, I obeyed. I didn't want Martha to come to the house. Martha pays me no mind. She was always there.

Martha came to the rescue when I was admitted into a mental institution. Victor called Martha and told her that I was found wandering the streets around their neighborhood. He told her that the ambulance came and took me.

I was admitted in the institution because I just kept saying, "My sister and my kids".

Martha told her supervisor that she had an emergency at home.

She was released from her duties and sent to help her family...

When Martha reached my house, she found Victor very relaxed watching T.V. My kids were quiet but got happy when they saw their "Aunt Martha".

Martha asked Victor, "Where is my sister"? he just replied in the hospital. "I am the husband, and no information will be given to you or your brothers".

Martha got so furious and started calling my parents and the rest of the family. She told Victor that if he didn't give her any information that she was going to the police.

He told her to calm down and the next day they went to the mental institution to pick me up...

My sister spoke to the doctors and told them all that she was going to take care of me and the kids until I recovered. The doctors were surprised because Victor told them that I had no family.

Let me tell you that Victor had lots of plans. He wanted to bring his sister and her family into the house. His sister was going to take care of the kids. According to Victor, I was an unfit mother in a mental institution.

Martha was in charge...

My sister was an angel sent from heaven. Martha took care of me and my family when I was release from the mental institution. She even enrolled the kids in a Summer program where they learned how to swim.

Martha slowly got rid of the medication that the doctor prescribed.

This is what we did: Martha would take me to my bedroom. She would close the door. She flushed two pills every six hours. She would report to Victor and of that I took the pills and was fast asleep. He was very happy...

I just relaxed without any pills away from Victor and the kids.

Do you want to know what was so strange? Victor was coming home everyday while I was sick. He didn't trust Martha...

Martha set schedules...

It was easy talking to my sister. I was feeling better and stronger each day.

We went to the pool every day. While sitting under the sun, Martha was questioning me about the day I was sent to that crazy institution.

Martha said, "Audrey, we have to plan how to get rid of Victor". I replied, "what do you mean"?

"I want to kill him", she said.

Martha contacted a hit man from Australia. She met him when she was on a mission. This Aussie was her only friend. He was also the best hit man…

The plan was that he would follow Victor after work. He chose a day that I would be away with Martha and the kids. We went to an amusement. A whole day away from my house.

When we returned, police officers were all over the place. Neighbors call 911 because they heard gun shots. The officers found Victor tight down spread eagle on the ground. Victor was naked with a shot on his head, another on his private parts and another shot on his chest. Victor died instantly…

The police investigators questioned my sister Martha and me. We told them that we were away at an amusement park. I also told them that Victor was always away on trips, and that I had no idea of his activities.

The cops believed my story. Their faces showed pity for me. They saw in front of them a fragile abused person….

For the next three months my relatives protected me and cared for the whole family until I was clear from any suspicious.

I spent my time reading books on psychology, relationships, and self-esteem. I wanted to understand people better. I wanted to understand myself. I even joined a gym and started losing a few pounds a week.

I began to question: How could I let another human being treat me like this? Why did I accept this behavior? What was wrong with me?

I knew that what he did was wrong. Violence is not acceptable in any form, however, I realized, it was all about me. I was so desperate to have someone to love me that I compromised myself.

I was scared and felt fear about pursuing my dreams. What if I failed? What would other people think of me? I couldn't do it on my own. I needed someone. Anyone. I wasn't good enough. Victor reinforced those negative self-images I had about myself.

It is important to define domestic violence because as a young person I did not know about it or see the signs. Domestic violence covers a wide range of abusive behaviors committed in the context of intimate relationships such as those involving family members, children, partners, ex-partners, or caregivers.

It can include many types of behavior or threats, including physical violence, sexual abuse, emotional abuse, verbal abuse and intimidation.

Some of my friends also experienced abuses, but not as bad as me. I didn't tell anyone because of the shame. When I asked them what they did, they would say to women in violent relationships, "always hold a vision of a better life" …

All I remember that they kept repeating that I am not a victim. Also, they informed me that I can find help, which I didn't.

Looking back and saw that this experience taught me courage. Having the courage to leave my negative thoughts. I learned to be on my own and more importantly, I was getting the courage to love myself.

I made a commitment to myself that I will and grow mentally and physically. I was not going to let that experience stop me from having a wonderful life.

I am a good person and have great potentials. I could do anything I wanted in my life.

My passion is to travel….

I have saved enough money to explore this wonderful world. I will travel to my parents' homeland where I was born.

I am alive! I could wear short skirts, polish my nails and listen to music. I am laughing again. I reconnected with family and friends. I studied and became a lawyer. I feel at peace within myself no guilt. I don't need a man to define me…

STORY 2

Tough Love

What does tough love mean in a romantic relationship? It means looking out for one another's physical health. It also means that you are looking out for your partner's emotional happiness.

Tough love can be difficult. It can be even more difficult to take, but it's important to remember that at the end of the day, tough love is a form of love.

Not all love can be supportive and enthusiastic, especially if there is a problem in a relationship. If someone has done something that hurt their partner it is not love.

There wasn't any explosive fight or huge issue that encouraged Geraldine to start looking for help. She always told her family and friends that her relationship with Jim was great…

It was mostly continuing the breakup of everyday life. It always left Geraldine with little energy, time, and emotional space to invest in her relationship.

"Nothing is wrong in my relationship", Geraldine would tell her relatives. "We don't fight that much", "we communicate openly, and we have sex once or twice a week".

Geraldine saw that there was no spark in their marriage. It isn't there anymore. We don't feel excited about each other the way we used to be. We don't do many things that move us away from our normal routines.

We're both tired and just uninterested to do anything to change it. We're the exact definition of being in a pit. I had low expectations.

I thought to myself "The best-case scenario is we may develop a couple good habits. It will help us connect again, but it's unlikely."

Geraldine had a long talk with Jim. They decided to have their own chat sessions on their own. No marriage counselor....

Geraldine asked Jim the first three things he noticed about her when they met....

Jim said, "when we were introduced, at a bar, I thought you were gorgeous, and very smart. You also looked charming and had a nice smile".

We both laughed. We talked about that night and reminisced on some stories. We hadn't thought them in a while.

Then, Geraldine started talking about what she noticed about him... She was lost for words. She didn't really know her husband or what really attracted her to him....

Jim was a stranger. Geraldine stayed married for the wrong reason. She didn't want to be alone.

Geraldine wanted to go shopping. Jim made sure she just had a couple of dollars. She wasn't allowed to buy without his permission.

Jim was always controlling her.

Geraldine asked for simple necessary things around the house. Victor was the best husband in the world according to everyone. He was the provider. That wasn't tough love. It was manipulation.

Geraldine was just a mother, a housewife and the cleaning lady.....

STORY 3

Puppy Love

It was a glorious and colorful autumn morning in the streets of New York. Since it was a holiday, everyone was out shopping.

They had just passed a coffee shop. Gladys was laughing and was pulling Paul inside a coffee shop. She was saying, "Come on, let's be simple and get some pumpkin pie and coffee!"

Let me tell you that I don't like coffee Paul stated. He never had. Gladys handed Paul a cup and looked into his eyes while he tried it. It was the best thing he had ever tasted.

They had feelings for each other, and they are about to find it out....

My hand still tingled where Gladys grabbed it.

As we walked through Central Park with our drinks, a light drizzle began to fall. Gladys pulled out an umbrella from her bag. I pulled up my hood and hunched my shoulders.

"Don't be silly," Gladys giggled, pulling me under the umbrella with her. I couldn't help but laugh. Her laugh is contagious.

As the sun started to shine again, Gladys pulled me down to sit on a bench. She beamed down at me. All I could do was to gaze back at her affectionately.

"Well, Paul..." Gladys began. I knew this tone of voice, it's dangerous.

"Who do you like?" She whispered, and I looked away. I wanted to say, 'you, you, a thousand times you. You're the only one I can ever think about. You're gorgeous and sweet and funny and...'

Instead, I shrugged my shoulders and looked down at my cup.

Gladys looked at me with a thoughtful smile. "If I tell you mine, will you tell me yours?"

"Okay." Paul said.

"The person I like is you."

Paul dropped his drink!

STORY 4

Pepito

Mr. Goldberg and his wife were a very happy to move from a big city to the quiet life in the country. The people there were very humble and caring.

Esther was having emotional changes. She couldn't explain to anyone especially her husband. Sometimes she was happy and other times, very sad. She was happy when she was around people. The minute they left their house or a gathering a sad feeling started dominating her body and soul.

Mr. Goldberg was different because he had his books and all his friends at the library.

One day, Esther told her husband she wanted a bird or dog. Mr. Goldberg didn't like animals. He told her that she can buy herself a bird….

Esther got up the next day very happy. She headed to a pet shop not too far from their house.

While looking for the best bird, she noticed a tiny African grey parrot. The bird was only a couple of days old. Esther never had a bird; however, she was sure this was the right one.

She bought all the necessary accessories for the bird. She got a very huge cage. The store owner explained that the bird was going to grow fast. And guess what? It sure did.

Esther taught him how to sing. That bird imitated her all the time. Sometimes Mr. Goldberg didn't know if the bird was talking or his wife.

He hated that bird because it never kept quiet. Esther, in the other hand, was a happy trooper. Esther decided to name the bird, Pepito. She like the sound of it.

Many years went by and Mr. Goldberg and Pepito never became friends. Pepito only had one owner and that was Esther.

Pepito was so smart that he knew when Esther was sick. Esther had lung cancer and didn't want her husband to know it. She was always caring for the bird that Mr. Goldberg never notice any changes in his wife's behavior.

One morning, Mr. Goldberg got up to make breakfast. He noticed that his wife didn't move. He got closer to the bed and found out that his wife has died in her sleep.

Mr. Goldberg was very sad. He was walking around like a robot. He didn't want to go to the library or meet with his groups.

It took months for Mr. Goldberg slowly get back to reality……

Mr. Goldberg didn't even try to be Pepito's friend. Pepito didn't care either about Mr. Goldberg. Pepito got fed but that was it. There was no bond of any kind between man and bird….

The lonely old man, Mr. Goldberg, started a new routine after Esther died….

Mr. Goldberg started his day at the library. It was a brief walk from his home. It was conveniently situated at the top of the main street near the market. That was the house that he and his wife purchased after they both retired.

When they first moved, Mr. Goldberg joined a local writing group which met at the library. He would spend many happy and creative hours at the library. He never bothered her to ask Esther if she wanted to go to the library. It was all about him and his new acquired friends.

He told his wife that it was good to do his creative writing among friends. Mr. Goldberg never invited Esther to any celebrations or special events. She was always alone…

English was an English Professor. Literature was her passion. Mr. Goldberg met her in one of his books signing many years ago. He thought Esther didn't like books, however, Esther tried to be part of his group, but her never bothered to ask her nor included her in his plans.

Sadly, it was all gone now. People had moved away, lost interest, or died. He was the only one left of the old crowd. He and the chief librarian, Mrs. Prieto, who was approaching retirement. Mrs. Prieto had a soft spot for Mr. Goldberg. She had known his wife, Esther. She enjoyed talking to both.

Mr. Goldberg was like a permanent fixture at the library. He always sat in his corner, reading the newspaper.

After endless hours at the library, Mr. Goldberg finished reading the paper and started looking for hat, scarf and phone. He then will walk across the street to "Mama's Café" for his morning coffee. It was the only pleasure he had in life but a real pleasure indeed.

He arrived home at about noon, unlocked the door and stepped into the hall.

"Hello," called a cheerful voice, that sounded very much like his own. It was Pepito, the African grey parrot. Mr. Goldberg moved it from the living room to the hall because of its constant interruptions to his television programs.

It had been Esther's idea to buy one, and now she was gone. He really wanted no part of that bird, but he was stuck with it.

"Hello," said the parrot again.

"Get lost," was what Mr. Goldberg wanted to say, but he could imagine the expected effects if he did. He ignored the parrot and walked through to the kitchen, to make himself a sandwich. He coughed several times. The parrot coughed back.

"Hello," it called. "Would you like a cup of tea?" Mr. Goldberg came back from the kitchen holding a packet of seeds and filled up the parrot's feeder. "Hello," it said again, Mr. Goldberg sighed.

Mr. Goldberg was thinking about the little job he had planned for the afternoon. He heard scratching noises in the attic last night. It was October and he guessed that the mice had left their summer quarters in the in the garden. Now, they were making themselves comfortable in the attic. They were getting ready for the winter.

The noises had come from above his bedroom which was behind the cottage.

He changed into a pair of overalls, put on a disposable dust mask and recovered the bar that released the attic hatch from the hook on the wall of his utility room.

"That's the ticket my friend," said the parrot. Mr. Goldberg lifted the metal bar in his hands as he walked pass the bird.

"Hello," it said.

Mr. Goldberg opened the hatch and let the ladder down. He climbed up into the attic carrying his traps and a small quantity of peanut butter in an empty margarine box: he had read that mouse preferred it to cheese.

He heard the parrot calling from below, "That's the ticket my friend."

It was very uncomfortable in the attic; it had been a hot day. He stepped carefully across to where the beams inclined down and joined with the ceiling beams. He then knelt and crawled into a narrow space. He lay down sweating on the floor. He then began to lay his traps, pushing them into the attic.

Mr. Goldberg was beginning to feel weak. The heat in the attic was taking over. It was then that the heart attack struck. His chest cramped. It felt as if it was being crushed by an enormous crab's claw. He lay back breathless. Mr. Goldberg tried so hard to call for help, however, there was no one around only his crazy bird.

"What's the time?" called the parrot.

Mr. Goldberg fell into a place between sleeping and waking, heat and cold, and called for help when he had the strength.

Mrs. Pietro walked by Mr. Goldberg's house on her way home from the library. She hadn't seen him for two days. She decided to visit him. She wanted to see if he was alright.

Mrs. Pietro walked up the path and knocked on the door.

"Hello," called a voice.

"Hello," she called back, "Are you alright, Mr. Goldberg?" she heard coughing.

"Help me," called Mr. Goldberg from the attic, but his voice was too weak. Mrs. Pietro didn't hear him. The parrot cocked its head. All she could hear was that crazy bird....

"What's the time?" it called.

"About five," called Mrs. Pietro. The parrot coughed again. "Are you sure you're alright? I'm on my way home, do you need anything?"

"Would you like a cup of tea?" asked the parrot.

"Help me," called Mr. Goldberg faintly…

"No thanks, I'm on my way home, George is expecting me."

"That's the ticket my friend," said the parrot.

Mrs. Pietro walked back up the front path and went home.

Two more days passed and by this time Mr. Goldberg was dead. He lay rigid and drying in the heat of the attic. Mrs. Pietro knocked at the door of the cottage.

"Hello," she called.

"Hello," said Pepito.

"Are you alright, Mr. Goldberg? You're not coughing as much, you sound better."

"That's the ticket my friend"

She shrugged, turned and continued her way home.

Another two days passed, and Mrs. Pietro knocked again, "Hello."

Pepito, standing on its perch, looked at its empty water bottle and empty feeder. It raised a leg, cocked its head on one side and began to scratch it.

"Help me,' it called loudly, "help me." ….

STORY 5

Summer Romance

It was a warm summer afternoon and there was just a glimpse of the sun above the horizon…

Dolores felt a slight breeze, brushing lightly against her skin. She could feel her dark brown hair flowing with the direction of the wind as she went around and around on the carousel. She closed her eyes and listened to the carnival music.

In the background, Dolores could also hear people talking and laughing. Even with her eyes closed, she could still see the joyful faces of children. Their eyes are wide open with excitement. Their parents were watching them carefully and happily.

Dolores smiled, capturing the moment. She made sure to mentally write down all the details in my head, so she could retell it exactly to her parents.

It has been nearly a week since Dolores saw her parents. It would be another month or two until she would see them again. Before leaving,

Her parents made her promise to call them once a week. Their 25th anniversary was last week, as her gift, she decided to go and stay with her aunt in Ohio for the summer.

As her mind wandered to her home back in New York, she felt the carousel slowly come to a stop. Dolores gently opened her eyes and let out a happy sigh. She laughed as she struggled to get off her carousel horse. She was feeling dizzy, therefore, she went to find a place to sit.

As Dolore sat down on a nearby bench, her eyes swept the carnival for a hot dog stand. She saw one.

Dolores began walking towards it. Halfway there, knowing she was supposed to call her aunt at 9:30. She decided to see what time it was. She looked down in her bag and began searching for her phone.

Suddenly, she ran into someone. "Sorry ", she looked up unexpectedly into the stunning brown eyes of a gorgeous stranger. He looked about her age, if not a year older. He was an inch taller than her. No words could even begin to describe him.

Dolores' heart was pounding. She tried to catch her breath. Just when she thought he couldn't get any hotter, the Gorgeous Stranger smiled, making his eyes twinkle.

Finally catching my breath again, Dolores tried to speak again…

"Sorry, I wasn't watching where I was going, he laughed, and then smiled again. "Don't be", he said. Even the sound of his voice made her heart explode. He held out his hand.

"I'm Leonard, by the way "I held out my hand, meeting his. "Dolores", she replied, matching his smile. "Do you live around here? I don't think I have seen you before"?

"No, I am just visiting my Aunt Rita for the summer. I live in New York. What about you?" Dolores asked. "I moved here about four years ago from New Jersey. I have lived here for some time. How long are you staying with your aunt?" His eyes seemed to sink into mine; making as if I really mattered.

My heart fluttered as though it were a butterfly trying to escape. The strange, yet amazing thing was, that, even though it was breath taking, I loved the feeling of excitement.

I wanted to jump up and scream, as though a lively volcano had erupted. Dolores could feel it building inside of her, as his eyes continued to stare into hers.

Dolores loved the way he asked her questions. It was hard to concentrate on anything when he was staring at her.

Dolores looked at Leonard and told him that she was going to stay for the summer. He smiled again." Cool, maybe we can hang out sometime. I could show you around town, if you would like", he said.

"Oh yes, I would like that very much" ....

"When would y- ", Dolores started to ask, but suddenly she was cut off. "Leonard! I've been looking all over for you"

Dolores turned to see who rudely interrupted her and saw a beautiful brunette walking toward them with two almost as equally gorgeous girls. One tall and the other one was average height. The tall one was also brunette, but the average height one was a light brown hair.

Judging by the way the beautiful brunette was walking just slightly ahead of them, Dolores could tell she was the leader of their group.

Dolores also, noticed by the look she was giving he that she wasn't too fond her.

Dolores just knew that she wasn't welcome. She also senses that they hated her guts. She sighed. They all seemed to walk in harmony. They were walking their way around as if they owned the place. Each of them thought they were better than everyone else. Their eyes weren't exactly friendly.

As they got closer, Dolores could see two guys with them, who seemed to trail the other two like puppies, obviously their boyfriends.

Dolores, realized at this point, that the leader didn't seem to have a boyfriend, but apparently wanted one, by the seducing look she was giving Leonard.

Dolores stomach turned...

"Hey Eva, Laura, hey Carmin. What's up Juan, Carlos?" Leonard said to them all, giving Dolores an apologetic look.

As a result, the leader was Eva, the two behind her were Laura and Carmin, and the guys were Juan and Carlos, Dolores thought, hoping that she could remember which is which.

As they reached where Dolores and Leonard were standing, Eva went and stood by Leonard; very close, Dolores added, while the others sort of circled around.

Eve wrapped her arms around Leonard. "Where have you been, we looked all over for you!" she said. She gave Dolores a dirty look. "Who are you"?

Dolores just smiled, but she was tempted to laugh when she saw that her little grin seemed to annoy Eva. Leonard, however, seemed to look amused again.

Dolores told herself that she would remain neutral if anything should happen. "Hi, I'm visiting from New York. I am just here for the summer". Nice, Dolores smiled to herself.

Dolores just hope that she could stay calm for the rest of the night…

STORY 6

Six Feet Under

Naydeen left the bathroom and went downstairs in a hurry. Into the kitchen she went only to find it smokey with a bad burned smell…

Her mom, Carmen, was standing over the stove fanning a frying pan that was issuing puffs of smoke with a dishtowel. Her 13-year-old brother, Johnny was opening windows trying to help.

The smoke detector started beeping loudly. Naydeen quickly pulled a chair out and unscrewed it from the ceiling.

Once she did that, the noise stopped. Her Mom took the pan over to the sink and turned the water on, making the smoke stop with a sizzle noise. Her mom then turned and seemed to notice Naydeen for the first time.

"Oh, good morning my little princess, how did you sleep?" She asked, like if nothing even happened. Naydeen shook her head slowly and stepped down from the chair.

Sometimes she thought that her mother might be crazy, but she loves her no matter what.

"What happened mom"? Naydeen asked and set the smoke detector on the counter.

"Hmm? Oh right, you see I was trying to make you and Johnny a spinach omelet, but I wasn't paying attention. I guess they got a little burned." She said and gestured to the black crusty pan.

"Just a little." Naydeen mumbled. Naydeen tried to tell her that cereal was fine, but Carmen wouldn't listen. Johnny said nothing. He just went for a box of Corn flakes.

Carmen made a face. "Cereal is not good breakfast, it's full of sugar and who knows what else, plus it doesn't fill you up." she said and frowned. Johnny rolled his eyes and dug into his Corn flakes.

"It's okay mom, we like cereal, and next time you want to make us breakfast try something simpler, like toast", Naydeen said and hugged her shoulders. "Alright" Carmen sighed.

You see, Naydeen's parents have been divorced for a while. Dad was the one who could cook, and Carmen has trouble with it…

Johnny and Naydeen live with Carmen most of the time. They spend every Wednesday with their dad and his wife Sonia.

A year after Naydeen's parents got divorced, her dad married Sonia. Sonia was pregnant that's the reason her dad married Sonia. They love each other of course, but that was the main reason they got married.

Three months after their wedding along came her half-sister, Cathy. She's over two years old now.

Naydeen sat down at the table and poured a glass of juice…

"Anything happening today at school?" Carmen asked. Johnny just shrugged with his mouth full of cereal.

"Not really, but there is a party tonight at Willie's house." Naydeen said. "Which Willie, the one who wears all that black cape all the time, or the volleyball captain?" Carmen asked while handing Johnny l a napkin.

Naydeen laughed. "The volleyball one." "Do you want to go, because you can if you want." Carmen said.

Naydeen thought about it. She likes Willie. Everyone knows him because of how great his parties are. "Yeah, I might if I'm in the mood." Naydeen said.

After breakfast Naydeen got dressed, in comfortable jeans, blue fitted blouse, and sandals, it was her usual outfit.

When she was ready, Johnny, and her got into the car and left…

Carmen and Naydeen took turns taking and picking up Johnny from school. This morning was Naydeen to take John to school.

"Have a good day." Naydeen said to Johnny. He waved.

At her school, Naydeen parked. She checked her hair in the mirror. It was back to its natural frizz. As always, Naydeen used that stupid straightener. This morning, she didn't. She got out of the car and went to class.

Naydeen really was in no mood of doing any type of schoolwork. Her mind was in Lala land. She wasn't prepared for her class because she didn't do the homework assignment.

Naydeen parents' divorce has messed her up. She did her chores at home because it was routine. She has lots of problems when it comes to sleep. She was fast asleep in class all the time.

Also, she began to use crack. Her mom or dad had no idea she was in deep trouble...

That day, Naydeen just wanted to run off and never come back. The classes were boring. She kept looking at the clock on the wall. The minutes or even hours took forever.

Finally, school was over for the day. Naydeen was there physically, but not mentally. She just wanted to leave that horrible building. She saw a couple of her friends and she waved at them.

When Naydeen got to the parking lot, she ran to my car. She started smoking and was feeling great! Naydeen smoked until everything was fuzzy. She started the car and drove off.

Once in the highway, Naydeen was flying. Cars were beeping as they passed her. She had mixed feeling at that point. She started driving faster and faster until she hit a pick-up truck...

Naydeen fell her body floating. People trying to help me or something. She kept yelling that she was fine. No one responded or paid attention.

Next thing Naydeen knew was that she placed in a coffin and was buried six feet under...

Life is too short to waste it. Enjoy everyday as if it is your last. Spend more time with family and friends. If you have a situation in school or your job etc. get help.

STORY 7

An old Buddy

Melinda laid her bag down gently on the sand and bent over to grab a towel from it.

The sound of the waves crashed in the near distance as the sun kissed my exposed neck. Melinda unrolled the towel and spread it out, setting the bag on the bottom left corner to keep it from blowing away.

"This is a great spot. The tide shouldn't come too close. We can build a fire right here." Raymond moved his hands in circular motions around the plot of beach he was referring to.

"Great," Melinda replied. The 'spot' was about 20 feet from the boardwalk, one of the only spaces not already filled by other bodies.

Melinda slid her sandals off. She then tossed her towel on her chair. As she crouched down to get comfortable, Melinda felt the rough texture of the towel against her bare skin, clustering underneath her knees. It was making sitting more difficult than necessary. Melinda dropped one hip on top of the ground and stretched her feet out behind her. Her toes were grazing the hot sand.

It was the middle of August, and the beach was buzzing with people. Families with kids were scattered across the sand, their sun tents and coolers marking their little slice of paradise. People were flying kites, their bright colors creating broken rainbows in the sky.

One can also hear music was blasting from several areas. Each device was playing a different tune. Each begging to be louder than its neighbor. It was anything but relaxing to Melinda.

Raymond had been the one to suggest going to the beach for the weekend. He thought it would be the perfect getaway from the stress of their lives. They had been trying to have a baby but weren't having any luck. Raymond was devastated by this situation. Melinda, in the other hand, was absolutely thrilled. Her birth control had not failed her yet…

"Look at all these kids". Raymond, wish they had their own little guys with them right now. He opened the folding chairs they had brought and was looking around the beach to catch a glimpse of all the children as he sat down.

"Yeah," Melinda replied.

"Sure, is a nice day.", said Raymond.

"Is sure is," Melinda said as she sat up to grab her book out of her bag.

"Maybe if she started reading, he would stop talking". Melinda thought.

"It's pretty warm. I am going to dip my feet in the water. Do you want to join me?" Raymond stood up from his chair and began taking his shirt off.

"No, thanks. I'm going to catch up on my reading. Have fun."

Melinda opened her book to a random page. She waited for Raymond to head towards the water. Melinda tossed her book to the side and laid down as soon as Raymond was out of sight.

"Linda?"

Melinda quickly opened my eyes. Nobody had called her Linda since college.

"Carlos?" I reached for my cover-up, suddenly embarrassed to be showing so much skin.

"I can't believe it. You look even better than I remember."

"Look who's talking." Melinda stood up, trying to calmly fix my hair along the way.

Carlos Silva. My Carlos Silva. That is all Melinda could say….

"How are you? What have you been up to?" He took his sunglasses off and slid them into his shirt pocket.

Then, he put a hand to his face to shield the sun moments later. His blue eyes sparkled brighter than the ocean.

"I'm good. I'm great. Really great. How are you?" Melinda tripped over her words, trying to remember how to speak.

Carlos laughed. "I'm doing okay as well. Where are you located these days?"

"I'm in New York. Came down just for the weekend to getaway. What about you?"

He stared out at the ocean. "I live here, actually."

Melinda felt a sharp pain in my chest. He had settled down and it wasn't with her.

"That's great, Carlos. That's really great." Melinda forced a smile.

"Yeah, it has been quite wonderful. I suppose you can say I told you so."

He playfully punched her in the arm.

Melinda wanted to say, go fuck yourself, but she bit her tongue...

Carlos and Melinda had a long-term relationship for almost eight years. They spent their last summer together at the beach. They ate and made love. They cuddled up very close to a bonfire roasting marshmallow at night.

Carlos and Melinda rode bikes through the small town. They enjoyed eating snow cones as they walked at the park. Carlos even taught her to surf, and she taught him to cook.

They spoke a lot about their childhood. They also shared their dreams for the future.

It was the best summer of their life. They didn't want it to end, however, things changed when Melinda proposed settling down and starting a family. Carlos had decided not to settle down.

Carlos wanted to travel the world by himself. He wanted to go to new places, and experience new things without her. He couldn't imagine being stuck in one place for the rest of his life. In his life, Melinda didn't have a place. That was 16 years ago.

"Well, time does have a way of changing your mind." Melinda had crossed her arms over her chest. she wanted their conversation to end.

"Yes, it really does."

He glanced behind him at a small child who was running his way.

"Slow down, sweety. You know we don't run on the pavement."

The little girl stopped at Carlos' side, wrapping her arms around his leg.

"Who's this lady, daddy?"

The pain in her chest rushed back.

"This is an old friend. Her name is Linda."

"Melinda," she quickly corrected him.

"Yes, Melinda. This is my daughter, Beverly."

"Hi, Beverly. Nice to meet you." It was not nice to meet her, but you can't tell a seven-year-old you wish you'd never met them.

"I should probably be getting back. It was really great seeing you, Linda...Melinda." He bent over and picked up Beverly, resting her on his side.

"Me too."

Melinda stood there for a moment, watching him walk away into the crowd of people.

"Who was that?" Raymond kissed her on the back of her neck which had started sweating either from the heat or rage, she wasn't sure.

"Just an old buddy from college," I replied.

STORY 8

A Tale from the Heart

Emma, a young student from a Catholic school asked her teacher, "Why did you become a religious person?"

The teacher began telling Emma a heartwarming love story...

Mrs. Emely Warren began: Many years ago, when I was a about your age, I was in love with a young man named Henry. He came from a well to do family. I was, in the other hand, was poor.

Henry and I began seeing each other in secrecy. We couldn't go to the movies or even amusement parks. We quickly developed a deep connection with each other.

Unfortunately, Henry's family found out about our secret meetings. Henry's family was not at all in agreement with the relationship. They even threatened to enroll Henry at a university overseas and far away from me.

Even though Ms. Warren came from a poor background, she was well educated...

Henry begged Emma to go away with him. She didn't have any money. She knew she couldn't go with him. This meant they would be separated from each other.

Henry repeatedly told Emely Warren that she was the love of his life. He will try everything in his power to keep that lovely relationship alive.

They both had fallen so in love with each other that they didn't want to end their forbidden romance. They both decided to run away.

In great secrecy, they planned their escape and set their plans into action. When Henry's family finally found out about their escape, the two-love bird were far away.

You know, after their escape, the two love birds never returned to their hometown. They joined a church, took holy orders and began traveling the world for various humanitarian missions. They spent 50 years together traveling. They were together yes, but not as man and wife. They were together serving God.

It is so ironic that two individuals, in love, never even kissed. They were just happy sharing each other company.

Henry and Emma finally got married. It was shortly before Henry died due to a severe heart attack...

STORY 9

The Accident

Every day about 8 a.m., Gloria takes her daughter Sandy to school. This morning was no different...

Sandy was fourteen years old. She was very popular girl in school. Sometimes that drove Gloria crazy because she had to take her daughter from one school activity to the next.

Half of the time Gloria was a walking zombie. Taking care of a house and working in her own flower shop was no joke. You see, Sandy's father was killed in Iraq, therefore, Gloria was a single parent.

When Gloria was driving Sandy to school, in a rainy and gloomy day, she saw a shocking car crash. The accident was serious, so she got out of her car to see if she could help.

There were two cars involved in the accident. One of the cars, a Yaris, quickly started to catch fire. She immediately checked if there were passengers left in the car. Gloria called the cops immediately...

All the sudden, she saw an unconscious fourteen-year-old boy in one of the cars. Without hesitating, she pulled the car door open and brought the boy to safety. He was brought to a hospital where Gloria and her daughter visited him several times. Both mother and daughter helped the boy recover.

As time passed by, Gloria noticed that her daughter started to go to the hospital by herself. The two teens were falling in love....

Sandy told her mother that she began to like Willie the minute she saw him many months before the accident. Sandy recognized

Willie right away. They were in the same school and took some classes together. Sandy really helped Willie recover faster than expected.

Unfortunately, both Willie's parent died after a week in the hospital. Willie was left in his aunt's care. He wasn't told about his parent's death until he was fully recovered.

Every afternoon, right after school, Sandy would visit Willie and put him update with schoolwork.

Willie had a happy life with his aunt and cousin. He graduated from high school and got scholarship to Harvard University. Sandy also received a scholarship, and both enter Harvard in the year2017.

They graduated from Harvard University and became lawyers. They opened a law firm in the state of New York.

I forgot to inform you that they got married and had a set of twins….

STORY 10

A Loving Father

Carmela thought that she had the perfect family. Since she was a young girl, her parents always gave her everything she needed and much more....

One day Carmela found a worn-down diary in a toolbox that belong to her dad. It was his diary. He wrote it about the time he was only 16 years old.

Carmela, unconditionally, loves her dad, who is not only the best dad but also a loving and kind husband. It wasn't easy for her to open the diary. Eventually, she became so curious about his life that she decided to read it.

The last entry in the diary was a short paragraph. It was wildly scribbled down. It said that at the time of writing the entry, that he was 16 years old and an alcoholic.

He went on describing that he dropped out from high school with a criminal record. Her dad also noted in the entry that one month later he would become a teen father.

At that point, Carmela began to cry. She was crying because her father became a changed man when he found out that he was going to be a father.

In those notes, he also made a promise to himself that he would set his life straight. He would become the father for his little daughter that he never had...

STORY 11

The Immigrant

Tomas Nevarez, that's his name. A name that had been announced all over the world. He had won the Lottery; the publicity stunt that had become a periodic tradition.

Tomas didn't intend on winning so much money. He got the ticket because his girlfriend was making a big deal about it. She told him that he was going to win big time.

Tomas just laughed. It seemed to make her happy that he bought the ticket.

The thing is that Tomas didn't consider himself lucky to be getting an "all expenses" paid trip for an "out of this world adventure."

He won, and that was a billion to one odd that would happen...

Now, Tomas is going to be an upper class in society. He was going to go to California. He will be famous for as long as he was up there. He was going to be there with the rich famous.

Tomas Nevarez will be forgotten the moment he touches bottom.

Reality is that the real millionaire would have lots of real important data to share with the world. All Toma could say was how weird it is to be with the rich and famous.

Tomas was acting as enthusiastic as he could. He hadn't paid much attention to the well displayed information on trips and interviews. He was going to attend many gatherings.

This trip wasn't a run-of-the-park nor was it a quick run to store. It was to be the fifteenth days away from his friends and family.

Tomas Nevarez destination was to conquer the world…

This was not just any place; it was Hollywood California. This trip was 'special.' It was a state just about the size of two or three town put together.

When Tomas got to California, he was able to walk around town easily. "What wouldn't be easy would be talking to people," he thought. He had no knowledge of the English language.

"Yeah", this was that kind of place where they looked down at Hispanics.

They didn't want their town to go down in price. Those racists had no idea of how smart Hispanics are.

As Tomas started walking towards a coffee shop, a patrol car stopped him. He asked him for his papers. Tomas had no idea what those papers were. He only had the key to his room. The officers got annoyed with him and pushed Tomas into the patrol car.

That was the first time he felt so lonely in his life. Back home, Tomas had so many friends. Here in California, he was called an immigrant.

Tomas didn't know why he was called an immigrant. He was very puzzled.

Tomas tried to tell the police officer that he won the lottery. The whole precinct laughed at him. Tomas wasn't doing well at all with his poor English.

A couple of hours went by. No one came for him. The cops didn't even give him food or anything to drink. They decided to turn on the TV. The news was about to begin. They were all surprised to see Tomas' face on TV.

The reporters were just giving information about him! Even the major and a whole staff from his country came to the TV station. They stated that Tomas was very important person. They wanted to know where he was.

Slowly, the cops turned to him. They tried to be nice, but it was too late…

They got Tomas a translator that explained how much money he has won. He was also going to present some cash to a poor sector in California.

Now, Tomas decided to go to another state where everyone was treated equally. He chose New York.

His fiancé, Milly, flew down to New York to meet him. He went to Spanish Harlem and gave money to all the Hispanics that were living in bad housing.

The New York City Major thank Tomas and informed him that he had plenty of relatives and friends in New York...

Tomas couldn't believe his eyes when he saw Milly. There were all his lost relatives that moved to the city that never sleep for a better life.

Tomas Nevarez was proud to report to everyone that he was given a medal for helping the poor. The police, firemen, and doctors were present at that press conference.

He told the press that he wanted to see students and teachers there. "Why?" Tomas was asked, because they are the future. Tomas told the press that we must tell the young ones to respect everyone no matter what their nationality or income was.

The reporters asked Tomas, "what were his plans now that he was in New York?" He smiled and told them that the first thing he was going to do was to go back to school and learn English.

He then told everyone that he was going to marry the love of my life, Milly. With Milly at his side, he knew that he wasn't lonely anymore.

They had a lovely wedding in Central Park. The invitation was for the rich as well as the poor.

By the way, the reason Tomas didn't have or didn't know about carrying papers around in California, was that he is an American Citizen. He was born in Puerto Rico. Puerto Rican are not immigrants. They relocate or migrate to the United States.

STORY 12

A Bizarre Love Story

Aida's breathing was deep and steady. She was running through a dark and dense forest holding her mother's kitchen knife. Her dress was torn down. Also, her legs, hands and her face were cut by the tree branches.

"Stop you are the victim", said the forest while burying its thorns in her.

"Stop and wait for the big brave man to save you", shouted the animals in the forest.

"Go back to be the innocent little girl we used to know", the strangers whispered with a shocking mumble.

It was wrong, Aida knew it, they knew it and even her lover knew it.

That is the only way you can go on with life. You must marry Junior. He is a smart man. "Don't go ruining it for all of us, her family warned her.

"You need to wait for us to save you", said her parents. with a commanding voice.

"You don't have the right to change anything in my life." Aida told her grandmother.

"You are wearing red; you know what that means right"? "Blame your new boyfriend. He is the one that brought the wine in the nearby liquor store". "You asked for it, stop complaining and carry on with your part of the deal", said Lourdes her grandmother.

Aida simply listened, for so many years. The story is being told so many times. This was a true and sorrow story...

She didn't want to disappoint her family or make them angry or even sad.

Not anymore...

She did her part in the plan that was made for her. She played her cards right.

Junior was not far away from her. She could see him running after her. He was panicking and hysterical. His breathing short and fast. White foam was forming around his mouth. His big, impressive eyes were now nothing but sheer horror.

She was faster than him and much stronger than he had ever been.

She was the predator, and he was the prey.

"Can you hear me?" She screamed.

"Can you see me?" She roars as a lioness.

He falls exhausted, nothing was left of him. She looked at him, he was weak and very pathetic.

The forest was quiet and very dark. Nothing or nobody will ask her to stop. Not anymore.

Everyone knew the truth....

STORY 13

The following four stories are about my father and grandfather. I didn't change the names because I want people to know who they were. They were American Soldiers serving our nation with pride.

Father and Son fighting for the Same Cause

In the early spring, in 1950, The Puerto Rico Army National Guard was training every soldier harder than ever. Everyone knew that soon the National Guard would be mobilized.

My mother and grandmother were sad during those days because they knew that every member in my family will be deployed to Korea.

Since my mother was pregnant with her second child, she was too big to work around the house. My grandmother, Guadalupe, let her rest because my mother was due soon. This time, both my grandmother Guadalupe and my great-grandmother had a bad feeling about this child.

My mother was always too tired and didn't want to eat. I guess my mom was always sick because she didn't see my father often enough...

On October 20, 1950, my mother went into labor for more hours than expected. She gave birth to another baby girl, my sister Adelin.

My grandmother Lupe and great grandma Dolores were happy because the baby was small, but healthy.

Digna, my mother, wanted to know if my father was around. My father and grandfather were doing drill at Lucille Field base known today as Fort Allen in Juana Diaz, Puerto Rico.

Both my father and grandfather were happy because the new baby was doing well. They wanted to go home, but all passes were denied.

Juan Jose Pagan Rodriguez, my dad, got very angry when he was told that he couldn't go to Ponce to see his family. He just wanted an hour pass to see his wife and daughter. The answer from the commander was no….

My father decided to jump the fence…

So, when his unit went on break, he started walking very fast. There were sugar cane fields before reaching the main road. As soon as he reached the street, a car stopped and to my father's surprise, it was his commander. The commander looked at him and told him to get in the car. The young Sergeant was surprised because he was escorted to Ponce to see his family.

The commander told him to stay the rest of the evening, but to return to the base the following day. My mother was very happy to see him. Adelin and I were beside my mom when my dad arrived. The whole family had a wonderful night together.

During the months that followed, things were very rough. Lots of soldiers were sent to Korea. My grandfather and my father were waiting for their orders…

Our nation was facing one of the worst times of that era. Puerto Rico was waiting and willing to fight in Korea.

I am proud to say, that my father, CSM Juan José Pagán Rodriguez, of the Puerto Rico Army National Guard and my grandfather, Staff Sergeant Julio Pagán Torres, now both deceased, were among those brave soldiers fighting for our country in one of the bloodiest conflicts.

STORY 14

Getting Deployed

In order to understand the commotion that was going on in the states and Puerto Rico, I will give you some facts of what our soldiers were facing during that time....

On July 1, 1950, the Army's 24th Infantry Division became the first U.S. troop to arrive in Korea. They were transferred from Japan passing through the Port of Pusan. The troops took up Positions in Taejon, about 75 miles south of Seoul. A couple of days later July 19, 1950, the 25th Infantry arrived followed by the 1st Marine Brigade and the 2nd Infantry Division in late July.

Things were getting worse in Korea that on July 20, 1950, the casualties were increasing. More than 2,400 men or 30% were reported dead. Taejon fell under the arms of the enemy.

All Americans and the rest of world were alarmed. This meant that many were going to be called to serve their country. The Reserves and the National Guard will be mobilized.

Puerto Rico, a beautiful island located in the Caribbean, and a Commonwealth of the United States, was getting ready. There was no cultural or language barrier holding those brave men. Those "Boricuas" were well trained. Three members of my family were in the National Army Guard. They knew that it won't be long for the guard to be call for active duty. All three were ready to serve their nation. They were Staff Sgt. Julio Pagan Torres, my grandfather, as signed to 65th Infantry 4 machine gun 30 calibers, Sgt. Juan J. Pagan Rodriguez, my father, assigned to 65th Infantry Heavy Mortal Co.

and the youngest, my uncle, Cpl. Julio Pagan Rodríguez was assigned to Artillery.

By early September, the new troops were combat ready in hardened fighting units. The Puerto Rican National Guard was mobilized on September 10, 1950. Every "Boricua's" family was worried because their loved ones will leave to an unknown land. Many have never been abroad. Now, they must face a lot of hardships.

It didn't take long for a humble family in Ponce to hear the worst news ever. Their sons and husbands must report for duty. This was awful because all three soldiers were assigned to infantry or artillery. The women were devastated when they heard the news on the radio.

Staff Sgt. Julio Pagan Torres and Sgt. Juan J. Pagan Rodriguez received their orders. Their unit, the 65th Infantry was being mobilized. Cpl. Julio Pagan Rodriguez wasn't called at this time.

The 65th Infantry was now divided. That meant father and son were separated. The 296 Infantry was sent to Tortuguero. They were di-vided into three groups, 2nd to Juana Diaz and the 3rd to Cayey.

STORY 15

Waiting For The Worst

Everything was moving too fast. The Puerto Rico National Guard was giving orders left and right. There was no question asked. It didn't matter if there were one sole survivor in a family. Men were needed to go abroad and fight for their country.

Sgt. Juan J. Pagán Rodriguez was ready to fight; however, he had a young wife and two young children. Sgt. Julio Pagán Torres had also young ones. They had a big problem. There was also a possibility that Cpl. Julio Pagán Rodriguez might be call for active duty. They wanted to serve, but they had a family.

The following day, both father and son decided to speak to their commander. The commander found it quite unusual for members of the same family to be called for active duty. He listened to their petition and wrote all the information given by my father and grandfather. He told Sgt. Juan Pagán Rodriguez that he was the one chosen to go to Korea and that Sgt. Julio Pagán Torres will stay in Puerto Ri-co.

What follows, will not only put you in tears, but will make you wonder…

In November 1950, Sgt. Juan J. Pagán Rodriguez said goodbye to his beloved wife and family. He was only 22 years old but was fully aware of his commitment. His father promised him that he would take care of the whole family. Sgt. Juan J. Pagán Rodriguez just said, "Bendición Papito" and got on the bus…

Many "Boricuas" were also leaving Puerto Rico. This was the saddest day for the whole island. Saying goodbye was very hard. The 65th Infantry had already sent soldiers to Korea. Those first infantry soldiers made history throughout the nation. They were known as "The Borinqueneers" The 65th Infantry Regiment started the assault on January 31, 1951.

NO WORD FROM SGT JUAN PAGAN RODRIGUEZ

The Pagán family was very confused during this crisis because right after Sgt. Juan J. Pagán Rodriguez left Puerto Rico, his father Staff Sgt. Julio Pagán received new orders. These orders stated that he was leaving for Korea in December 1950.

This was the worst Christmas gift that anyone could receive.

Now, Staff Sgt. Julio Pagán Torres was also leaving his family. He told his wife, Guadalupe, "No te apures, todo va a salir bien". He couldn't face his daughter in law, Digna. She was holding her youngest daughter Adelin.

Digna was too upset to say goodbye. Sgt. Juan J. Pagán Rodriguez left the island months before and no one knew his whereabouts. The so many visits to the Red Cross were made in vain.

Sgt. Julio Pagán Torres even went to his commander for an answer of his previous visit. The commander apologized for the awful mess and stated that he was sorry. He told Sgt. Pagán Torres those orders were revoked because they got to Washington too late. Communication was very slow in those days…….

ILL FEELINGS IN THE FRONT LINES

Sgt. Juan J. Pagán Rodriguez was already fighting in the front lines. He got to Korea in January 1951 and at this point he was uneasy. He had been away from his family for nearly two months and no news was received.

It was hard to get anything where he was stationed. His new acquired family was his buddies, fellow "BORICUAS". All of them were waiting for any kind of news from Puerto Rico.

In Ponce, Puerto Rico, things weren't that great. With the breadwinner gone, it wasn't easy to raise all those children. Guadalupe and Digna had to go to the Red Cross. They wanted to hear news from their husbands. The Red Cross assured them that both father and son were fine. Food and emergency money were provided. Digna was worried because the youngest daughter was very ill. Adelin was a very fragile child and needed medical attention.

When the Red Cross saw the baby, they referred her to the best doctors. The child was well taken cared and recovered within months.

By the end of February, troops were sent to the front lines once again....

STORY 16

In Korea

One morning, Sgt. Juan Jose Pagán Rodriguez was ordered to take a couple of guys to a designated area. Sgt. Pagán Rodriguez briefed his men and started walking.

It was a cold bitter day and a lot of snow on the ground. The young soldiers were still trying to get used to that weather. They were all melancholy because they missed their sunny and warm Puerto Rico. Many had suffered from frost bites. It wasn't easy keeping those soldiers motivated. They haven't heard anything from their families in months.

As they were walking, Sgt. Pagán Rodriguez started telling funny stories. The soldiers felt at ease. They reached their destination point. There were many wounded and others were suffering from the cold. Sgt. Pagán Rodriguez and his Troop relieved those men.

The fire never seized. Sgt. Pagán Rodriguez has been on his post for nearly a week. He was hungry and so were his men. They needed clean uniforms and chow.

Sgt. Juan J. Pagán Rodriguez kept fighting even though he didn't receive any news from Puerto Rico.

Suddenly, he received a message. He was ordered to report to his Commander. The young sergeant was surprised, but at the same time was happy to take a shower and change his uniform. He was escorted to his superior and to his surprise there was Staff Sergeant Julio Pagán Torres waiting for him.

Words couldn't describe the emotion that those two human beings were feeling. Tears of joy were rolling down their faces. Sgt. Pagán Rodriguez asked his father about the family. He was also puzzled and questioning his father's arrival…both….in Korea…

The Commander of the 65th Infantry told both father and son that they would have to wait for new orders. He also told them that they will leave for Puerto Rico soon….

Those orders never came. Sgt. Juan J. Pagán Rodriguez was once again separated from his father……

A couple of days have gone by….

Sgt. Juan J. Pagán Rodriguez and his men were going to another camp site.

They had a couple of jeeps with plenty of supply. Sgt. Pagán Rodriguez saw a troop right in front of him. They were going to the same unit.

At that point, Sgt. Juan Pagán Rodriguez got the surprise of his life. His father, Staff Sgt. Julio Pagán Torres was among those men! He called his father, and both rode on the same jeep.

Once they arrived at their designated area, their new commandant called them. This time he gave them written orders. That was the best news Sgt. Pagán Rodriguez had received. He was going home, and his father was going with him safe and sound.

Sgt. Pagán Rodriguez and Staff Sgt. Julio Pagán Torres didn't want to be part of the big reception that was waiting for them in Puerto Ri-co.….

They were the first father and son wearing the same uniform and fighting for the same cause, but they just wanted to see their family.

They went to Ponce without being noticed. A taxi driver was the only witness when they reached home. There were a few gathered in front of the house. None of them were aware that a taxi had stopped there.

The two sergeants got off the taxi very quietly and opened the gate. Digna and Guadalupe started running once they saw them. It was a great day for the Pagán Family.

The Korean War brought Puerto Rican soldiers their greatest visibility, highest awards and most punishing losses. There were 43, 434 Puerto Ricans in this war and 39, 591 of them were volunteers.

The 65th Infantry was chosen to guard the nation. They received awards for their bravery. It was also the last group of soldiers to leave the combat zone...

Some bullets were whizzing by them as they boarded the ship to evacuate........

For that a great SALUTE TO OUR "BORICUA" Korean's Heroes. We will never forget them.

Staff Sergeant Julio Pagán Torres and Sergeant Juan J. Pagán Rodríguez were the first father and son to serve the nation. They were in combat together and together returned to Puerto Rico.

CSM Juan J. Pagán Rodriguez was very proud of being a soldier during the Korean Conflict...

CSM JUAN J. PAGAN RODRIGUEZ
This poem is dedicated to my dad
Born 01/29/1929 Died 03/28/2020

MY HERO

In choosing of becoming an NCO…
You accepted many responsibilities
In choosing of becoming a father…
You accepted many responsibilities
You are a role model, a trainer and a loving father…\

My hero…

As I sit here, thoughts of yesteryears come to mind…
You my father and the soldier…
Dealing with your family
Dealing with your troop…
Both tasks closely related and hard
An Army Non-Commissioned Officer and a father
Of four…
Your wisdom of many years made you a great leader…
Your wisdom of many years made you the father you are…
I salute you dear father…
I salute you for all the years
You devoted to us and to our nation…
May God bless you…
And May God bless America always!

STORY 17

The Surgery

Monica was a beautiful little girl that needed a heart operation. She came from a very poor family; therefore, it was hard to get the money right away. All the neighbors and classmates made collections throughout a small village in South America.

When a surgeon operated Monica, complications started to arise. She lost a lot of blood and needed a blood transfusion. However, she had blood type A+, which wasn't available in the hospital.

The surgeon, therefore, asked the Monica's parents if their son who was type A+ as well, could donate blood. They agreed...

The doctors explained to Julian that it was important for him to agree with the blood transfusion. It was a matter of life and death. Julian, seemingly afraid, sat a couple of moments in silence until he finally agreed.

He got up and hugged his parents, wishing them goodbye...

After the nurses had taken the blood from him, he whispered anxiously if they knew how many minutes he had left to live. He was absolutely convinced that he was going to die so that his sister could live, and he was willing to do so.

When the nurses realized that the Julian thought he was going to die, they cheered him up. They explained to him that he had many wonderful and joyful decades left to live....

STORY 18

City Life

This is a typical scene in big cities now a day...

After passing a cracked sidewalk, there was a telephone pole with layers of flyers in rainbow of colors. There were also patches of dry brown grass that stood next a ten-foot-high concrete block wall, caked with dozens of coats of paint. You can also see a small shrine at the foot of it, with burnt out candles, dead flowers and a few soggy teddy bears. One word of graffiti filled the wall on the background which said: Rest in Peace!

City life didn't appeal to everyone with the rising crime and drugs on every city block. Luisa was one of them. Especially after what happened to Roberto. All he was guilty of was being in the wrong place at the wrong time...

As the bus pulled in, Luisa was just thinking if this was her chance to escape or would she pick up her suitcases and head home as she did so many times. No way, she thought. When she was about to board the bus, she saw her sister, Carmen, running towards her.

"You can't leave. You can't leave," she kept shouting, but Luisa ignored her. Luisa knew at that point that there was nothing she could do. Carmen just walked away.

Once the bus reached its destination, Luisa got off. She walked to her friend Tata's house. Tata had left the city almost a year earlier with her parents. She got a job and just moved into her own apartment. The apartment was big enough for only for one person, but she did tell Luisa that she could stay with her until she got a job and a place to live.

When Luisa arrived, Tata was at the door waiting for her. Both were in tears as they hugged. Apart from being Luisa's best friend, Tata was also Roberto's sister. This was the first time they had seen each other since the funeral. He was very popular. Many turned out to pay their respects.

After making their way up to the apartment, Tata put on the tea kettle. She also had freshly baked bread. Tata set a small table with the teacups. Luisa was relieved to have something to eat. She was hungry after her long journey.

They then began to chat about old times. While chatting, Tata gave Luisa some surprising news about the person they thought responsible for Roberto's death. He had recently moved to the area where Roberto used to live. That guy was now living just streets away from the scene of the crime, so she thought. He may have been found not guilty where a court was concerned, but Luisa and Tata believed that he was still to be blame.

After their conversation, Rosa escorted Luisa to the only bedroom in the tiny apartment. Tata had set a dresser so that Luisa can use it. As she unpacked, Luisa couldn't help but wonder why the killer had moved to the same neighborhood where Roberto used to live. She hoped she wouldn't have to bump into him.

A few days later, on her way to the Job Center, Luisa saw the killer. He was fooling around with some girl instead of looking where he was going. How could he laugh and joke like that after what he had done to Roberto? Luisa also wanted to know why this guy was in this part of town. Something is wrong. She decided that she was going to get even.

Luisa began to walk very fast towards the Job center. She was beginning to plot her revenge. Luisa was very determined and wasn't afraid to get even with this loser. She made it to the job center and got a job at a boutique not too far from Tata's apartment.

The following day, while doing some shopping, Luisa realized it wasn't going to be too difficult to find Mr. Loser. She wasn't surprised to see him coming out of a bar. She caught up with him. As she was walking past him, Luisa let her bag fall to the ground. He eagerly helped her pick it up and gave it to her.

"There you go," he said, handing her the package. Then, noticing a coffee shop across the street, he asked her if she would like to have coffee with him. This guy had no idea who was Luisa. He was just staring at a gorgeous girl in front of him.

After a few minutes, Luisa replied, "All right" …

The coffee shop was kind of cozy. The people were all very friendly not like the big city where she used to live. Luisa was very surprised about how nice this guy was behaving. He was quite a charmer. He also seems very educated. He told her that his name was Jaime and that he lives with his parents.

After leaving the coffee shop, he walked with Luisa to Tata's apartment. Once in front of the building, Luisa was hoping Tata wasn't watching from the window. Just as she was about to leave him to make her way up to the apartment, he asked her if he could see her again. "If you want," she replied casually.

Jaime got very happy. He told Luisa that he will pick her up about eight in the evening. He also informed her that they would go for a drink. Luisa just answered, "OK." Luisa wasn't going to waste any time with Jaime. The only thing in her mind was to get her revenge…

When she got inside, Tata had just got out of the shower. Luisa was relieved because that meant that Tata didn't see her with Jaime. Tata was smiling and happier than ever because she had her best friend living with her. They had a delicious dinner prepared by Tata.

After that, Luisa got ready to go to the night club. Tata had already gone out for the evening. Luisa was feeling kind of guilty because she didn't want to lie or make any excuses about what she was about to do.

Just after eight, the intercom buzzed. She went down to meet Jaime. He was really a nice-looking man. They made the perfect couple. They were getting on so well that she was beginning to think he was a nice person, but she knew better.

After coming out of the night club, he walked her home. She asked him in for coffee. He accepted. This was her chance to get even, but before her key could turn in the lock, the door started opening from the inside. Luisa was confused. She thought Tata had arrived home early. Luisa was surprised when the door fully opened. It wasn't Tata she saw...

"Carmen, what are you doing here?" "I thought I would pay you a visit. I couldn't stand being at home without you. The neighbor across the hall gave me the spare key. It is OK, isn't it?" "Of Course, it is."

Luisa at that point remembered that she was with Jaime. She hoped that Carmen wouldn't recognize him, but it was too late.

"Luisa, what the hell are you doing with him?" "What does she mean by that?" he asked with a puzzled expression. "You are the one who was responsible for what happened to Roberto. That's what she means." He looked at Luisa stunned, then left. "Thanks, Carmen, you've scared him away." She thought that would be the last she would see him.

The next day, Jaime was sitting on a bench with a girl. It was the same girl Luisa had seen him with when she was on her way to the Job Center. Jaime left the girl and came over to talk Luisa. All Luisa could say was to please keep away from her. She didn't want any part with Jaime.

Luisa looked at Jaime and said, "'Does your girlfriend know what you are capable of?" she asked him. "She's my sister, and if you are referring to what happened to Roberto, I wasn't to blame.' There is so much I want to tell you. Please give a chance to explain what went on that city street so many miles away.

He began telling Luisa what really happened the day Roberto died. He told her that he was on his way to his house, when he saw a couple of members of a local gang forcing Roberto into a van because he wouldn't hand over money they demanded. Then, realizing he was a witness, they dragged him into the van as well. The van took off at speed, crashing against a concrete wall. All got out except him. He was left fatally injured. When the police arrived, the gang members said that he was the one that was driving, and that it was his fault that Roberto was dead.

"You're lying," Luisa yelled after he had finished explaining.

Three days later an automobile pulled up and parked beside the concrete wall. The driver opened the door but did not get out of the car. Although her face was in shadow, it was easy to tell she was sad. There was something about how she turned away from the sun and rested the weight of her hands on the steering wheel, something about her silent calmness, that caused Luisa to sigh. The young girl watched the driver lean out of the car and stretch her hand out towards one of the burned-out candles.

Luisa returned to Tata's town to sort things out. She went out in search of Jaime. Jaime was in no mood to talk to Luisa. He had suffered enough. Jaime's sister tried so hard to explain to Luisa that Jaime was innocent. "No, he's not," Luisa said.

Jaime's sister never gave up. She kept insisting that Jaime was innocent. "Why do you think he moved here? To escape from the gang, that's why. See tomorrow's paper, then you'll know it is true." I know that you won't believe anything that the newspaper writes.

The following day, Luisa bought a newspaper. All over the front page it was stated that Jaime was innocent. It was explained that the others involved in the crash had been charged with Roberto's death. Luisa started shouting that Jaime was telling the truth after all. She decided to go and apologize for her behavior.

Luisa decided to go to Jaime's house. His sister answered the door. She had an angry look on her face. She began yelling at Luisa. "He's not here," she said, after Luisa asked if she could speak to him. 'Where is he, then?' Luisa asked. "He's gone." "Where?"

I don't know. He left without a word. If it wasn't for you sticking your nose in our affairs, Jaime would still be here, she said, before slamming the door at Luisa's face.

Luisa couldn't feel any worse making her way back to Tata's apartment. All that she could hope, for now, was that Jaime turn up safe and not become another victim.

Luisa wasn't a religious person, however, she started praying for Jaime's safety. She had so many mixed feelings about the whole situation.

A couple of months have gone by since Jaime's disappearance. Luisa now has her own place. She is very happy to be living with her sister Carmen. She thought about Roberto and Tata. That was in the past. She is trying so hard to start a new chapter in her life. It isn't easy starting all over again…

One day, as Luisa was preparing for work, she heard her phone ring. She answered the phone and to her surprise it was Jaime. She couldn't believe this was happening after so many months. She finally heard his Jaime's voice. He is alive and wanted to be her friend. He told her to please meet him at the coffee shop where they could talk. She agreed.…

STORY 19

The City that Never Sleeps

It was a Saturday afternoon and raining in New York...

Out on the streets of Manhattan, Annette could see tourists trying to hail cabs and failing.

Above in the grey skies, airplanes dropped through the storm at Guardia and Kennedy Airports to leave or pick up their passengers.

At Citi Field, in Queens, after the covers were finally rolled away, the Mets gained out a precious win on a sacrifice fly in the bottom of the ninth.

In London, five time zones east, Prince Harry and Meghan Markle pledged their everlasting devotion to each other in a fizzle of international splendor.

On this day, Annette wanted to devote her time to love. She could feel it fill the city's streets and even on the trains under the streets.

Open love or even secret love Annette was willing to have. You, see, her long-time boyfriend, Josh, left her. She was all alone.

It has been over a month since Josh left their apartment. He went to live with one of his coworkers. Josh, the typical loser...

Annette wanted and needed physical love or even spiritual love. Any type of love will do. She needed love on every point of the scale.

Today Annette was very depressed. She wanted love and excitement...

The romance wanders around like fog in the city. Not "romance," of course, in the old-fashioned, idealized sense of the word. It is just perfectly appointed young couples spinning happily through the streets while teenagers sang in street corners.

What Annette didn't know was that there was a romance waiting just around the corner....

The real world of love does not require youth choreography or even necessarily couples. Annette was going to get it soon. She was going to get love very direct, tough and flexible.

As Annette was taking her stroll for a few minutes, she saw a young man just about her age. He was simply looking around. Perhaps he was only looking for a fast fling.

Annette was totally unaware to all of this. She came from a well to do family and very proper. She trusted everyone...

Annette saw the guy at the corner and wanted to meet him. She was obviously walking around and came to feel as if she was part of the scenery.

The young man was amused of the way Annette was dressed and carried herself. Very attractive, good taste in clothing and look hungry for an adventure...

Bob was the young man's name. He waited until Annette reached the corner. Once there, Annette introduced herself. Bob, in the other hand, took his time. He was observing her.

Finally, he introduced himself. It started to rain again. This time, it was a heavy rain with lots of wind. Bob showed his good manners. He invited Annette to his apartment right across from where they were talking. Annette hesitated but agreed to go with him.

He lived on the third floor. It was only a studio apartment...

As they walked into the small apartment, one could see a bed and only man stuff. Very neatly and well decorated.

Bob offered Annette a drink. It was, of course, cheap liquor. She said anything will be ok. Bob handed a glass of whiskey on the rock. Annette drank it very fast. He gave her another glass, this time a full glass. Once again, down it went.

Bob was enjoying every moment of this delicate little creature in front of him. The perfect bait for a rainy afternoon....

Annette started looking at Bob in a very romantic way. Bob really stared at her for a long time.

He decided to have a glass of whiskey. He started to get a buzz. Annette was looking ready for action.

Bob said, "let's go to bed". Annette, answered, "yes my love".

She started taking her cloth off rapidly. Bob was doing the same.

Once in bed, Bob started feeling her breast, legs and finally touching her private parts. This was making Annette very excited. She wanted more and fast. Bob whispered in a very sweet voice, "be patient my little angel". "You will get all the love you have been requesting".

Annette was so drunk that she wasn't aware what she was getting into. She was really enjoying herself. No one had ever made her feel this way. She was in heaven….

She kept begging Bob for more. Bob was an expert at this sort of game. Rich girl coming to the city for just lust not love. He knew them all….

When it was over, it was almost 12 midnight. Annette has been with this stranger for over six hours. She couldn't believe it.

Annette got dressed very quickly. She must catch a taxi and head home. Bob offered to take her home. Annette simply said no and left….

STORY 20

Loving world history

By the time Amy got to her locker Alice was there waiting. "You're not mad at me, are you?" She asked right away.

"Why, should I be?" Amy asked while opening the locker. "Well, no, but you seemed upset this morning on the phone." She said and stole a piece of gum from her bag.

"I'm not upset, but I was a little annoyed that you wanted me to watch Eddie, like if he's going to cheat on me the first chance he gets." I said and started walking to class with Alice next to me.

"Hey, I never said that he was, and I don't think he would, you trust him. It's Molly I don't trust." She explained. Amy nodded her head in agreement. "She's such a slut." Alice continued.

Just then Eddie came around the corner and picked me up in one of his bears hugs he was known for.

"Hey" Alice called Noris." Eddie joked over her shoulder. "Oh, ha Eddie, see you at lunch." She said and gave Amy a look.

Eddie sat me down and kissed me. Just like everything else about Eddie, his kisses are unique. Sweet and tender, but firm and so good at the same time.

"How's your morning been?" he asked and took my hand. By the time we got to the math class Alice had told Eddie all about the omelet fiasco. The cook had her day off and her mom went into the kitchen to make breakfast.

Bad mistake…

Eddie sat Alice down at the desk next to him. He was trying to stop laughing. "I'm glad you think my mom almost setting my kitchen on fire is amusing." Alice said with some sarcasm. He shrugged. "Sorry, it's just that I can't see your mom doing something like that, she's so funny." he laughed. Alice smiled because it was true.

The rest of the morning went by without any kind of incidents. It looked like a regular day of school, until world history class.

Alice was not usually a complainer, but she hated this class. It has the worst location in the whole school, therefore, when you're bored you have nothing to look out the window.

Alice is a good student averaging A's and B's, but this is the only class She has received lower than a C.

Alice thinks that the work is dry and pointless making it nearly impossible to focus. The thing everyone hates about the history class is the teacher, Mr. Green. He's the biggest ass in the world. Ironic that his name is Green, huh? One turns green when anyone sees him. Alice thinks that Mr. Green by making his students' lives horrible is his mission in life.

When Alice got to her desk, saw that Mr. Green had already handed out yesterday's test scores.

To Alice surprise, she got a C-. Jerk. She studied forever for that test. Leaning over to see the score Alice got Eddie gives her a sympathetic shrug.

Right before the bell rang Molly walks in wearing stupid booty shorts and a tight pink tank top. It's 50 degrees out and that's what she's wearing. Ugh. She walks to her desk, eyes searching the class until she spots Eddie. She gives him a flirty little wave. He was looking into his bag and didn't see Alice. Amy was right, she wants my boyfriend. Great.

"Alright class, you'll see that I have already handed out your tests from yesterday, as you can see most of you didn't do so well." Mr. Green said in his hollow voice. Alice sweared his eyes lingered on he when he said the last part.

He went on about how he's disappointed with the class, blah blah blah. Alice tuned him out for most of the class. She stared at the clock on the wall.

Alice started looking around the room. That's when she saw Molly writing a note and passing it to the girl next to her. Molly asked the girl to pass the note to Eddie.

Alice got pissed. She leaned forward and intercepted it before Eddie notice any communication between Molly and the girl.

Alice waited for Mr. Green to turn his back to the class. Alice had taken the note from the girl. The note read: Hey cutie, "Do you want to go to get some ice cream after class.?"

"I'm sad. Think you could lend a shoulder to cry on?".

Alice shoves the note in her pocket and try not to jump over her desk to fight with Molly.

Alice was so focused on attacking Molly that she missed the question Mr. Green just asked her. "Um, could you repeat that please?" She asked, even though she knew that he won't.

"Ms. Rivas, is my class not interesting enough for you?" He asks loudly. Everyone is staring, Molly is smiling. "Uh no sir, that's not it-" He interrupts even louder.

"Perhaps you would like to finish your daydreaming in detention?" Alice said nothing. "You've wasted enough of my time today Ms. Rivas. Go to the detention room right now." He said and wrote a slip.

Alice took it and walked slowly, wasting as much time as she could…

When she got there, she gave the slip to the teacher and sat down.

After 20 long minutes, the bell rang for lunch.

Alice headed for the cafeteria. She sat at a table with Eddie and Amy. There were also some of their close friends.

Alice put her face down on the table, hating Mr. Green. Eddie let her cry a bit. "It's Okay sweety everyone hates him." he said like he could read her mind.

Alice laughed and began to feel better. "It's not just him." Alice said and sat up. Molly too." Alice said and watched his face for his reaction. He frowned.

"What did she do?" he asked. Alice looked at Amy for help. She nodded and explained to Eddie what she told me on the phone this morning, all except the part about how I should watch him of course.

When Alice was done, he sighed. "Come on Alice, you don't know for sure that she even said any of that. It could have just been gossip." He said.

Amy glanced at her. Alice pulled out the note from class and gave it to him. He read it then, surprisingly, laughed. "Wow she's really putting herself out there isn't she?" He said and laughed again.

Eddie has an adorable laugh, but right then it was getting on her nerves.

Alice stared at Eddie. "You don't think this is something to worry about?" Alice asked, frustrated.

Eddie held his hand under her chin and looked into her eyes. "There is nothing to worry about, I love you, not her, okay?" He said with a smile. "Okay." Alice sighed.

Eddie then leaned down and kissed Alice. "Are you going to Bobby's party tonight?" Alice asked when he pulled away.

"Nah, I have practice tonight." Eddie said. "I hate that my boyfriend is a popular player." Alice said with a smile.

Eddie shrugged, smiling back. "Are you going?" Eddie asked. "After the day I've had, I could use a party", said Alice.

Alice went to the party and was happy to see all her friends. Sometimes is good to relaxed after the mess she encountered...

STORY 21

The Punch

When one is a teenager, anything upset you...

This happened, to Annie, one day after school. Annie was driving home feeling tired. She was still angry about an incident that happened in her English class.

Oh well. It's not like Annie got an after-school detention or anything. Ms. Pappas gave her extra homework on purpose. Ms. Pappas thought that she could ruin her night, ha!

Annie was going to ignore her extra homework. To Annie, it wasn't a big deal to fail English. She was doing fine in all her other classes.

When she got home, the second she stepped out of my car, her neighbor's huge dog, Blackie came running full speed towards her.

It jumped up and down. Blackie started licking her neck. "Blackie!" Annie yelled. She also tried to shove him off. Blackie was covered with mud. Now her jeans and t-shirt are covered with pawprints. She must change for the party anyway.

After a struggle with Blackie, Annie managed to force him off by throwing a stick. He ran after it.

Annie hurried towards the front porch. She got inside and slammed the door.

Her mom was at work and Ruben was still in school. She had the house all to herself. Annie kicked off her shoes, grab a bag of chips, and flop down on the couch. She turned on the TV and surfed through the channels until I got to MTV. A reality show was on.

It was showing an episode about summer romances. She fell asleep before the program ended.

Next thing she knew her mom and Ruben came through the front door complaining about Blackie...

The Price is Right was on by this time. Annie sat up and changed the channel. "How was your day, Annie?" Mom asked from the kitchen. Ruben jumped on the couch and turned on his Nintendo game.

"Ms. Pappas sent me to detention before lunch." Annie said and wandered into the kitchen with her. Her mom was unloading groceries, therefore, Annie helped.

"Oh, that's not good, what happened?" She asked, concerned. Annie said that she wasn't paying attention in class.

Ms. Pappas got pissed, then sent me to detention.

"I've had a lot of meetings with her, I can understand why you weren't listening to her." Mom said. Annie laughed.

After the groceries were put away, Annie went upstairs and searched through her closet for something to wear to the party.

Mary called her and said that she would pick her up around nine. She also informed Annie what she was going to wear. Annie had decided to go with a black baby doll t-shirt, and a short jean skirt and black heels. She went on about her skirt. That wasn't anywhere near as short as the ones Mary usually wears. They up ended their conversation.

Annie got dressed and waited for Mary. It was a little after nine when Mary pulled up in her car and beeped. Before they left, mom them stopped Annie.

Mom said, "Annie, please promise me that if you or Mary drink any alcohol you won't drive." Mom said while hugging them. They promise her mom and told her not to worry. They said that Willie's parties aren't usually that wild. They assured her. She shrugged. "Call me if you have any problems!" Mom yelled out.

Inside the car, Michael Jackson was blasting. Mary is obsessed with Michael Jackson. Annie is not knocking pop, but she is more of a heavy metal rock fan.

Mary approved of her outfit and gave her a thumbs up. As they drove, Lily beeped Annie. She didn't tell Mary.

At Willie's, the party was already in full swing. There were tons of people and the music loud. Willie was at the front door handing out designated driver bracelets.

"Hey guys, glad you could come." Willie said. Mary grabbed a bracelet and followed Annie inside. "You're not drinking?" Annie asked her over the music. "No, I have to babysit my cousins in the morning. I really don't need a hangover." She explained. I'm not a big drinker but Willie always has the best punch, spiced of course.

Annie grabbed a cup of it and walked through the crowd talking and dancing with different friends…

"Hey, I'm going to go talk to Ray for a while." said Mary. Ray was her latest crush. Her crushes never really last longer than a week or two.

"Have fun." Annie said with a wink. She rolled her eyes and walked over to him. Annie watched them talk briefly before going for another cup of punch.

Annie was almost done with her third cup before she decided to stop. Who likes hangovers anyway?

"Hi Annie, having fun?" Wanda asked. I knew Wanda because she was Mary's neighbor, and she has math with her. "Having a pretty good time, and you?" Annie asked feeling a buzz from the punch that was kicking in. Wanda grinned and held up her own cup of punch. "Oh yeah." She replied.

They talked for a bit before her friends started yelling from the stairs. "Be right there!" Wanda called back.

"Oh gosh Annie, I totally forgot to ask, do you want to play a game with us?" Wanda asked, her voice was slightly slurred.

"Well, I don't know" "Come on, please?" She interrupted. Annie glanced around for Mary. She saw her on a couch laughing with Ray. Annie decided to go with Wanda and her friends.

They went upstairs to a less crowded room with a big screen TV and a large, cushioned couch. The music wasn't as loud up there. There were a lot of the people chilling in different bedrooms doing who knows what.

They sat down on the couch. "So, what's the game?" Annie asked. "We're going to play 7 minutes in Paradise." A girl named Judy said. Annie got the impression that Judy was the leader of their group.

"Oh...Well I have a boyfriend so I'm out." Annie said frowning. "Please play Annie! "Wanda begged. "I can't, like I said, I have a boyfriend." Annie continued.

Wanda sighed. "Tell me uh, Annie, is your boyfriend here?" Judy asked, talking to Annie for the first time.

"No.." Annie said slowly. "You like to have fun, right?" She asked, smiling a little. "Of course, but-" "Then what could playing possibly hurt?" Annie pressed her lips considering.

Maybe it was the buzz she had, or something else but it didn't seem like such a bad idea to play.

Judy had already sent Wanda and some guy to the last empty bedroom. Someone would knock on the door when time was up. "So that's it then, you're playing." Judy said like it was final.

"Um. If I play, I don't have to uh, kiss anyone do I?" Annie asked. How naive is that? Ha ha. "What? Oh yeah sure, do whatever you want." Judy said.

If Annie hadn't been buzzed, she would have noticed the sarcasm in Judy voice, but she didn't. Annie was still thinking it over when Judy got up and locked the door.

"Hmm...Oh hey! Hey Mark come here for a second, I need you!" Judy called. Silence. "Please?" She called again after getting no response.

The second this Mark came into the room Annie had the impulse to straighten her outfit. He was gorgeous! He had brown hair that went a little past his ears, perfect nose, and dark eyes that looked black from where Annie was standing. He was wearing a long-sleeved gray shirt and dark blue jeans. His hands were in his pockets as he looked around the room.

"Would you mind doing me a little favor?" Judy asked him. He gave her an annoyed look. "Please?" She asked while tilting her head to the side. Looked like a flirty thing, I don't know.

"What do you want me to do?" He asked unkindly. "Well, we happen to be playing 7 minutes and I need a handsome guy for my friend over there." She said and gestured towards Annie.

Mark glanced at Annie briefly then looked away, making Annie feel shy.

"So... if you play, it will mean a lot-" said Judy "I'll play." He Mark said and walked out. Judy grinned at Annie.

Annie slowly followed both down the hall feeling nervous. Judy opened a door and turned on a light, then turned to Annie.

"Sorry I couldn't get you guys a bedroom, they're all uh, occupied." Judy said with a sly smile. It was a linen closet with only a couple shelves. It was clean luckily.

"I'll let you know when time is up." She said while pushing Mark and Annie inside and closing the door. Annie heard her walk away.

Annie looked shyly at her shoes.

"So, I-" Before Annie could finish her sentence or even think, Mark had put his arms around her waist. He then pulled Annie towards him and began kissing her fiercely.

At this point, Annie was completely frozen with shock...Well almost completely. Her hands had involuntarily dug into his thick hair keeping his face secured to hers.

Annie couldn't focus because everywhere his hands or lips touched her, it burned. Burned in a really great way. Making Annie want more. While one handheld her, his other crept up her leg and dug into her thigh making Annie moan.

Annie wrapped her legs around his waist. She wasn't in control of herself anymore. His hand left her thigh and went behind and under her skirt. Mark pressed his fingers in her keeping her very still.

Mark then pulled away from her lips and instead he began kissing slowly down her throat.

Annie tried to calm her breathing but failed. There was a loud knock on the door. They both froze...

"Times up!" Judy called. Mark brought his face up to her and stared into her eyes for a moment. Then he dropped his hands and turned without looking back. Mark walked out of the closet leaving Annie in shock...

STORY 22

Damage Control

Liz heart was pounding while she stared at Alberto. Liz couldn't believe that Alberto had simply walked out of their long-time relation. Oh my God...

What in the world just happened? Did Alberto leave her? Without an explanation? Damn!

Liz had to get out of her house and see if any of her friends knew about Alberto.

Liz slammed the door. Out of my way she yelled at her brother. She nearly stumbling and was falling. Liz rushed down the stairs past Milly and Jane's curious faces. They were all puzzled. Alberto was nowhere to be seen.

She went in a pub and scanned the crowd until I found Lillian. She was standing near the door talking to Tony. Liz clumsily pushed her way through everyone until she got to her.

"Oh, hey Liz, where have you been?" Lillian asked. "Uh, it doesn't matter, can we go somewhere?" Liz asked quickly fighting away all thoughts. She stared at Liz like she was an idiot.

"Um...Please?" Liz asked, feeling annoyed. Liz didn't have time to stand there while she stared at her like that. Lillian turned to Tony, said goodnight, and both girls left.

Lillian didn't speak to Liz the whole ride home, which was out of character for her. It's not like Liz would have been able to talk anyway. Liz was too consumed by thoughts of what happened with

Alberto. Lillian was confused. She dropped Liz off without a single word, then sped away.

Apparently, Liz pissed off her best friend somehow. Great.

Mom and Ben were asleep. Liz quietly made her way up to her room and passed out on her bed hoping she wouldn't have any dreams. Liz only wanted to sleep. She will deal with everything tomorrow.

The next morning, Liz woke up feeling like absolute crap. She must have had whiskey at the pub than she remembers. She got up and checked her messages fighting the urge to vomit the whole time. Two missed calls from Sonia. She only wanted to talk to Alberto, the love of her life. So, she thought....

Damn. She started freaking out. Why in the world would Alberto leave her? Liz was also wondering if Alberto had a new romance.

Liz had only one boyfriend. That boyfriend was Alberto. She only had kissed Alberto. He wanted more....

Stupid. Stupid. Stupid. Many times, he asked her to have sex. That would be the only way she can prove her love to him....

Now, is all over. She sighed and took an Aleve for her headache.

Liz called Lillian to see if she heard anything from Alberto. No answer. She tried again and still got no answer. It was only 10:30 a.m. She knew she was up. She had to go to her part time job early.

Liz guess Lillian is ignoring her, wonderful...

Liz started pacing around her bedroom. Okay, here's the facts: She got very drunk at the pub, made out with a gorgeous stranger and enjoyed every second of it...crap! Liz pissed Alberto off. Liz needs to do some major damage control.

What should she take care of first? Hmm...I suppose calling Lillian would be the easiest thing. She started thinking that maybe one of Alberto's friends were at the pub and saw her go into the with Allen. Of course, most of his friends were with Alberto. They were celebrating Sam's birthday. Liz knows no one could have seen anything, she hoped.

Liz picks up her cell and dial Sam's number. She was feeling nervous. "Mm hello?" He said drowsily. He must still be in bed. "Hey sleepyhead." Liz said hesitantly. "Oh, good morning beautiful." He replied. He didn't sound upset or mad. Liz sighed in relief.

"How was the party, anything wild happen?" Liz asked. Something wild happened in pub. Liz thought, then ground her teeth together.

They talked for a little while before she told him she had stuff to do. "Alright, see you, Liz." He said. Liz smiled. She hung up.

One thing out of the way, Liz said…

Once again, Liz tried to call Lillian. She still wasn't answering her phone. Liz gave up for a little while and got dressed. She went downstairs.

In the living room, her mom and Ben were on the couch watching cartoons. That's usually how Saturdays are at her house. Liz plopped down in the middle of them. She kept calling Lillian. Liz was hoping she would get annoyed and just answer.

Finally, after almost an hour of calling she answered. "What?!" She practically yelled. Liz got up and went out onto the front porch.

"Hey, don't yell at me, I wouldn't constantly be calling if you had answered the first time." Liz said. "What do you want?" Lillian asked, milder this time.

"First of all, why are you so mad at me?" "I have to go. I'm at work." She said. "Don't you dare hanging up on me without an explanation." She was silent for a moment before she sighed and spoke in a nicer tone.

"Come on Liz, last night was the first time Tony and I have had a chance to really talk and if you hadn't come over practically pushing me out the pub, he might have asked me out." She explained.

Liz rolled her eyes. Here she thought she was mad over some huge thing and it's about not getting asked out.

Liz told her that Alberto left her….

STORY 23

Let the Music Play

Marian got to the mall and went straight to the music store. It's one of her favorite stores to shop. That store has everything. It has Music, DVDs, magazines, what more do you really need though Marian.

In the store she looked around but didn't see Charlie. Marian was going to give Jane another call. She believes that she was lying. Marian turned around a corner and there, sitting crossed legged on the ground, was Charlie. It had been, what, maybe 12 hours since Marian last saw him. How in that short amount of time he had forgotten her.

He was so passionate. Wow....

Charlie was wearing black jeans and a white t-shirt; his super blonde hair was messy but still sexy.

Marian wondered briefly if that blonde was natural. He was reading the back of a cd so he didn't see her standing there. Marian was staring at him like a creep.

Marian took a deep breath and walked in front of him. He put the cd down. He saw her shoes and slowly looked up at her. It made her feel...I don't know...Strange having him look at her the way he was right now.

Once his eyes made it to her face, he half smiled but didn't say anything. Marian would have said something but him smiling like that made it hard to breathe.

Finally, Marian had to break the silence. "Um hi." she said uncertainly. Nothing from him except that smile. She tried again.

"So, I just" ... "Do you like music?" He interrupted. She was caught off guard. "Uh yeah, who doesn't?" Marian replied, a little out of breath.

Unexpectedly he grabbed her hand and pulled Marian down next to him. "Here listen to this." He said and took off the headphones and put them on her.

If I you thought I had been out of breath a few seconds ago, that was nothing compared to now...

His hands so close to her face. He leaned back and started the music. Marian heard the music, but she wasn't understanding any of the lyrics. Too worked up. God, I don't even know this guy and he makes her feel like this, how is that even possible? Charlie watched her face while the song played through...

Again, Marian tried to focus but with a hot guy watching her is hard to ignore. The song finished.

"Want to listen another one?" He asked. She was about to say yes but stopped and remembered the reason she came here in the first place.

She took the headphones off and gave them back to charlie. "No thanks, I came to talk to you actually." I said. He looked slightly confused. "How in the world did you know I was here?" He asked, turning to look at her.

Marian noticed while they were sitting on the floor that his eyes are dark blue. So dark that the irises almost blend in with his pupil.

Oh my God, she has been staring at him, examining his eyes this whole time like a weirdo. He cleared his throat and looked away, releasing her from his stare. She blushed, embarrassed.

"I, uh, knew you were going to be here because I called Jane." Marian explained. He shook his head. "She knows my every move." He mumbled under his breath.

"So, what did you want to talk about?" He asked looking at her again. Marian took a deep breath and kept her eyes on her hands while she spoke.

"Well, I need talk about our science project. What ever happened in the lab wasn't my fault. It would never happen again."

She said quietly. "What are you- oh right, the explosion. Ha, that was fun." He said with a laugh.

Marian looked up at him instantly getting angry. "It's not funny, I have a reputation." she said. He stopped laughing but still had a grin.

God, he looked sexy with that grin...Focus! "So, let me get this straight, what I think you're saying is that you are some kind of 'nerd'. You are always proper and never get in trouble. You came here to talk about, what exactly?" He asked.

"I really want to be your lab partner. When I played that stupid game in class, I had no idea that I could lose my scholarship. I'm not about to lose it over you or anybody. So, I'm asking that you don't say anything to anyone that it was my idea." Marian pleaded.

He didn't say anything for a few seconds. "What's your name?" He asked unexpectedly. "You don't even know my name?" Marian asked in disbelief. He has been in the same class for almost a month, and he doesn't know her damn name. Geez. "We didn't see each other exactly in the lab or around school." He said and grinned.

Marian sighed. "My name is Marian." He nodded slowly. "It's nice to officially meet you Marian, I'm Charlie." He said and shook her hand. He then stood up and smiled down at me. "Don't worry about the whole scenario in class. I won't say anything " He grinned before continuing. "You owe me." He said and walked away...

STORY 24

Prince Charming

The weekend went by without incidents. Rita spent it at home with her mom. Elizabeth came over for a little while on Sunday. Rita wanted to tell her all about what happened at the picnic so bad, but every time she tried, she was overwhelmed by guilt and thoughts of her looking at her like she was a trashy slut.

I've always told Elizabeth everything, but what if she judged me? I couldn't handle that. The guilt was even worse every time Sam called.

Rita hoped that on Monday the guilt would be easier to deal with, and things would go back to normal.

On Monday morning, Rita was brushing her teeth before going to work. Her mom came into the bathroom. She works at a Veterinary clinic as a receptionist, so she was wearing pink scrubs with pictures of kittens. Her frizzy blonde hair was pulled back in a ponytail.

"I need you to pick up Rickie from school and drop him off at your father's house." She said. Rita works at the mall in a general store, probably one of the easiest jobs in the world.

"Is everything alright Rita, you seem like something's been bothering you." She observed. She checked her make up in the mirror, waiting for her response. Rita spit some toothpaste out before answering. "I'm fine mom, don't worry." "Okay sweety, have a good day." She said and gave her a kiss on the cheek before leaving.

At work, Sam was waiting for her by her locker. She paused when she saw him. She took a deep breath then continued.

"Hey beautiful." He said and pulled her into a hug. "Did you see the game on Sunday? Totally awesome." He said, clearly thrilled.

She laughed. "Yeah, I did, all it is with you guys is football, football, oh, and football." I teased him.

"Not exactly, it's football and you." He said and kissed her. She leaned more into him, not feeling as guilty when he held her. She wrapped her arms around his neck, having to stand on her tiptoes to do it. He's so much taller than she is. He pulled his lips from mine, raising an eyebrow.

"What's gotten into you?" He asked with a laugh. "Um, nothing I just missed you, that's all." I said and pulled away. So, I'm a liar, oh well.

Rita really wants to have sex with Sam....

After lunch, Rita was looking for Mr. Smith, the supervisor. She had planned to surprise Sam.

"I'm thinking of going to the spa after work and getting a manicure, I haven't in a long time, want to come, my treat." Sharon asked. "No, I have to work late today, anyway, my nails are a lost cause." Rita said while looking at her own nails, or stubs to be more exact. Sharon laughed. "Woah, who is that?" She said and pointed.

Rita looked up in the direction she was pointing. Low and behold there was the most gorgeous man she has ever seen.

He was near office door talking to some of his friends. Rita never realized that he was working in the same store with her. Damn. She quickly tried to change the subject.

"Mr. Smith is late, I need to talk to him." Rita said and started walking fast.

Rita bit her lips nervously and watched Sharon approach the stranger. I couldn't hear what they were saying but something she said made him smile.

Rita tried not to be seen by the stranger. She didn't want to come off as a retard. So, she hid behind two tall guys from the store across the way.

She peeked around them in time to see Sharon walking away from stranger. Rita sighed in relief. She happened to glance back over in the stranger's direction. He was looking back at her. "Crap!" Rita gasped.

The guys she was standing behind both turned and looked at her, confused. "Uh sorry." Rita mumbled and stalked away from them. She sat down on a bench, feeling like an idiot.

A tap on her shoulder made Rita jump. She turned to see the stranger standing there with a smirk on his face.

"So, is uh, whitestream a friend of yours?" He asked, nodding to Sharon, who was talking to Megan.

Rita stood up and faced him. "Yes, she's my best friend actually, so what do you want?" Rita asked, the question coming out meaner than she intended. "Hey what's up with the attitude?" He asked with a laugh.

Rita sighed. "Sorry, but I can't be seen talking to you, I have a boyfriend." He shrugged. "Yeah, you've mentioned the 'boyfriend', does he not allow you to talk to other people?" He asked, a little sarcasm in his tone. Rita got angry.

"Why don't you mind your own business and stay away from me." Rita said and started walking away. "Oh, come on what happened to us at the picnic? I thought we might have a chance of becoming friends." He said while following her. Rita turned around to say something and almost ended up walking right into him.

"Considering how we met, I don't think it's possible for us to even be friends." Rita said and put her hands on her hips. "What? Oh, you mean because of the kissing?" He asked, a huge smirk on his face. Rita was majorly blushing, she didn't answer, just stared at her shoes.

"Come on Rita, that's even more reason for us to be friends, all the pressure is off now that we already made out at the picnic" "Shh!" Rita hissed while making sure nobody she knew was around them. He smiled.

God, all this guy did was smile. Not that she minded, his smile was gorgeous. "Not so loud." She warned, still checking around. He sighed. "Listen Rita, a lot of people go to picnic and play around with others. It's not a big deal." He said with another shrug. It was like he was trying to make her feel better. Weird. Rita looked up at him while he continued.

"Stop beating yourself up over nothing and let's be friends." ...

STORY 25

Halloween

The Halloween dance had really left Iris feeling like crap.

Iris was lying on her bed wanting to just forget the whole thing. It was as if had even happened. She rolled over and stuck her face into a pillow.

First Larry leaves her there to be his friends' personal driver. Then Allen drops her for Adele.

Unfortunately, Iris was more upset about the second thing. Adele had called her a few times, probably to tell her how fantastic her night had gone with Larry.

She didn't know, she didn't answer. If she had answered her calls, she would have been very upset.

She hates being angry with her best friend, especially when she doesn't even know she is angry.

Her mom was at work, she had left early. Louis was downstairs playing his Xbox. Iris was in bed wishing she could redo the past two months.

Tonight, Halloween, her mom had asked her if she could give out candy to the kids that came to the door.

Trick or treaters, little monsters were coming to her house asking for candy. It was just what she needed to deal with today.

Her dad had sent her a picture of Lilly in her costume on my phone. She was going to be a ladybug. She did look adorable, but even that didn't do much to improve Iris mood.

It was nearly noon when Iris finally left her bedroom. Lying in bed was depressing her.

Iris went downstairs and chilled on the couch with Louis.

"Want to play with me?" Louis asked, gesturing to the Xbox. "No thanks Louis." Iris replied weakly. He examined her. "You okay sis?" He asked, looking concerned. Iris loves Louis so much. He's like the perfect brother.

After her parents got divorced Iris and Louis sort of banned together, taking care of each other when were depressed or upset. Iris smiled.

"Just had a bad night." Iris said. He frowned. "Did Larry do something, because if he did, I'll beat him up if you'd like." He said and winked.

Iris and Louis both laughed. "Naw, I'm fine." Iris said and patted the top of his head. Iris watched him play Halo for a long time. They had lunch then went back to the living room and put on TV. SpongeBob was on. "You ever notice how many facial expressions Spongebob has?" Iris asked with a laugh. "Yeah." Louis replied with a grin. It was starting to get late in the day.

Both Louis and Iris were still in their pajamas. Talk about a wasted day...

About 5 PM, there was a knock on the front door. Iris sighed and went to it. Probably some of the first kids to get candy. Iris opened the door to see Allen standing on the porch. Iris stared at him totally surprised.

"Trick or treat." Allen said with a smile. My eyes narrowed. "What? you are not going to offer me some candy?" Allen asked, smile fading slightly.

"How did you know this was my house?" Iris asked rudely. Seeing his handsome face just made her feel hurt all over again. She knew she had no right to feel that way, He's not my boyfriend. He frowned at my tone.

"Allen asked Adele. I told her that I needed to talk to you," he said. Adele, of course. Now Iris was really pissed. They talked about her.

"So... Can I come in?" He asked when Iris didn't say anything else. "No." Iris simply answered.

Allen sighed. "Okay Iris, something is obviously wrong, so instead of just glaring at me, why don't you tell me what it is?" said Allen.

He looked kind disappointed that Iris hadn't invited him in. Good. "I don't really want to talk to you Allen or see you for that matter. If you could just leave, I'd be a lot happier." Said Iris and started to close the door.

Allen put his foot in the way to block it. "I'm not leaving until I know what exactly I did to piss you off like this." He said, a bit of impatience in his tone. Iris chewed on the inside of my cheek not meeting his eyes.

What could Iris possibly say? I'm mad because my best friend likes you, and I think you might like her back? Seeing her arms around your neck makes me feel sick?

Lately Iris wish Larry didn't exist so I could be with you? God, this suck. "Oh." He mumbled suddenly.

Iris looked up at him. "You're mad because...Yeah, I see now." He was talking to himself. "This has to do with Adele, doesn't it?" He asked gently. "No." Iris said quickly, but her eyes dropped to the ground. He sighed deeply. "Iris, are you upset that I danced with her?" He asked.

"I um, well I think that if you two are going to date then just say so." I made up, avoiding the question. Iris wants him to know that she has a thing for him.

Allen looked at her for a long time that Iris finally had to ask what he was thinking about.

"Well...I was just thinking about the first football game. How mad you were at me. Last night, I guessed I flatter myself to think that you were maybe, a bit jealous of Adele." He explained quietly.

"You think I'm jealous?" I asked, stunned. Apparently, Iris wasn't as good at hiding her crush on him as she thought. He shrugged, staring at her, watching her reaction. "I'm not jealous Larry." Allen lied.

"It's weird having my friends like each other, that's all, I'm not sure of how to handle it." Iris continued. "You...You do like her, right?" Iris asked, hoping her voice wouldn't give away how bad the question was burning inside her.

"Who? Oh Adele, oh yeah course, what's not to like?" He asked with a shrug. Iris felt like a deflated balloon at hearing his words.

An ache started in her chest, painful, too hard for her to continue with this conversation, so I asked the first question I could think of. "So why did you come to my house again?"

Iris voice even sounded toneless. "Uh, right, see I wanted to ask if you'd like to go trick or treating with me?" He said, a small smile returning to his face. "But if you're already planning on staying home, it's not a big deal." He said, his eyes roaming over her pajamas. I blushed.

"Actually, I didn't get dressed today." I said, embarrassed. He smiled more genuinely this time. "Great. Would you like to come with me then?" He asked hopefully. Iris considered. It sounded so much better than staying home to pass out candy to little brats.

Iris started for the stairs when she noticed Allen following her. Iris turned, feeling her face get hot. "Um, wait down here while I change." Iris said. He raised an eyebrow.

"I can't wait in your room?" He asked, confused. Iris stared at him; cheeks probably close to catching fire now. "No, That's where I'm getting dressed." Iris mumbled uncomfortably.

"I'll come with you; I won't look." Allen said with the most mischievous look she ever seen. Iris smacked his arm. "Go!" She said. He laughed and went back down the stairs.

Did he think he could just come and watch her get dressed? He has some nerve. The thought of Allen in her bedroom while she was getting naked... Iris was close to fainting.

She found some black jeans and a warm long sleeved brown shirt. She combed her hair through, lounging on the couch all day had done nothing good for her hair. Iris grabbed her jacket and went downstairs.

Allen was sitting next to Louis on the couch, both laughing. smiled at the scene. Allen looked up and met my eyes with a smile. "Ready? "He asked. "Yeah, um you don't mind if I got out with Allen for a little while do you Louis?" I asked, unsure. Louis shrugged.

"You can handle passing out candy?" He rolled his eyes. "Go have some fun Iris, I can figure out how to pass candy out to little kids, besides, you need to have some fun sis after all the moping around you did today." Louis said.

Allen raised an eyebrow. Iris quickly hangs around the door. They both laughed again. Allen followed Iris outside, down the steps to the sidewalk. "Which way?" Iris asked, determined not to meet his eyes. He pointed and she started in that direction. They passed a few houses but didn't stop right away.

"Here." Allen said and gave her one of the masks. Iris glanced up to see that his was already on. Iris tried to repress a smile but failed. Damn him for making her feel better. She pulled the mask on, and Allen led the way up to the first house.

After almost half an hour, their pockets were full of candy. They should have grabbed a bag or something. Ha. "So... You were moping around today?" Allen asked, his voice muffled by the mask. Iris wondered when he was going to bring that up.

Iris sighed. "No... Well sort of I guess." Iris said and sighed again. "May I ask why?" Iris bit lip before answering. "Well, Larry did leave me at the dance early."

Allen turned his masked face in my direction. "Huh, you know what, I wouldn't have left you at the dance if I had been your date." he said thoughtfully. Iris frowned, but of course, he couldn't see. "You did leave me though." Iris pointed out quietly.

"What? No, I didn't." He said, surprised. "Oh yes you did, you stopped dancing with me to go with Adele." Iris explained, feeling embarrassed to have to say it.

"Oh...I suppose so, but I wasn't your date." Allen said, almost sounding angry. They were quiet for little bit. Finally, he sighed.

"Even though I wasn't your date, I apologize for leaving you alone." He said in a formal voice. Iris couldn't help but smile. Iris got the feeling Allen didn't like having people angry at him, even over little things.

Iris suddenly felt stupid for spending the whole day moping. So, he danced with Adele, big deal. I'm going to have a long talk with myself later about what's worth getting upset over and what's not.

They went to tons of houses. There was an old lady that was feeling bad for them because she didn't have candy. She gave them money instead.

They eventually had enough candy to eat until Christmas. Iris decided to go back to her house. When they got there, Allen he hesitated on the front porch. Iris pulled off her mask and gave it back to him. He kept his own though. Not sure why.

"Tonight, was really a lot of fun." Iris said, mostly to fill the silence that had taken over. This would be the part where they would kiss goodnight if this was a date, but it wasn't. It was just them standing there awkwardly instead.

"Yeah." Allen replied, nodding his head. Iris felt ridiculous talking to him with that mask on his face. "See you at school then?" Iris said and smiled a little. He pulled his mask off and stared at his feet briefly before meeting my curious eyes.

Something in his expression made her heart speed up. Like he wanted to say something, or perhaps do something. He was chewing on his lip, very sexy by the way.

Iris felt like she couldn't move. She was staring into his eyes feeling lost. He leaned towards her, slow motion it felt like. His eyes never leaving mine. Just as he was inches away, she happened to come to her senses and turned her head away.

His lips ended up just barely touching her cheek, but that was enough to make it burn nicely. Why hadn't that burning feeling just been a figment of my imagination in the closet? Why did it feel the same when she was sober? Damn! Damn! Damn! He jerked away from her quickly. "I, um I don't know what came over me Iris! I'm sorry, it won't happen again. I promise!" He said fast, making the words kind of blur together.

We both pointedly looked in different directions, both blushing. Iris had never seen Alle blush before, huh. It made him seem less like supermodel and more, Iris didn't know, more human, down to earth. You know what I mean? She had to take a few deep breaths before responding.

"It's okay Allen, really, nothing happened. I'm not mad, it's... Just normal, right?" Iris said, trying my best to make things less awkward. He nodded slowly, not looking at me though.

"Anyway, let's just forget about it, we are teenagers after all." Iris said with a shaky laugh. She was trying to make it seem like joke. God I'm an idiot. Allen returned her smile, but it seemed forced.

"Yeah, you're right, just stupid kids, see you on Monday, kay?" He asked, finally meeting my eyes. Iris nodded, relieved. She went inside the house the minute he walked away, and practically fell onto the couch.

Louis gave her a look, but sensing she didn't want to talk about it, he didn't say anything. What a great brother.

She couldn't believe that Allen just tried to kiss her. Iris wanted to kiss him too…

STORY 26

Sixteen and Never Been Kissed

November was turning in colder and with more rain than October....

Henry and Louise have been pretty much in silent and agreed not to mention or talk about what happened between them.

Unfortunately, Louise blushed a lot more when she was around Henry. He seemed to have chilled out a bit and inappropriate with his jokes. He hasn't told anyone about their encountered in the locker room. Louise wanted to keep her mind off what happened between them.

Not that spending time with her old boyfriend was a punishment, however, spending so much time with him, especially time alone together, she felt like she was giving him the wrong idea.

Louise hated feeling like a tease every time they stopped making out. He constantly reassured her that he wasn't angry, but come on, she was like an Ice Princess.

She did want to have sex obviously; she was only sixteen. She was controlling her hormones. Many times, she thought about sleeping with her ex-boyfriend, all the time, but lately the mere thought of actually doing it scared her a bit.

What if she got pregnant? Stuck with a kid in high school? This was always on her mind...

Louise has watched enough Teen Moms to know she didn't want that. She didn't want caught a disease. Louise trusted her ex completely. That was in the past.

Even though Louise was a young teenager, she was well aware of having intercourse and the consequences. It's the possibility of getting sick disease that she didn't trust. Those were both minor concerns to her.

The thing that worried Louise most was sleeping with ex and then…What exactly? What if he got bored and left her? What if she realized she was the one bored?

Louise really loved, Milton, her ex-boyfriend. Milton was her first love. God, she must had watched way too much reality television…

Let me tell what happened to Louise to change her mind about sleeping around at a young age….

It's a Saturday night and Milton and Louise are together, at his house. They were making out on the couch. Milton has two older brothers, both already moved out and going to college. His father is a small-time lawyer, and his mother showcases houses. She sets homes for sale up with furniture, so they look nice to potential buyers or something. They're both nice and, also, at work.

Milton is kissing Louise under her chin when Louise happened to glance around the living room. Both of Milton's dogs are sitting next to the couch staring at them. Louise began to feel all awkward. They're animals, but still...

"Um, Milton?" she said, shifting uncomfortably. "Yeah?" "The dogs, they're um, watching us." Louise mumble.

Milton raised his head and laugh. "Don't worry sweety, they don't care." He said and leaned down to kiss her, but Louise held up her hand. "They might not care, but I do." she said and sat up.

Milton rolls next to Louise looking disappointed. Lately that's usually his expression though. She feels bad yet again for not giving Milton what he wants. It's hard to let down the people you love. "I'm sorry." Louise whispers.

Louise always apologizing after they make out has started to become routine. Milton sighs and shakes his head…

"Louise, you need to seriously stop saying you're sorry all the time, If you're not ready, that's that." He said. Louise could detect the disappointment that had been in his expression. They sat on the couch next to each other in silence for a while.

"So... What do we do now?" Louise asked, feeling irritated. He glances at her because of her tone. "A movie maybe?" He suggests. Headlight's flash across the living room wall.

One of his parents is home. He checks out the window and groans. "Damn, it's my mom." Louise stands up and straighten her shirt.

"Hey, you don't have to leave yet, mom won't mind if you stay." He says and grabs my hand.

Louise looks at him. "I know, but I should probably get home, stuff to do." she say. He stands up and wraps his arms around her waist. Louise leans into him, he's so warm.

"How about I come over tomorrow night and we can rent a movie, just the two of us, what do you say?" She smiles, feeling better. "Sure thing." Louise says and tilts her head up for a kiss.

Just as his lips touch hers his mom comes through the door. Louise steps away from Milton unhappily.

"Oh, hi Louise." She says with a small smile. Her hair is all windblown. The dogs are barking like crazy trying to get her attention.

"Hello Mrs. Brown." Louise says and returns her smile.

After a few minutes of the usual chit chat, How is school? How's your family? Louise says goodbye to Milton and goes home.

When Louise gets home, her phone rings. It's Henry. She hesitates, just for a moment, before answering. "Hello?" He sighs deeply before speaking. "I'm lonely."

Louise goes up to her bedroom and lays on the bed, feeling like this conversation might take a while. "What are you doing?" Louise asks, finding a magazine. "Chilling on my bed, being lonely." He says.

Louise feels bad because he does sound kind of depressed.

"That's weird, I'm chilling on my bed too." "Oh really? Hmm... What are you wearing?" He asks, Louise knows he's smiling. She smiles too.

"Tonight's the night I usually put on my leather cat woman suit and dance around my room." Louise answers dramatically...

"Cat woman suit, huh? With the whip and everything?" He asked eagerly. She laughed. He joined her.

Once his laughter died away, he sighed again. "So why are you so lonely?" Louise asked. Louise doesn't like Aaron sad. "Well, I called most of my friends, they all have stuff to do, and frankly, being all by myself at my house sucks." He said. "Where are your parents?" He doesn't answer.

"Henry? You still there?" "My parents are, you know, busy and stuff." He said indifferently. Louise got the impression that he didn't want to talk about his parents, so I dropped it.

"Is there something you want me to do?" Louise asked. "You could come over, keep me company." He said. Louise bit her lips. Henry and her, in his empty house together. Not a good idea. He seemed to realize it was a bad idea too.

"Right, um, that's not going to happen." He said, sounding embarrassed. "Yeah." Neither of us spoke for a minute. "So... Do you have any plans for tomorrow?" He asked. Louise jumped on the change of subject gratefully.

"Actually, Milton is going to come over around seven or so, we're going to watch a movie." she said. "Oh." He mumbled. Louise felt bad again. "Do you have any plans?" she asked, already knowing the answer. "Nope. Well, I will if my friends stop avoiding me." He said.

Louise could hear some resentment. She wonders why they were avoiding Henry. Another long silence between them. Louise hated Henry being alone and sad. It made the ache in her chest hurt even more.

"I didn't want to say anything, but my friends are actually kind of pissed at you." He said, pulling Louise from her thoughts.

"What?" I asked, totally surprised. "Because of the stupid party, they don't like how I, how did they put it, 'came to your rescue', yeah." He explained.

Great, now Louise felt even worse, she was the reason Henry was alone and sad....

"But you didn't do anything wrong! That guy was drunk, and he kept knocking into me. You only stopped things from getting bad." Louise tried to reason.

He laughed bitterly. "Apparently my friends aren't very big fans of your boyfriend or his friends for that matter." He said. "Maybe you should get new friends." Louise suggested angrily. "You think?" he said sarcastically.

Louise played back against her pillows trying to calm down. He sighed. "Don't get angry." He said. "Too late." Louise replied. "My friends...They're not as bad as you're probably thinking right now, just, a lot of shit has happened between them.

Your boyfriend excluded of course." He added hastily. Louise sighed. "Okay, whatever, but I think they're jerks for being mad at you." Louise said, feeling the anger slowly leave. "Yeah, Henry agrees."

"Hey Henry?" "Yes?" "Would you...Would you like to join Milton and I tomorrow night to watch a movie?" Louise asked. He seemed to think it over.

"I don't know Louise; I got the impression that it was going to be a movie for two." He said. It was, but she felt bad. "No, you can come too." Louise insisted. "Uh, I'm not really sure...Milton probably won't want me there." He said. "I want you to come, okay?" Louise said, trying to be forceful.

"Well then, how could I refuse?" Henry said, Louise could tell he was smiling.

Finally, Louise had been the one to cheer him up for once.

Louise got up the next morning. She made sure it was okay for both Milton and Henry could come over. Her mom said yes. She always says yes.

Louise spent most of the morning in her room trying to get dressed and ready. She changed outfits like five times before deciding on a pair of dyed jeans and a white V-neck shirt.

She helped mom around the house doing a bunch of chores and stuff to make sure the house was clean. They had dinner and about six. Louise loaded the dishwasher when they were finished.

There was nothing left to do but wait for her friends...

Louise started to get nervous. She hadn't told Milton that Henry was coming over. She hoped he wouldn't be angry.

A little after seven there was a knock on the door. Louise opened it to find Henry smiling...

"Hey, I know I'm early, but I brought snacks!" He said and held up a bag of pretzels and a pack of mountain dew. "Thanks." Louise said and pointed to the end table in the living room. He walked over and dropped his snacks onto the table.

Her mom came in from the kitchen. "Oh hello, you must be Louise's friend Henry." She said smiling. Henry returned her smile with an even more friendly one and shook her hand. "Nice to meet you Ms. Reid, I should have known that Louise being so beautiful, of course she'd have to have an even more beautiful mother." He said in his most sweet, sexy voice. Her mom blushed slightly.

Louise bit her lip. He called me beautiful. Oh God. "Well thank you very much. Louise, could I talk to you really quick." Mom said. She went and sat on the couch to give us some privacy. "Yeah mom?" "I have to work early in the morning, so I'll be in bed, if you need anything just holler.

Oh, and sweetheart, that boy-" She nodded to the living room. "Is a major cutie." She said and gave me a wink. Louise sighed, rolling her eyes. "I know." She chuckled, understanding. She left to her bedroom and closed the door.

Louise sat down on the couch, making sure there was a decent amount of space between Henry and her.

"So what movie are we going to watch?" He asked, folding his arms over his chest. Louise shrugged. "I don't know, we're just going to go through the movie rentals on demand." she said. He nodded.

Neither of them spoke for a moment. "You didn't tell Milton I was coming tonight, did you?" He guessed. Louise shook her head, making him laugh. "Will he be mad?" "I really hope not." she said and glanced at the door because there was a knock.

Louise got up and opened the door. Milton pulled her into a tight hug right away.

"Hey, ready for a good night?" He asked, smiling his adorable little half smile. Louise felt guilty. "Um, you don't mind if someone joins us, do you?" she asked hesitantly. "Who, Louis?" "Uh no, um, my friend Henry." she said.

Milton followed her eyes to the couch. Henry waved smiling pleasantly. "Oh." Milton said. His smile seemed to have vanished in an instant. "I'm sorry, he was lonely, and his friends are mad at him for helping us at the dance, I felt guilty." I explained quietly.

Milton didn't say anything, just looked at her. She met his stare, hoping he could see how sorry she was.

Finally, he sighed and went into the living room. He plopped down on the couch and patted the spot in the middle of them. Louise let out a sigh of relief and sat down.

Milton put his arm around her shoulders, making Louise feel a little irritated. It was as if he was trying to show Henry that she was taken.

"Sorry for interrupting your night, but when Louise asked me to come, I mean, could you say no to her?" Henry said. He was clearly asking for trouble.

Milton pretended he didn't hear him and turned on the TV. Louise stepped on Henry's foot without Milton seeing a thing. Henry just grinned. Milton scrolled through all the movies making suggestions.

"Hmm...How about that one movie with Russel Crowe, you know, the newest one?" "The Next Three Days?" Louise asked. "Yup that's the one." Milton said and waited.

What a random movie selection. "Sounds good to me." Louise said and curled more into his Milton's side.

"Alright then." He put it on and turned off the lamp. As the movie played, Louise couldn't help but feel like it was more of a movie for couples. The guy is willing to do whatever takes to get his wife out of prison because he loves her so much. Come on. It was an odd experience to watch a movie with your boyfriend on one side, and your friend/the guy you made out with in school.

The movie ended at 10. Mom was sound asleep, and Louis was spending the night at dad's house. Henry clapped at the credits. "Great movie, definitely better than I expected. Russel Crowe, good actor, gotten a bit pudgy though, still a cool dude." Henry said and smiled at Milton and Louise.

Milton looked at him like he wasn't sure of what to think of him. Louise sighed. "Now I have to use the bathroom which is... Where?" Henry asked and stood, stretching as he did. "Last door down the hall." Louise said yawning. He nodded and left.

"Finally, a moment alone." Milton said and pulled Louise against his chest. "Sorry the night didn't go as you probably planned." Louise said.

"What, spending the night with my girlfriend and her odd friend? That's exactly how I wanted to spend this night." He said sarcastically and kissed her neck. "He's not odd." Louise said, a little defensively.

Milton raised an eyebrow. "Well, okay maybe he's just a tiny bit odd, but he's really cool once you get to know him." she said with a smile. "Speaking of getting to know him, how did you guys become friends?" Milton asked, puzzled. "Uh, we talked some in gym, like I said, he's cool." Louise said.

"Whatever, kiss me." Milton said making her laugh. His lips were more fierce than normal, not that she minded. Milton wasn't usually too, wild. He was calm and collected almost all the time.

Louise's hands clenched the front of his shirt. His hand gripped the back of her neck making her moan slightly. "Woah, uh sorry." She pulled away from Milton to see Henry turn his back on them.

Louise blushed deeply and slid off Milton's lap. "I'm going to get going, thanks for letting me join movie night." Henry said and started for the door. "Wait, you don't have to go yet." Louise said halfheartedly.

Henry gave her a smile. "Naw I'm tired, thanks though. Good night." He said and walked out the door.

Louise sat back next to Milton feeling annoyed. Henry says he's so lonely but leaves as quick as he can. Milton and Louise kissed in front of him, big deal…

Louise wondered if their kissing upset him or something. Sigh. Milton was smiling, like he was satisfied.

"Hmm…Looks like it's just you and me now." Milton said and tried to kiss her again. Louise moved out of his way. "What's wrong?" He asked, surprised. "Did you know Henry was coming back from the bathroom when you kissed me?" she asked, starting to get pissed. He looked guilty.

"Why did you do that Milton?" she demanded. "Come on Louise, the guy has a crush on you, it's obvious. I just thought I should remind him you're taken." He said.

Louise could tell he was on the edge of anger too. "That wasn't very nice." she said. We glared at each other.

After a while of glaring silence Milton sighed. "I should go home." He said and got off the couch. "Can I at least have a goodbye hug?" He asked awkwardly. Louise just looked up at him. "Please Louise? You know, I could die on my way with you being mad at me." He pointed out. She grinded her teeth but got up and hugged him anyway.

Milton wrapped his arms tightly around her. "Sorry for making you mad, really. I won't do anything like that again." He said quietly. "Promise?" "Yeah, I promise." he said. Louise sighed. "Okay fine, you're forgiven." she said. "Good. I love you, Louise." He said and kissed her forehead. "I love you too Milton."

He leaned down and kissed her one last time before leaving for the night. Louise felt kind of put out. Milton thought Henry had a crush on her. He obviously didn't know Henry.

STORY 27

The Complicated Teenager

Maggie spends Saturdays with Tina, and Sundays with Mike. She has long phone conversations with Anthony almost every night...

Maggie is a very busy girl. She works at a grocery store on random weekdays and stays with her dad as much as possible. She has decided to put the whole 'Anthony's having a crush on her thing' out of her mind. It just seemed so impossible for him to crush on a girl like her.

Anthony is a strange individual. He never dated anyone, which was weird. He constantly has girls around him; he'd laugh and flirt with them, but when it came down to dating any of them, he didn't.

Tina was still completely obsessed with him. Tony had gotten a new girlfriend so her chances of her getting with him were reduced.

Tina had started talking about possibly getting a job at the grocery store with Maggie, which, it would be cool to have her best friend there, but that would mean her spending even more time pestering her about Anthony.

Maggie kind of hoped that Anthony would start dating someone at least, just to get Tina off her back. Well...No actually, Louise did not want Anthony with someone. To be clearer, with someone other than her.

God. Being a teenager is so complicated. There are always stupid feelings and hormones making one mess out of you.

It was almost Thanksgiving. Maggie was going to spend it with her mom. Her dad was going out of town on business trip and won't be back for some time.

Mike was also leaving for a couple of days to see his grandparents. Thanksgiving was a week away. Her mom is never really prepared for anything. They still didn't have any food for the big dinner. Maggie was going to the store to pick up all the stuff we needed.

Mike was busy packing with his family, so I asked Anthony to come with her to the store. He hadn't mentioned any plans with his family, so he was free, plus he made things so much more fun.

He showed up at her house at 9 a.m. Maggie likes doing things early, save the rest of her day. Her mom was still sleeping.

Maggie got in her car, Anthony in the passenger's seat. "Where are we all going?" He asked once they pulled out of the driveway. "Market, and the post office for my mom." Maggie said and checked her side mirror. Safety first. "Cool. Hey, do you think we could make a quick little stop before the other stuff." He asked.

"Sure, where to?" Maggie asked and glanced at him. He was smiling a little. "There's an um, body shop down the street from the drug store." He said. "Body shop?" she said, raising an eyebrow. "Well tattoo shop actually." He muttered and looked out the window.

Maggie stared at him in shock. She remembered to keep her eyes on the road. "You're getting a tattoo? Albert, are you sure you want to do that, I mean, you're not even eighteen yet, you might regret it." Maggie tried to reason. He laughed. "I've done a lot of things I regret Maggie, but that's not the point. Besides, stop freaking out I'm not getting a tattoo, I was thinking about getting a piercing. They do both at the shop." He said.

"Oh." Maggie mumbled. A piercing wasn't as bad I suppose, if he didn't like it, he could always take it out.

Maggie felt relieved. "So... What do you want to get pierced?" she asked hesitantly. "Oh, probably my bottom lip." he said. "Your lip? But you have nice lips!" she said without thinking.

He looked over at her. Her face turned red. He laughed. "Yeah, I do have pretty nice-looking lips, is what you probably meant." He said still chuckling. Maggie nodded mutely, feeling incredibly embarrassed. "Anyway, I've wanted a piercing for a long time, I figured today was a good day to do it." He continued. They drove in silence for a bit until she pulled up to the tattoo shop.

"Anthony, don't you need permission from your parents to get a piercing?" Maggie. "Don't worry about it, I know the chick who does the stuff." He said and held open the shop's door for her.

They went inside. It was a typical tattoo place, pictures of examples on the walls, some couches to wait for your turn. There was only one other person in there getting work done on his arm.

They went up to the counter. A girl with spiked neon blue hair came out of the back room. When she saw Anthony, she grinned.

"Hey blondie-boy, I was wondering when you would come in here." She said and slung her arm around his shoulder.

Just that simple touch between them made Maggie's hands ball up into fists. Jealousy is a bitch…

"Hey Barbie, sorry I haven't been around in a while, but I'm back and I'd like to get my lip pierced." He said. She surveyed his face, making Maggie even more jealous.

"Hmm, I always seen you more as an ink guy rather than a metal face." She mused. She glanced at Maggie then back to Anthony. "Oh right, Barbie this my good friend Maggie." he said, smiling in her direction. She smiled and nodded to her. Maggie gave a smile in return.

"You want your lip done then, huh?" She said and stepped away from him. Maggie sighed. "Yep, can you do it today, or do I have to come back?" He asked, following her to the back of the shop. Maggie followed as well. "Of course, I can do it today, it's not like I have anything else to do!" She laughed and gestured to the almost empty shop.

"Damn holiday, makes everyone leave town or spend time with their family. Nobody wants any body art!" She said sarcastically. She gestured to a special reclining chair for Anthony to sit. Maggie sat next to him.

"I'll get my things and be right back, just stay put." Barbie said and went back to the front of the shop, leaving just Anthony and Maggie.

"Having any second thoughts?" Maggie asked hopefully. She didn't really like the idea of Anthony's lip being somewhat ruined. He shook his head looking amused. "Are you sure?" He laughed. "I'm absolutely sure Maggie, chill."

Barbie came back into the room holding this instrument with a large needle at the end. Maggie shivered involuntarily.

"Before I stick you, you need to pick out a piercing to put in to keep the hole open. You can get a new one in a week." She said and held out a metal tray full of different rings.

"Hmm, Maggie can you pick one out for me? I don't really care." He said. Maggie leaned over and examined the tray. She picked a black sliver ring and gave it to Barbie. "Good choice." She grinned.

"Alrighty then Anthony, sit back and don't move. I'm not going to lie, it's going to hurt a little bit, but I know you are tough." She said while patting his shoulder.

He did as she said. Barbie held the needle up to Anthony's mouth. That's the time Maggie had to look away. Needles, Ugh. There was a slight click noise and Barbie sat back.

Maggie thought it was safe to look. Anthony was massaging around his mouth, and the ring she had picked out was now placed on the bottom left side of his lip. Even though the area was kind of puffy he looked, well, damn good.

Barbie gave him a small hand mirror to examine his face. "Well, what do you think?" She asked. He nodded his head. "Awesome Barbie, seriously, I really like it." He said and grinned, then winced slightly. "Good I'm glad you do, and since you've been my only customer, like all day, I'm not even going to charge you." She said. "No, I can pay-" She interrupted him by shaking her head. "Nope buddy, this one's on the house." She gave him some liquid stuff to keep his piercing clean and they left.

As they drove to the market Anthony was smiling to himself...

STORY 28

Giving Thanks

The week went by quickly. Everyone was leaving the city to visit their relatives....

Mayra got a call from many of her friends. They all wished her and her family a Happy Thanksgiving before leaving.

Mayra had called Billy almost every day to make sure he hadn't changed his mind about coming over for dinner.

She had talked to him into coming early to watch the big game with her brother. Mayra guessed she was quite persistent. Oh well, there's a lot of worse things she could be.

On Thanksgiving morning Mayra and her mom got up extra early to start preparing dinner. For some unknown reason, everybody eats early on this specific holiday.

Mayra had put on a pair of gray jeans and a shirt. It had tiny painted handprints all over it to represent turkeys.

Mayra had never been much of a cook but of course, neither was her mom. They kind of just guessed what to do with the food and ingredients.

Since that complete fiasco was still somewhat fresh in her mind, Mayra handled all the stuff that involved the stove and oven, while her mom stirred and mixed. Luckily there was only going to be four of them eating. She couldn't imagine cooking like this for a whole bunch of people. Soon everything was baking and all we had to do was wait for it to be done.

When Mayra told her mom about Angelo joining them, she didn't mind in the slightest. She thinks because he called her beautiful when he came one afternoon after school. He had won some major points.

He showed up exactly the time she asked him. The time was right before football started. The four of us gathered into the living room around the TV to watch.

Her mom spent most of the game answering phone calls from various family members. Ben was seated in between Angelo and her. She was relieved of that especially since he had gotten that his new hair cut. He had gotten quite a bit hotter.

Mayra didn't need to be right up against him. Ben had told Angelo how cool he thought the hair cut was. Her mom had also mentioned that it suited him nicely.

How many mothers compliment haircuts? During half time Ben joined mom in the kitchen to get things ready, since the food was almost finished.

Mayra had to admit that she was having a really good time. "Thanks for inviting me." Angelo said, giving her a grateful smile.

"See, I promised you would." Mayra replied. She felt happy to have made Angelo happy. As corny as that sounds.

"What is Willy doing today?" He asked, stretching out next to her. "He's out of town with his mom and dad visiting his grandparents and stuff." she said. "Sounds great." Angelo replied.

Mayra knew Angelo disliked Willy. Willy was still Mayra's boyfriend, the guy she loves. She didn't exactly like Angelo's tone.

"It is great actually." Mayra said, not angrily, but close enough. Angelo rolled his eyes. He stretched out again, his joints popping as he did.

He eyed her curiously. "What's wrong?" "I just don't like that sound." I mumbled. "What sound? This?" He asked and cracked his knuckles. again. "Angelo don't, I hate that." He laughed. "You hate the sound of joints and stuff cracking?" He asked and cracked each finger. Mayra slapped his arm. "I'm serious! Stop doing that or I will resort to more violence!" She threatened Angelo.

He raised his eyebrows. "I will stop if you tell me why you hate it so much." He said. She thought it over, the gave in. "When I was ten, my older cousin Ray pinned me to the ground and cracked all my fingers back resulting in me having to go to the ER because of a sprain. He always did that kind of stuff. Now, every time I hear that cracking sound it brings back crappy memories." She explained, feeling embarrassed. She had never actually told anyone about that before, except Mary. Angelo stared at her.

Mayra looked away at the TV screen. "Wow, what a shit head. What ever happened to him?" He asked. "Well, my mom was pissed, and told my aunt off and said if Ray ever touched me again, she'd call the police.

That was the only time Mayra had seen her mom that angry." Mayra said. Angelo's lips were pressed, as if he was thinking. "You know what, that story actually just made me want to find this Ray and give him a good swift kick in the ass"

"Oh, hey mom!" Mayra said, talking over Angelo before he finished his sentence. "Dinner is done, you two can come and get some now." She said and gestured for them to come into the kitchen.

The food had turned out delicious. They all ate until they were full…

STORY 29

The Bra

Every girl has that one bra, that when she wears it, she feels like a tramp...

Hector came home early from visiting his grandparents. He couldn't wait to get back to his house. Apparently, his grandpa hadn't been in the mood for houseguests. The poor old man has been sick for years. He even hated himself. He was tired of life itself....

Hector called Becky the second he got home. He told her that he had to unpack. Then he would come over.

Becky still had another day of vacation before school started. She was surprised by how badly she wanted to see Hector. It felt like a physical need.

That made Becky feel good. She was only going to look at William as a friend. The way it should have been. No, more long phone conversations, just texting. Maybe a couple phone calls- No!

She was close enough to William. No more holidays together either. As much as she hated the idea of William alone, having him spend time with her family just made him even more a part of her life. Of course, she didn't want to shove him away completely, just a respectable distance.

Becky also decided that whatever might be going on between him and Jean was none of her business. She thinks that's quite a bit of progress.

Hector was home and she would be getting in some much-needed time with him.

Her parents were working as usual. Benny was at his friend's house for the afternoon. The house was all for her. Not that she minds. While she waited for Hector, Becky spent awhile in her closet.

A few months ago, she had taken a trip by herself, to Victoria Secret. Probably one of the most embarrassing experiences of her life. The salesgirls made her blush every time they suggested that she should try some items on.

She had gone there specifically for some new bra and pantie combinations. Something for Hector to see her in. Becky wasn't usually so bold. She thought that her age is making her more confident, if you can believe that.

When Hector and Becky had first started dating, she was so shy. She would barely kiss him. Now, she can't get enough of his kisses. Wow, that sounded so slutty. Ha.

Now, as she sat in her closet, Becky examined the dark purple and black bra and pantie set she had bought that day. She had never worn them. Becky always felt too...I don't know, weird. It was like, if I put them on, it felt as if she was being easy. As if the second she put them on she was going to have sex. Becky knows, it's a stupid thing to fear. She is not always a sensible person.

Becky was contemplating whether she should wear them underneath her clothes in case things went a certain way with Hector when he came over.

She wasn't sure if today was the day they would finally make love. Ugh, that phrase makes her toes curl. Again, another odd thing about her. Becky feels more comfortable saying 'slept together' rather than 'make love'. She didn't know why. Maybe Hector was thinking along the same lines as she did.

Becky's stomach felt kind of hollow just thinking about today being the day they would do it. Even though it's against her better judgement, she put the bra/pantie set on. They don't feel any different, well, maybe the panties do, but other than that she feels the same.

She fixed her hair and makeup slowly then made her way downstairs into the kitchen. Becky had no idea why she went to the kitchen. Maybe for some water to calm her nerves. She can't remember.

She is overreacting, but she can't help it. Becky watches out the window feeling very far away. It had snowed a lot during las two weeks. She shivered for no reason. A couple neighbors came home and left. It was still early in the afternoon.

Becky was too frozen for her chair to turn. She wanted to look at the clock to know for sure what time it was. She watched and waited for what must've been twenty minutes before Hector's gray truck pulled into the driveway. Becky felt her pulse quicken. She needed to get a grip, seriously. She didn't need to have a heart attack this early in my life.

It felt like slow motion as I got up and walked to the front door. A moment later he knocked. Becky took several deep breaths before opening it. The second the door was opened Hector's face split into a huge sexy smile.

"Hey beautiful." He said. Becky flung her arms around his neck, kissing every free inch of him. He wrapped his arms tightly around her waist. "Wow, you miss me that much?" He laughed. "Nope." She lied and looked up at him. He kissed her lips and she felt like she had been holding her breath for a long time.

Now, she could breathe again. Becky pulled back smiling, what she assumed to be a very dopey smile.

"It feels as if we've been apart forever, which is weird because it hasn't even been a full week." He mused, still holding her. "I know what you mean- oh my gosh! Did you get a haircut?" She asked, surprised. He grinned and ran a free hand through his much shorter than usual hair. "Yep, mom insisted. She said I looked like a hobo. You like it?" he asked.

Becky bit her lips and nodded, wanting very much to be touch. He sighed. "Here, I can tell you want to." he muttered and bent his head forward. She ran her hand over his entire head loving how soft it felt.

"I love it." She said when he stood straight. "Good, I'm glad. Now where were we?" he said and kissed her hard. Becky did a little hop to wrap her legs around his waist and felt him carry her over to the couch.

Once there he laid her down. He went to pull away, but she held on, so he came down with her. He let out a breathless chuckle. "You're so wild today baby." "Not that I care." he added.

Becky raised an eyebrow. "Do you want to do something else? She heard chess is very fun-" he cut her off with another hard kiss. She wept a moan.

All the things she was experiencing were crazy. Like how she had mentioned with William she felt burning. Well with Hector, it was like a cooling sensation that left her shivering for more. "I should go away longer next time." He mumbled against her lips. She disagreed. She never wanted Hector to leave again. Having him here felt complete. A flash of William's face went through her mind. She pushed it away instantly. Almost complete, her mind corrected itself.

The urgency was fading away now, but she tried her best to hold onto it. Damn William for not even being here and ruining the mood.

Hector could sense Becky wasn't as into it now and pulled back to look at her…

"Are you okay Becky?" He asked. His lips had gotten a little puffy from making out, and his new haircut was totally messed up thanks to her. She ignored the question and raised herself up a bit. "I wanted to show you something." She mumbled. He looked curious. "Alright, show me." he said….

Becky slowly unbuttoned the top few buttons of her shirt making his eyebrows raise questions. She prayed for her face not to turn red. Becky could never be a stripper, that was for sure.

Once the buttons were free her purple bra was exposed. "I uh, got this for um, you know, something special." She whispered, not meeting Hector's eyes. He placed a finger under her chin, so she had to look at him.

"Something special?" he repeated. Becky nodded. He glanced down at the bra then back at her. "For the first time we…?" He didn't finish his sentence. She knew what he meant and nodded. He looked from the bra to me repeatedly before taking a deep breath.

"Becky, I love you, but I don't think today is the right day." he said. It seemed to take all his will power to say it. For a moment she let his words sink in.

Then, unexpectedly her eyes began to tear up. He looked utterly bewildered…

"Becky! Becky please don't cry! What did I do?" he asked franticly. "Oh Hector! Thank you! You have no idea how worried I was! I love you too, but I didn't want to do it today." she cried feeling crushing relief.

He pulled her to his chest and hugged her. "Damn, you really freaked me out, I thought you were angry with me." He laughed. Relief in his voice too. She wiped her eyes and started to feel kind of stupid.

STORY 30

Heavenly Body

Wanting to jump off the moon with him….

Since Billie and Adler had decided, to finally be together, Helen have been doing her best not to worry or randomly freak out. She kept her word and didn't mention anything about it to Maria. Helen had felt bad about it at first, keeping a secret from her best friend…

Just the way Adler had acted gave it away. Helen went to ask her what was up, and she'd instantly pretend. Helen hadn't even spoken. Which was very unlike her. She loves to talk.

They had a free period one day at school Mr. Goodman, her math teacher, had food poisoning and was home sick. So, the two of us were kind of just walking around campus like many other students. It was cold, but it was better than being in school.

"I wonder if that chick from biology really is pregnant." Carmela said. I shrugged. "She could be, I always see her surrounded by guys." Hellen replied. "I hope she isn't I'll feel so bad if she is. Her life is going to be ruined." Adler said sadly. Helen felt a pain of fear for herself. What has she got pregnant? "I don't think her life will be ruined, just put on hold for a while." Helen tried to reason. Adler laughed. "Put on hold forever is more like it." She said and hugged her arms around her shoulders to keep warm.

"Yeah, I suppose. "Helen mumbled. "Is there something wrong Helen, you haven't been acting normal lately." Adler said, looking concerned. "I could ask you the same question actually, you've been acting pretty strange yourself." Helen said.

Adler chewed on the side of her cheek and looked away from Hellen. "Come on Adler, you can tell me what's wrong." Helen said. She took a deep breath and looked back at her. "Will you promise not to get mad or freak or anything?" Adler asked, making her nervous.

"Um..." "You have to promise!" Adler said, a little louder. "Okay fine! I promise not to get mad or freak. Happy?" Helen said sarcastically. She nodded.

"Alright, the reason I've been acting different is...is well, I've sort of been seeing Billie." She admitted quietly. "Uh, what do you mean exactly about 'seeing Billie?" Helen asked. "Going on dates and stuff, and, um, kissing too." She said and smiled sheepishly. Hellen stomach seemed to have disappeared. It was a very unpleasant sort of feeling.

At first, I wanted to scream and curse at Adler, but the next second I felt rather numb. They had been going on dates and... and kissing behind her back. Some friends. She had been watching Helen's face, which she had carefully made sure it didn't show any kind of emotion. "That's...Why, why didn't you tell me?" Helen asked, toneless. She let out a sigh of relief, apparently thinking she wasn't mad.

"Well, it was kind of Billie's idea. He said you would probably be upset if you found out, so we've had to keep it quiet." She explained. Hellen nodded mechanically. Billie's idea. Great.

"How long has this been going on?" Helen asked. She seemed to think about it for a long moment before answering. "After the first football game, he hadn't asked me out, so I cornered him one afternoon and asked him out on another date." She said, then smiled.

"Wow." Helen muttered. "I know right? Me ask Billie out, I have no idea where all my confidence came from that day." She said shaking her head.

Helen felt slightly sick. "And Billie didn't want me to know?" Helen asked, the anger was starting now. Adler could tell. "Hey, I'm really sorry I didn't tell you. I kept feeling like the worst friend in the world for keeping it from you. But it's out in the open now." She said, her smile faltered at Hellen's expression.

"Are you angry? Oh, please don't be angry!" Helen stared off into the parking lot feeling the anger burning a hole through her.

She had felt bad for him for being alone! That jerk! She let him spend Thanksgiving with her family! He should've just spent it with Adler, then they could have had a wonderful little time together! Oh, when I see Billie again... "Helen please talk to me." Adler pleaded. Helen sucked in a deep breath through her clenched teeth and glanced at her. Helen could tell her lack of speech was upsetting her. Not that she really cared right now.

"So, is he what, your boyfriend now?" Helen asked quietly. She nodded. "Okay then, thank you for telling me the truth Adler, really. I'm glad I know now." Helen said and gave her the best fake smile she could manage.

Helen looked severely relieved. Even though at this moment she couldn't even stand to be near Adler. She would put on the best show. Sure, she had been dating Billie in secret, but she told her the truth. Adler couldn't be that mad at her. Since she first seen Billie, she's said she wanted him. She never lied about that.

I'm the one who's always kept that inside but Billie on the other hand is a different story. He's the one who wanted to keep their little relationship in the dark. Like a coward. Helen felt used now. Billie had used her.

The day seemed to drag on forever. Helen wanted to get to gym to talk, or well, to unleash her fury on Billie. Helen just wished there was a way to not have Adler there. It would be kind of obvious that she had lied about not being mad if she started yelling at Billie right in front of her.

As they walked to gym the secretary's voice came over the intercom. "Adler Byrd to the office now." I looked at Adler. She smacked her palm to her forehead. "Oh crap, I totally forgot about my dentist appointment." She said.

Helen couldn't believe her luck. Adler started to go but stopped and looked back at her. "Are we okay?" She asked hesitantly. Helen stared at her for a moment. "Yeah Adler, we're okay." Helen said. She nodded and left.

Helen hurried to gym. Mr. Schwartz had gotten to the point of not really knowing what activity/sport to start us on since it was almost the end of the semester. So, he's just been making us do laps. He's such a lazy teacher.

Helen spotted Billie instantly. Which is easy considering he's the only platinum blonde haired person in the whole school. He wasn't doing laps like everyone else, just watching.

Helen marched toward him. Before she got there his lips turned down in a grimace and he gripped his chest slightly. Her steps hesitated momentarily. "Billie?" Helen asked cautiously, making him jump. He hadn't seen her walk up. He turned and smiled. "Hey Helen." He said. He sounded a tiny bit breathless. "What's wrong?" Helen demanded. He raised an eyebrow. "Nothing, why do you ask?" They stared at each other. Okay, if he was going to pretend nothing happened so was, she. Hellen crossed her arms over her chest and glared up at him.

"So, Adler told me some interesting news earlier." Helen started. He didn't say anything, so she continued. "Don't you want to know what that interesting news is?" He shrugged. Helen was getting even more pissed by the second.

"Apparently you've been dating my best friend for a while in secret." Helen said quietly. She looked at his face waiting for him to deny it, to say anything really, but he didn't. He just looked back at Helen, no emotion. "Wow, you're not even going to try to deny it." Helen said while shaking her head.

"How could you-" "Okay just stop right there." He said, interrupting her. "We're not going to do this. Not going to do some big fight thing where you accuse me and yell at me, nope, not going to happen." He said.

Helen eyes widened. "You've been lying to me, having my best friend lie to me-" "Yes it was stupid of me to hide it from you, I'll admit. I've felt guilty but I knew what would happen if I told you the truth. I'm really very sorry I kept it from you, just didn't want to hurt your feelings." He sighed.

Helen bit her lips, wanting very much to insult him but she didn't. He sighed again. He turned to her and asked, "Do you want to jump off the moon with me?

STORY 31

The club

December 24.... That was going to be the day Eddie and Delia finally will consummate their relationship....

They have no idea why that was the day they decided on really have sex for the first time. They were discussing the whole thing and Delia just randomly spit out that date. Still had a decent number of nerves but that was to be expected. Right? Anyway.

After a night on the roof with Kermit, Delia spent a lot of time thinking about how strangely he had entered her life, and now he was a, well, not a huge part, but a big part of it now.

Even though she couldn't stand it, he was still dating other girls. Luckily, he seemed to understand how much she disapproved so whenever just the two of them spent time together he didn't talk about it.

Delia was so relieved when he said he'd keep it to himself. Did she really need to hear him gush about his new girlfriend, who also happened to be her best friend? No. Emma was a bit trickier though. Like Delia said before, she loves to talk. They once had an hour-long conversation just about true friendship....

If she can go on that long about something she doesn't really care about, can you imagine the amount of time Delia has to hear about Kermit?

"Do you have to work tonight?" Eddie asked. They were leaning against her locker holding hands. "Yeah, pretty much every night this week." I sighed. "That sucks, oh hey man!" He fists bumps one of his friends as he passes them. "Why does it seem like you never have to work?"

Delia asked, annoyed. He grins.

Eddie works at Hollister at the mall. He doesn't really shop there but when he does, he gets her good deals. Eddie is the kind of the perfect person to work at a store like Hollister. He is tall, built and hot.

"Did you hear about Miranda?" Delia asked. He shrugged. Miranda was the first girl Eddie ever slept with. He told Delia about it when they first got together. Her mom worked with her mom at the vet clinic and heard that they moved out of town a couple days ago. "Are you sad at all?" Delia asked when Eddie didn't reply. He examined our intertwined hands. "Not really, we haven't even talked in like, a year. Plus, why would I miss her when I have you?" he said and gave her a smile. I smiled back.

Eddie's had much more experience with love and sex than her. He's never admitted exactly how many girls he's been with; she doesn't really want to know anyway. If she did know she would constantly see the girls and think of how they've seen her boyfriend naked. Sigh.

"So have you, uh, talked to that one guy lately?" he asked hesitantly.

Delia raised an eyebrow. "You mean Kermit?" He cringed a little but nodded. "Yeah, I've talked to him, he is my friend after all." Delia said. He glanced down at me. Probably because she sounded defensive. "Why do you ask?"

He was about to answer when Holly walked up and interrupted. "Hey Eddie." She said, all flirty. "Oh, uh, hi Holly." He said awkwardly. She glanced briefly at her like she was some disgusting bug then back at Eddie. "I just wanted to say your last game was great, you're such a good player." She said. Delia glared furiously. How dare she flirt so obviously right in front of her. Just then Emma walked up, followed by Kermit. They were holding hands. Oh God.

"What's going on?" Emma asked when she noticed Holly. "Oh, hello Emma, is it time for a V-Club meeting?" Holly asked sneakily. Emma made a face. "V-Club? What the hell are you even talking about?" Emma demanded. "You don't even know about the special club you and your little friend are in?" Holly asked, gesturing to Delia. Emma waited. Holly let out a stupid little giggle. "This is just great! Emma and Delia, the two biggest members of the club and they don't even know what it is!" Holly laughed.

"Spit it out already so we can go on with our lives." Delia growled. "The V-Club, the precious pure little Virgins club." Holly said. Delia stared at Emma, and she looked back at her, and she knew what she was thinking.

Eddie realized that we were about to jump Holly a second before we tried, and he stepped between them.

"Woah! Come on guys don't even listen to her, a fight is not worth it." He was saying as we both tried to get around him. What a hypocrite, he was ready to start a fight at party last week...

Both girls were proud to be part of the V-Club. No one had any bad or dirty episode about them. At 16, they were clean and humble individuals.

STORY 32

In Love

Say that again, but this time without talking.

"I think I'm in love with Herbie." Pamela says out of the blue. It's Wednesday night and they are the café drinking hot chocolate. Wednesday night is still girls' fun night, but it was canceled due to Jenny throwing such a huge tantrum that it took both teams to calm her down. They're still actually in café trying to stop all her crying.

Awilda had just taken a drink of hot chocolate when Pamela said that and ended up burning her lip out of surprise. "Um what do you mean by 'in love' exactly?" Awilda asked while rubbing her mouth. She rolls her eyes. "Come on, you know what I'm talking about, I'm in love it's finally happened!" She said happily.

They stared at each other. Awilda honestly didn't quite know what to think of this information. Pamela couldn't be in love with Herbie. I mean...They've barely dated.

Plus, she always goes on about boys she supposedly loves. There was Trevor, a guy in our freshman year named Dennis, some guy we met at the mall once. The list goes on and on. "Will you just talk already; I can tell you want to say something skeptical." Awilda said. Pamela smiled a little. She knew her. "Well obviously I'm skeptical, this isn't the first time you've been in love now, is it?" Awilda asked. "Remember dear Lance?" She cringed.

Pamela used to be absolutely obsessed with Lance. When he came out of the closet it turned her world upside down. "I thought we agreed to never mention any of that ever again." Pamela said.

"Sorry." Awilda replied, grinning. "That doesn't count though, he was in a band, I was just a fan." She said dismissively. "Crazy fan." Awilda mumbled. Pamela ignored her. "Okay, how about Trevor? Dennis? Or-" "Fine!"

"But not this time, not with Herbie, it's totally different." She insisted. "How so?" Awilda asked. She thought about it for a moment. "Whenever we're together it just feels...I don't know, right. I can be myself with him. Like that's the way it should be. You ever feel that way with Samuel?" She asked. Awilda didn't answer.

"Uh, give yourself?" Pamela asked hesitantly. "

Awilda, he's going to be the first guy I make love to." She said quietly then looked away blushing. She was right. Awilda stared at the table, mind racing. Pamela wanted to sleep with my Herbie, ugh, he's not mine. That is the last thing that came to Awilda's little head......

STORY 33

The Ice Princess Strikes Again

Thursday morning Myrna was all set and ready to go to school and expose Iris' plans.

Myrna was getting dress for school when I realized she was sick. Her head hurts and she was coughing like a smoker. Myrna felt like absolute crap. She decided to stay home and went back to bed.

Myrna received lots of text messages from all her friends. She ignored them. Myrna laid in bed all day, took a shower, then went back to sleep for the night. It was a wasted day, but she needed rest.

The next day was Friday. Myrna still felt sick, but she had to go to school. She wasn't in her class work. Myrna wanted to stop her friend Gerry. She didn't want Gerry and Roy to start their romance.

It wasn't any of her business what they did together, but she could not overlook this situation. Not them sleeping together…

Myrna got to school and waited near my locker for any sign of Roy. She usually sees him in the hallway before class. No such luck this morning. She should have called him and told him. Myrna felt like this should be something she have to tell him in person.

'Oh, Gerry wants to have sex with you, please don't!' Yeah, hopefully Myrna would come up with something a little cleverer than that to say. She waited throughout the day looking for Roy.

Myrna was starting to get mad when she went to lunch didn't see Roy. She sat down at their table…

"Hey ' Gerry, where is Roy?" Myrna asked. "Oh, apparently he's home sick with the same crap you had. A bunch of kids are out sick actually." She explained.

Myrna felt depressed now. She was running out of chances to talk to him. The usual happiness she had on Fridays was ruined by this. On Saturday, Gerry was going to go to a motel with Roy...Ugh!

Myrna ended up giving her lunch to Jamie. She went home...

As soon as she got home, she called Roy. Myrna had to work, so she figured they could at the pet store to finally tell him.

It wasn't very nice to make Roy come all the way to the pet store just to talk to her, he was sick...

Thank God it was the weekend now. Plenty of time to sleep and recover. Myrna was at the counter organizing dog treats when Roy walked in. He didn't look sick, so it eased some of her guilt.

"Hey." He said. Myrna took a deep breath. "Hey yourself, thought you were sick." She said. He shrugged. "Not really, just didn't want to go to school."

Myrna glanced at his face. He was smiling slightly. He was wearing a leather jacket. She examined his face a little closer. She could see that he was exhausted just from walking from his car into the store. That worried her.

She was worried because Roy was losing too much weight and didn't care about school anymore. Something terrible was going on with Roy and she was going to find out......

STORY 34

Feeling Low

Sunday was a great day to call friends and family…

Daniela was ready to apologize to her friends. She was acting very strange in school and even at home with her family.

The first-person Daniela was going to call was Fred. She did care for him, but she wasn't ready for any serious commitment.

Monday morning class started as usual. She was late for class. On her way to her room, she saw Enrique.

"Hey." Daniella said. He gave a stiff nod while grabbing books from his locker. I sighed. "Enrique, please talk to me I'm really super sorry I forgot about our plans, I had a lot of stuff on my mind." She said. "Funny, you forgot about our plans, but you made sure Victoria's plans with that Ramon didn't follow through." Enrique said sarcastically.

Oh God, was he jealous or something?? "Come on Enrique. Give me a break. I didn't try to ruin things because of Carmen. She's my best friend, would you want her to get hurt?" Daniela demanded. He glared down at me. "Don't try to turn this around on me Daniela, you know I don't want anyone to get hurt.

"Daniela, just mind your own business. Stop getting so involved with other people's love." Enrique said.

It felt like forever until Daniela made it to my car. Once inside, before she had even put the keys in the ignition she started crying. Crying, because nothing had physically changed, and yet, nothing was the same now. It wasn't the same because Daniela had finally admitted something to me. She must keep away from other people's love affairs. She is not a kid anymore. Daniela must mind her own business that is the bottom line....

STORY 35

It's Christmas

Christmas in Cindy's house is usually spent, half at her dad's and the other half at her mom's. She loves this time of year. The snow, the decorations, it's all so pretty. It's a time for family, fun, happiness, and of course, love. Oh love. What would we do without it? Love can make you feel incredible and yet hurt you so much at the same time. Strange.

That's how Cindy was feeling as she helped her mom put up their tree. Her mom doesn't like evergreen trees, so they put it up only a couple days before Christmas. They take it down before new year's eve. She has a weird system for traditions. They don't go all out with stringed popcorn. They don't know anyone who still strings popcorn. They just put lights, a few ornaments, and of the star on top. Simple.

Tommy is sitting on the couch watching them do the work, lazy little brat. Cindy says that with love though. Mom put the star on and then stood back to admire it. "What a lovely tree, you two agree?" She asked, smiling at them.

"It's awesome mom." Tommy said. "Really awesome." Cindy added. Her mom went to start dinner, so Cindy sat with tommy on the couch.

Everyone was excited for the nice kind of long, break from school. I hadn't really been paying any attention to the conversations. Cindy was too messed up right now to care about anything. She loves

Byron. It was like a ball and chain around her ankles, no matter how hard she tries to remove it or run away from it, it's still there...

What is she going to do now? It's not like she told him how she feels. Cindy doubts he would ever somewhat feel the same about her. Guys like Byron don't go for girls like her. She is too plain and simple...

Cindy was feeling down. Her self esteem was very low. She saw all her friends happy but not her. She was a loser. Nobody has invited her to a Christmas party.

Cindy started walking down the street. She was very surprised to see so many homeless people in the cold. Then she saw one of her classmates. He was also walking very sad. They started chatting and forgetting about their loneliness. Cindy pointed out the homeless.

Her classmate Jerry told Cindy that he was going to give them something and he did....

"What did you give them?" Cindy asked, super curious. "Uh, a bunch of coupons for free smoothies from that new place." he said. Cindy laughed. After a moment he started to laugh with her. They both had a "Merry Christmas."

STORY 36

Just One Call

One night on his way home, Gary made eye contact with a gorgeous young woman named Lydia. He went back to his phone and didn't think much of it, but she came and sat next to him....

Gary got very nervous. He didn't say anything. After several stops, Lydia asked him if the bus was going to a certain stop. Gary gave her a quick, 'Yeah, the sign is over there,' trying to avoid being the creepy passenger that is more interested in the person than providing directions.

Lydia was persistent and kept asking him too many questions. She gave him her business card before Gary got off the bus. Lydia pointed out that her cell phone number wasn't on it. Gary laughed and told her that it was a joke. She didn't put the phone number because if you really cared, she would give it to the person that wanted it.

Gary gave Lydia his number. She called him and they spoke for several hours. Lydia sounded just like an investigator. Gary found that amusing. He told her that his name was Gary.

They went out a couple of nights. They always had great conversations.

Guess what? They have been dating ever since.

STORY 37

The Camp Band

Joseph had just finished training as an Army musician. He was assigned to a band. Boy, was he nervous. When he is nervous, he loses his appetite.

Joseph hadn't eaten much before his first performance, which involved standing on a parade square for about an hour and a half.

He blacked out and one of the other musicians saw him wobbling and caught him. His saxophone went flying in the air just before he fell.

It took three men to carry Joseph off the square. The first person he saw was Linda. That was when he came out of his dizzy spell.

Around him, there were all the musicians.

Linda was just standing next to the soldiers who caught him…

They have been together for over twelve years. But guess what? They have been married for eight! They have a five-year-old gorgeous daughter and a two-month baby.

STORY 38

Found Romance Instead

A few years ago, Awilda flew to Egypt for an archaeological dig. She used her field kit as her second carry-on...

Well, just her luck: after a 10-hour plane ride, Awilda discovered that the airline lost her luggage.

After filing her report, she wanted to get to a hotel to take a shower and long nap.

Awilda checked in asked the girl at the counter where to go to buy supplies and clothes.

She began explaining to girl her experience with my luggage. When she got back from her shopping trip, she found out that her 'roommates' had used her allotted towels.

Anyway, she returned to the front desk to ask for some towels. Just as the clerk was telling Awilda they didn't have any more towels, the cutest guy she has ever seen tapped her on her shoulder. He told her that he had some she could borrow. He also told her that he was visiting from Ireland. He always brought his own towels while traveling.

Apparently, he heard her story earlier and felt bad for me. Wished he could do more for her.

They went to his room to get the towels. As they were walking, he invited Awilda out for a drink to help improve her day.

The best decision in her life was saying yes! Why? Because that's, my dear friends, is how they met. They are presently married and living in Ireland.

STORY 39

The Cupid's Arrow

Bill and Kathy lived in the same college dorm for nearly two years. They have never met before until that day...

When they met, almost four months into the semester, he was doing his laundry. He realized that he needed seventy-five cents to finish his laundry.

He walked around the nearby lobby. He was checking to see if anyone may have any change. Kathy was sitting at a table with friends.

The funny thing is that Kathy had never carry her wallet when I am with friends around the dorm.

At that point she saw her wallet. She looked inside and there were three single quarters. Nothing more. Nothing less. Kathy let him have her quarters and they exchanged names and phone numbers.

Four years later, we were exchanging vows! Not a bad deal one would say! It only took Kathy seventy-five cents to find the love of her life...

Wait, did he ever pay her back?

STORY 40

Lost at Sea

Norberto was standing there just standing. He was looking right at Margaret with his horrifying blue eyes. He couldn't breathe.

At this point, Margaret couldn't move. She was paralyzed by Norberto's looks…

Norberto had sandy blond hair and blue eyes. His hair cut had the right length, but this gorgeous guy had a smile that could kill. His arms were crossed. Norberto had a sort of sluggish look about him.

Margaret knew better. He was ready but for what…

The year was 1454. They were standing in a dining hall. Everyone was waiting for the king to arrive. Lady Adela and Prince Felipe.

Let tell you some information about this young couple…

Norberto was the youngest of six brothers. Margaret was the oldest of three. Margaret's parents both died of a plague that happened in Spain.

Along with her younger sister Alison, Margaret decided to go to an unknown island. She was told that over there she will find her lost relatives.

When Margaret was about six, she remembers that her younger brother was lost at sea. Her brother was a sailor serving for the queen of Spain. There was no information given to her family about his whereabout.

It has been over twenty years now and Margaret never forgot her brother. This long journey that was making was to recover her lost brother.

The funny is that Norberto, this gorgeous guy that she just met, was going to the same island. On this same ship, the queen and prince of

Spain was going to claim a piece of land discovered a couple of years before.

Norberto and Margaret have been dining and dancing on a ship to an unknown island. They have fallen in love and are about to discover a big secret together when they are making their entrance on this unclaimed land....

STORY 41

The Unwanted

Skye had moved recently, and she hated her new house. She misses her friends a lot...

The alarm went off Gerard way's voice echoed in her room. She opened her eyes. The misery is setting in. There is no way she can escape it. Her aunt loves yelling at her making her life miserable.

Skye lays in bed staring at the ceiling. She looks at the clock and get up slowly staring at the light. There is a brown wall covered with posters and artwork her friends gave her.

She walks to her closet and picks out her usual black skinny jeans. She finds her missing t-shirt. She starts taking off her PJ's and changing into her clothes.

After she is dressed, Skye puts on her skeleton socks. She walks to the bathroom. She pulls her blue hair in a ponytail...

Skye is now ready to eat her breakfast a report to her new school. She doesn't want to go. Her aunt comes out of nowhere and starts screaming at her for no reason at all.

Skye is a very lonely girl that just loss her parents in a car accident. Now, she must live with her crazy aunt until she is 18 years old. Her life was great when her parents were alive.

Skye doesn't care to be alive. She wished that she could have died with her parents. Her so many dreams are now gone.

Her aunt Mary didn't want Skye either. The minute she saw her at the airport she told Skye that she is just there as a paying tenant. Mary will be receiving a lot of money for taking care of Skye.

Aunt Mary made a lousing breakfast of scramble eggs with burnt toast. She told Skye to clean up after she finished eating. Skye looked at the eggs and threw the whole breakfast in the garbage. she cleans the kitchen that was very messing indeed.

When she got to school, there were kids of all different sort of background. There was group called "The Losers". That was the group that caught Skye's eyes.

Her other classmates didn't approve of her crazy outfit or hair...

When school was over at 3 pm. Skye started walking to her crazy house. The Losers were waiting for her. She joined them. They had a car and invited her in for a drive.

Skye had nothing to lose. She got in a was really enjoying herself. One of the guys gave her a pill with a beer. Skye took the pill and the chaser was the beer.

In less that a mile from her house, the happy losers lost controlled of the car....

Skye was pronounced dead by one of the paramedical at the scene....

STORY 42

Missing

Naydeen Silva disappeared when was only three years old. Her parents reported her disappearance; however, she was never found....

It is over a year and no news about Naydeen. The nearby neighbors were puzzled because the parents stopped searching for her. This girl had two older sisters, Lucinda and Theresa. Both sisters witnessed the physical abuse that went on in their home. They also had a brother who was always terrified to say anything. They were afraid that they might get beaten as Naydeen.

When they were young, their father Chris, used to beat Lucinda, Theresa and their brother Gary. Now, they are teenagers, and they carried their terrible secret of what happened to them.

Lucinda was so sick and tired of lying about Naydeen that she decided to tell her best friend Julie.

Let me take you back in time....

It was beautiful Winter morning in December 1980. Mrs. Silva was preparing breakfast for her family. Her teenage children were getting ready to go to school. Naydeen being so young was already in the kitchen waiting for her breakfast.

Mr. Chris Silva was a very strict man. He was always yelling at his wife. Matilda always prepared his food on time. She was a very humble country lady. Matilda always obeyed her husband and never tried to contradict him. She kept the house clean and did her chores on time.

That winter morning was no difference. She got up at 5:00 am and started preparing breakfast and lunch for Chris and her three older children. Naydeen went to the kitchen as always. She was so closed to her mom that she wanted to help. Her mother told her that she was still too young. Naydeen was trying to set the table when she dropped a glass. Chris came into the room yelling at his wife. Matilda was stunned by her husband's anger. She thought that he was changing, but she was wrong. He took Naydeen by one arm a started hitting her repeatedly. The other children came running into the room and didn't dare to say or do anything.

After Naydeen's beating, Matilda went to the kitchen to finish breakfast and pack lunches for Chris and the other kids. Chris was still busy with Naydeen. Naydeen's fragile body was just lying on the floor. Chris went to his bedroom and found a suitcase. He placed Naydeen in it.

Chris went to the kitchen as if nothing happened. He told his teenage children that every was fine and to go to school. His wife just looked at him. He gave a very strange stare....

Right after breakfast, Lucinda, Theresa and Gary went to school. They were shivering and afraid to even talk to their friends. ....

At their house, Chris and Matilda were getting ready to go out. Chris told his wife that Naydeen was dead. Matilda didn't even check the body. She just followed her husband command. She got dress and got in their car. Chris placed the suitcase in the trunk.

Chris got in the driver's seat and without a word began driving. The couple was heading to the Catskill's Mountains upstate New York. It is a lovely place during any season. This was winter, therefore, there were a lot of skiing and skating going on.

There were plenty of people of all ages at a nearby resort. Chris kept driving until he was near the forest part of the mountain. As he got there, he made sure that not a single person was around. It was still early in the morning; therefore, all the events and that section of the mountain was closed.

Chris parked the car and told his wife to get out. Matilda obeyed as always. Chris took the suitcase out of the car and told his wife to make sure that the car was secure. They began walking very fast into the woods. They found a trail that led them deep into the mountain site.

When they were very high and no sign of humans, Chris dumped the suitcase and again told his wife to follow him...

They returned to their vehicle with no problem. No one has seen them. Chris and Matilda went home at exactly 10:00 a.m. Chris still said no word to his wife. He went into his room and starting pacing back and forth.

Chris was scheming something. He was trying to come up with an excuse of any kind to tell his boss. Chris wanted to make sure that he covered every angle.

At 10:30 a.m., Chris called his boss. He worked at a local law firm. Chris was a well-known lawyer. It was easy for him to tell lies and no one knew he was lying. He was lucky on that day because his boss was on vacation.

Chris spoke to his secretary and informed her that his youngest child was missing. Chris told his secretary that Naydeen went outside looking for her dog and never came back. The dog, Fluffy was found in the garage by his wife. That was a lie of course....

At about 2:00 p.m., Chris told his wife that they must report Naydeen's disappearance. They went to the police to report the disappearance of their three-year-old daughter. They were so concerned and convincing that the investigators almost broke down in tears.

The Police Department in Upstate New York started working on the case right away. They placed photos and information throughout the whole county. They also investigated neighbors and their children. The neighbors all cooperated because they had children of their own.

The whole neighborhood searched for days around the vicinity. Since the area was so closed to the highway, rumors started that maybe Naydeen was kidnapped.

Days turned into weeks and the searched never stopped....

The investigators, Agent Wilson and Agent Donahue started the case they told Chris and Matilda that their baby was going to be found. They never gave up....

In the Spring of 1982, Agent Wilson and Agent Donahue decided to close the case. Almost two years have gone by and no trace of Naydeen Silva.

After almost three years of searching, the strangest thing happened. Agent Wilson received a call from Juliet Brown. When the police investigator went to visit the Browns, they were puzzled with the information their oldest daughter stated.

Julie started spitting out all the stories that her friend Lucinda told her about her family.

This is what Julie informed the investigators:

"Lucinda used to tell me about the violence at home," Julie began her statement. The investigators were all ears. "But I knew she was holding back. There was always something she couldn't bring herself to say. I told her that if she couldn't say it out loud, she should write it down and give it to me instead. Lucinda was never really allowed out by herself, however, one day after school she gave me a note.

She wrote that she was going into town with her mom. She said they were going to the general store. So, I decided to go there, and started looking through clothes, always keeping my head down. I was looking through a shelf when Lucinda and her mom walked past me. Lucinda spotted me. She walked by and dropped a letter on the floor. I picked it up quickly and walked out of the shop as fast as I could."

Julie kept talking....

I couldn't believe it when I got home and read Lucinda's letter. describing Naydeen's murder. "I'd do anything to change that morning," Lucinda had written. "I wish I never seen it, but I did and Theresa and Gary too. We just sat there and watched. We even saw the suitcase they took her in. They knocked me over and smacked me because I saw everything."

Julie gave the two agents the two notes Lucinda has written. They then went straight to the Silva's house....

Chris and Matilda Silva were arrested for the murder of their young child. Chris told them that it was a fault accusation. The agents placed them under arrest with no bail whatsoever.

Later in court, Lucinda said that what she had written was purely fiction it was all "free-writing" that she had made up. Julie knew it was true. Julie was also ready to testify and was ready to reveal any secret that involved the Silva's family.

Julie went to see the investigators and told them that Lucinda was still afraid of her parents.

This is what Julie Brown on her second statement told the police:

"I met up with Lucinda in the park the next day," explained Julie, who graduated from high school and was studying psychology. "Lucinda was completely terrified. She was watching every car that drove past them thinking it might be her dad. I gave her a copy of the letter that she has given me. I said to her, "I want you to read it out loud to me". She couldn't do it. She broke down completely. She couldn't tell anyone the truth because Lucinda's parents used to threaten her that she would be next if she told anyone. She was a victim.

After that, Lucinda would talk about Naydeen. She had nice memories of them together as well as and everything they have gone through. She told me that Naydeen was treated the worst out of her sisters and brother.

According to Lucinda, she was the most 'trouble'. Naydeen sometimes wasn't allowed to eat and other times they would leave her outside in the rain. It was caused by things like her having a dog or speaking to strangers.

"The thing that triggered the argument that morning when Naydeen was killed was that she broke a glass."

When Lucinda's parents Chris and Matilda Silva were arrested on suspicion of murder and brought to trial in May 1982, Julie knew she had to do something. Lucinda told the police that her parents killed Naydeen, but Lucinda refused to admit the truth.

"Even though Lucinda had begged me not to, once the trial started, I called the police and told them that I had evidence. Lucinda had asked for the letters, but I had photocopied them. I also kept a diary. I was disappointed that Lucinda wouldn't speak up.

As soon as Mr. and Mrs. Silva had been charged, I said to Lucinda 'You're going to have to forget about your mom and dad. This trial is about your sister. You must stand up for her because nobody else is going to do anything."

The trial took place in Albany Supreme Court. From behind a screen, Lucinda's sister Mary told the jury what had happened: "My mom said to my dad, 'Just finish it here'." She went on to explain how they'd pushed Naydeen onto the sofa. How her mom reached for a bat. they both then stuffed in Naydeen in the suitcase. Mary said they held it in there, while her sister stopped moving. Naydeen wet herself because she was "struggling so much".

Lucinda refused to confirm Mary's story. Gary just stayed quiet through the whole trial.

Julie's evidence became crucial. Thinking back on the trial, Julie said, "It was very scary. I had kept the secret to protect Lucinda's life.

I just kept thinking that once you are a witness nobody is allowed to speak to you, so you feel very alone`. I knew I wasn't doing it for myself. I was doing it for Lucinda."

Finally, Lucinda's parents were found guilty of murder and sentenced to life in prison, with a minimum term of 25 years.

Julie stated that she wants to speak up on behalf of all the other women who are being controlled by their parents or partners. They are in danger just as Lucinda was. "The thing is these crimes are so hidden. You could walk past someone and never know what they're going through.

Some people also need the right help. Sometimes reaching out can make things worse. I really think this day is important for raising awareness. People like Lucinda have to get help before it's too late."

If you think this is the end of the story, you are wrong....

The Police Department always tries to solve any unsolved cases. Agent Wilson and Agent Donahue are now retired; however, their offspring are now law enforcement in the same unit as Wilson and Donahue.

They were assigned to the dead file section to see if they could come out with some unsolved mystery cases...

They found Naydeen's case....

They went back to the scene of the crime and guess what? They solved the case!

Since the Silva's case was all over the news, a report came from Wisconsin....

There is an elderly couple that claimed that they found Naydeen in the Catskill Mountains so many years ago.

The couple explained how the found the fragile little girl stuffed in a suitcase back in 1981.

That missing fragile child is now married to a doctor and has three grown children attending college.

STORY 43

Active Hormones

Anne was 18 years old when she has been dating her boyfriend Jeff for over a year. They started having sex very early in their relationship. He used condoms each time, however he was getting annoyed every time they had intercourse.

One-night Jeff asked Anne one question; "Are you afraid to go without condoms?" So, in the heat of the moment, already in position, she said "no."

Ever since then, he never wanted to wear them again; he said he couldn't feel anything with it. Sometimes Anne didn't want to be intimate in that matter, but somehow, he persuaded her. She wasn't on birth control.

A couple of weeks went by, and her period was late. Anne called Jeff.

Anne went on that she was never late. She also told him that she might be pregnant. They went to a local drugstore and picked up a pregnancy test.

As she took the test awaiting the results, the display read, "positive."

Anne was numb and couldn't process the reality. He asked her what she wanted to do. Her numbness was turning into confusion. She is thinking about how disappointed her mother would be.

Anne told Jeff that she couldn't have the baby. They decided to take a drive to see her cousin Andy.

Andy was Jeff's best. Jeff told Andy that Anne was pregnant. The first thing Andy asked Anne if she wanted to be a mother at 18? Andy kept telling her, "You know you can get rid of it". Anne emotions were drastically changing, and fear was rushing in. She told him I know…

Anne didn't' get rid of the baby at 18. She never saw Jeff again, but she kept making the same mistakes repeatedly. She kept dating losers.

Now, at the age of 42, all she was thinking was about her babies. She had seven and two grandchildren.

STORY 44

The Vulnerable Girl

Milly was only 15, and very vulnerable. She was thinking that she needed a boyfriend. So, she finally got one...

Milly was an only child. Her parents were always very protected. She didn't have any real friends. Milly only socializes in school.

One day, a guy in her class asked her out. She was so happy, however, there was a very serious situation involving her parents. They always told her that she was too young to have a boyfriend.

Milly didn't care or even thought about her parents. She was just happy with the idea of having a boyfriend. Of course, little did she know that they were the wrong boys. They were very immature and really were after only one thing, sex.

Milly wasn't ready. She always thought that she would save her virginity for her wedding night. Nevertheless, she surrendered and consented to keep him interested.

Shortly after she made an appointment with an OBGYN to get onto birth control. As is customary they did a pregnancy test on her, which came back negative.

After talking with the doctor, they decided to give the Depo-Provera injection. The depo shot gives you three months of medicine during which you have no period.

Milly was about a month and a half into my second dose, and she had been having some health problems. She had an appointment with her primary physician and due to being on depo pregnancy never came up.

Her doctors' prognosis was that her gallbladder needed to be removed. As a pre-surgery procedure, they brought Milly in to have an ultrasound of her gallbladder.

The strangest thing happened. Her gallbladder wasn't where it was supposed to be. So, the technician started to look around, which is when she found the little baby inside of her.

Milly was instantly overcome by so many emotions all at once; joy because she couldn't wait to become a mom. She was also angry because the boyfriend lost interest in her.

The technician took a couple of measurements, informed Milly that the baby was about twenty-three weeks old, she told her that the baby was a boy.

When her mom walked in the examining room and Milly told her that she was pregnant. Her mother simply said, "we'll talk about this at home" and she left.

When she got home from work that night, her parents and her sat down. They told her that she was going to have an abortion or find somewhere else to live.

My family had always been very tight, so this hit her like a ton of bricks. Being that she was so far along she had to think fast, as it was there were only a couple clinics in the state that would do a late term abortion.

The closest clinic that would do the procedure was still over an hour away, so her dad drove her to the clinic. Milly remembers seeing some people at the front of the building protesting the clinic's work and it made me feel horrible.

They entered in the back of the clinic and checked in. After signing consent forms and filling out some paperwork they took her back for another ultrasound and some other lab work. They then informed her that due to how far along she was the abortion would be a three-day process, and that she had to be sure this was what she wanted because once they started, there was no going back.

Milly told them that she was sure, and they got started. The first step was to insert several medicated "sticks" into her vaginal canal to start the dilation process. Then they said she was free to go, and to come back the next day.

For convenience her father got a hotel room for her to stay up there, and her sister stayed with her. Milly cried a little bit before she fell asleep that night.

The next day her sister took her back to the clinic where they removed the older pads and put in news ones and more of them. They told Milly that she would probably have some pretty bad cramps that night and sent us on our way. They were right. They were worse than any menstrual cramps.

The next morning, we went back into the clinic for the last time. Milly checked in…

They had her undress and they put her to sleep. When she woke up, she was no longer pregnant. They had her get dressed and they sent me home.

Milly never could bear children later in life….

STORY 45

Top of the World

They stepped inside the elevator and began their ascent, above the rest of the city…

The elevator was wood paneled with a dark reddish shine, and the doors were covered in gold leaf. Madison Avenue and 80th street, top of the world.

The doors finally opened to reveal a faintly lit hallway with three doors. Jeremy knocked on the first one to the right. A gorgeous girl wearing tight jeans and an even tighter black tank top opened the door. Her eyes, were green, seemed as though she came straight from a model agency.

Jeremy quickly introduced himself. He greeted her with a smile. As she walked up to introduce herself, she quickly turned her back to Angie and followed Jeremy deeper into the apartment.

"Jeremy, did you bring my cigarettes?" she whined as she trailed after him through the apartment and into the kitchen.

Angie paused a moment in the doorway to absorb the surrounding atmosphere of the apartment. I looked around in amazement the extravagant decorations of the house.

To her right, hung some sort of old portrait which could have dated back to the colonial America. The entire floor of the apartment was extravagantly covered with an immaculate white carpet. Angie thought that these kinds of apartments were merely myths.

Angie proceeded to explore the depths of the apartment in search of Jeremy. As she looked around, she noticed a door cracked open.

Angie peered inside and opened it slowly. There was indeterminable number of people on the bed watching a movie.

Angie stood there for a moment debating whether she should go in and introduce herself. She really was confused.

There was this guy that walked briskly to the door and closed it in her face. Angie decided not to go in. She hurried into the kitchen.

The kitchen was at least twice as large as any room in her house. Jeremy stood by an industrial sized fridge and signaled her towards him.

As Jeremy searched through the fridge he paused. He reached into his coat pulling out a pack of cigarettes. He tossed them to the floor in front of the gorgeous girl. She lunged fervently for the box and began to tear it open. Jeremy reached into the fridge and passed Angie a coke, while retrieving one for himself as well.

"I'm telling you man this girl is very rich—Just look around!" he exclaimed. Angie and Jeremy decided to leave....

Jeremy and Angie spent most of the taxi ride uptown revealing exactly "how rich this girl was."

Jeremy told Angie what went in the apartment because she didn't understand a thing.

Jeremy began his story...

Nelly walked over to Jeremy and looked at Angie carefully from head to toe.

"He looks like a messy homeless guy" she said decidedly. "What's his name?" she inquired.

Angie looked up, a little surprised.

"Jeremy meet Nora—Nora meet Jeremy," he said in a slightly restless way.

After this cordial introduction Jeremy quickly took a seat in front of the television. Angie smiled jovially at Nelly to show that she wasn't annoyed. The girl merely looked past her.

Angie remembers the coke Jeremy gave her. Both Angie and Jeremy remember that the girl looked up at them. For a split second, her eyes begged for sympathy and escape.

"Excuse me, Nora need a Perrier," she whined.

She quickly turned from them and went to the furthest point of the kitchen to get one.

Jeremy told Angie that the house looks ridiculous. Nora had no idea who Jeremy and Angie were. They were to social workers investigating Nora.

When Jeremy and Angie reached their office, in mid-Manhattan, they decided to call Nora's parents. They right away told them that their little girl needed their service.

Nora came from a wealthy background. She was only 18 years old and wanted to be on her own. She couldn't handle her own affairs and that is why Jeremy and Angie were sent to help her....

STORY 46

The Wrong Decision

Evelyn, my sister, had an abortion when she was 15 years old. She had no one talk about her situation. The baby wasn't growing right and likely wouldn't it survive. My friend found out somehow and told my family.

Beverly was still in shock about the whole situation. She was speechless and didn't want to start anything with Evelyn.

Their friends knew about it. Evelyn couldn't face them. The jerk who got her sister pregnant was emotionally abusive. Evelyn lost almost all her friends because of it.

Now, Evelyn goes to therapy every two weeks, but she never talks about what happens in her sessions or what they talk about. She usually wants to be alone after. She wasn't sure if she would still go to heaven.

Evelyn comes from a very religion family. She wasn't allowed to go out with boys. She didn't listen….

One lovely spring after, she left the house in a hurry. She met with Steven, her so call boyfriend.

Steven said to Evelyn on their way to a motel, "You and me are going to have the fun of our lives". "I love you and this is the only way you can prove to me that you love me with all your heart".

Evelyn was in love with Steve or had the desire to be with a man. Who knows what went on inside her tiny brain. She was too young and very innocent.

Once they got to the motel all the sweet talk coming from Steve was gone. He pushed Evelyn around the room. She was hurting badly. Steven was getting a lot of pleasure of this savage scenario.

Steven jumped on Evelyn and started inserting objects in her vagina. Evelyn was bleeding a lot. He was raping her. The more Evelyn scream, the more pleasure he receives....

Steven was 22 yrs. old. He was the son of a farmer. No education whatsoever. He wanted only young in experience girls to satisfy his animal instinct.

Steven looked at Evelyn and said, "You are mine and no one else". "You won't tell anyone about this or I will kill you and then I will kill myself". She just stayed quiet ....

A couple of months went by and Steven repeatably abused Evelyn. She wasn't a beautiful young girl anymore. She was only a destroyed young teenager with no hope and low self-esteem.

After a couple of months after their last encounter, Evelyn told Steven that she was pregnant. Steven stated that the baby wasn't his. To him, she was a tramp.

Evelyn started running away from Steve. Without looking at a car that was coming and hit her. The people around the area call an ambulance. She was rushed to a nearby clinic. There, she lost her baby. An abortion took place because the doctor saw that she was an abuse child....

It's been one year since she had the abortion, and she is still mad at Steven....

Steve disappeared from the neighbor or even the country. The local police still after Steven because he a very dangerous....

STORY 47

The Silence

There's a screaming inside Dolly's head. She knows it's her, but of course that doesn't change anything...

It's funny, how people always talk of that dry, critical part of you that just watches while your world caves in.

The writers, the poets and the psychologists can say so much with their smiling and sweet voices, but they don't know that even the ones who watch can scream. Oh, God, but they can scream so loud that nobody hears them.

Once, Dolly woke up in bed, and saw a crack of morning coming through her curtains. Two hours later, it's impossible to summon the fascination that a bit of light can take you into a trance.

After all, a sunny day it will help you with any depression level. It's far easier on the face; not even painful compared to trying to look neutral when it's facing you across the kitchen table as if the sunlight means something. Nobody really notices you when you're drinking coffee.

School isn't bad as these things go on as usual. The corners of your eyes get a lot of work, naturally, and you can spend a pleasant period spying out a teacher's sad smile: that mouth-up-eyes-down flicker that manages to lose itself on any other wayward charge.

It's not limited to the masters and matrons of wisdom, heaven knows; you know the look social services have perfected, the one that wants to help you.

If the teacher knows you care, you're allowed to comfort yourself with thoughts that a girl doesn't make her real friends 'till university anyway. A cup of tea can solve all her problems. Bags, though, not tea leaves – too bitter for children and adults alike.

The vastly superior Garden wins a battle with the television to hold sway over time and inattention, though each one clamors in it's own way.

Today Dolly was very focus in her biology class. She saw trees and bushes at a different anger. To her, it offers shade to fit her mood.

Dolly keeps telling her parents that she has problems sleeping. She guesses they don't care…

She also keeps saying that the sun slides away taking the sunset with it. Dolly has a way with words that no kids her age can even pronounce. Darkness is her worse enemy. Like most children she has a father who would stay beside for a while, until she discovered how misplaced her fears had been.

Dolly's parents think that she outgrew all those negative imagination. , but they are still there.

She is not afraid of the dark, anymore. She is not afraid of the nightmares either. It's the waking up from them she doesn't like. Screaming out in the dark used to bring them running, but she doesn't do that anymore…

Dolly learned to stay quiet. Silence is the key. No one will n ever know.

STORY 48

Remains of Dark Memories

The light steps made by John sank into the thick, muting cushion of snow without the faintest snatch of sound…

The flakes settled softly in his wake, swirling flurries of a gentle blindness, slowly, sweetly tucking away all slips of sound in the deep caress of forgotten dreams.

The late hours of evening had yet to pass over the day. John's worn leather soles, peeling away. He must do something soon. He has paused and settled their weight firmly to both feet.

A stray, still form during bustling bodies, collars up to the chin, cheeks flushed with cold, eyes beady and black.

John painted a queer picture in the middle of the shabby street, an oddly clear figure frozen in time, surrounded by the grey-blurred outlines of rushing passerby. Stepping closer to the building, the sound of his own footsteps crunching in the snow seemed suddenly more solid, and, as he pressed a battered hand to the frozen bricks of the towering old Grand Hotel before him.

A shiver ran down his spine, an empty echo sounded down the street.

Hours, or perhaps minutes later he still sat on his chair. John started looking again at his painting. He remembered that man, the superb quality of his tailored suit, the look of respect in his eyes. The way his eyebrows lifted in barely concealed a surprise.

The quirkiness of his mouth as though unsure whether he was permitted to smile. Perhaps it had only been a dream after all…

The next morning, an irritated demolition worker leapt angrily from his crane to see what had caused the delay, cursing as he pushed through the small crowd of workers around the condemned building. He stopped as he saw a man curled and small at the base of the old hotel and paused.

Soon however, the crowd dispersed, grew disinterested, resumed their tasks, and with the aid of a couple fellow workers. The body was hosted unceremoniously down an alley way and buried in a makeshift grave of snow.

As the building fell in crumbling ruin, and the carefully crafted might of the hotel crashed to the ground, empty echoes streamed down the snow-muted streets, lost on the ears of the deaf-toned passerby.

STORY 49

The Alien

On the first day of his new life in the new neighborhood, Mr. Drakes heard about the Green Man. The Green Man was built entirely of metal. He has no bones, no liver, and no kidneys!

Guess what? He was not a robot. His voice wasn't made up of controlled beeps or monographic measurements. He spoke with lucidity, like any other person would, and had hair and teeth.

When the Green Man goes to the window, he raises the ribbon effortlessly and looks out over the city. He only does this at night, when people aren't watching. If they are, any lights, he just simply stays still.

Sometimes he must look before peeking out of the window, otherwise, there'd be a big outcry of, "There's the Green Man!" from down below on the streets.

Grown-ups don't want to wake their children up, therefore, during the night is when the Green Man makes his every move. It is very sad that the neighbors never bother to get to know the Green Man. He was always alone. He never went to the store to get food or anything.

Some said that he is an Alien from Mars....

STORY 50

Four Eyes

When Johnny was ten years old, he started wearing glasses. Those glasses weren't prescribed. They had been his fathers as a child. His father fixed them so they could be fitted with stronger frames.

They magnified everything about his eyes, making them look dark and doughnut shaped. The one for his right eye was thicker since he had taken it out with a glue gun by mistake two years earlier.

Johnny could be likened to a pear in his many black spots, some on the whites of his eyes, some on his arms and knees, because he was born two months too early. His head was very deformed.

John kept Barbies in his basement under a white cloth, a frenetic pleasure. His father was president of the local chapter of his school district. Johnny would often have to play downstairs in a cold basement while they held their meetings in his house.

The poor four eyes kid was always alone. No one cared to check after him. To keep himself from being discovered, he hid behind an enormous broken chandelier that his mother had once loved.

Johnny was sent home from school with a letter stating that he was never to return to class. He was kept from other children because he scares them….

After a while, Johnny didn't care anymore. He invented games and even imaginary friends. He was always checking every so often to see if he was being watched through the oblong droplets of glass.

His father was a tall, skinny man whose face moved like a wooden puppet's. He always rested his coffee mug on his right knee and could not gain any weight no matter how much he ate.

Johnny even had names for his imaginary friends. He invited Tom known for his ability to peel little kids like skinned fruit. He was also somehow connected to everything adults weren't.

The word out in the street was "KEEP AWAY FROM FOUR EYES……

STORY 51

The Birth

At approximately 10:30 p.m. on Friday, January 15, 1949, Guadalupe and her mother, Dolores, were enjoying a pleasant breeze, when suddenly; they heard Digna from afar....

Guadalupe looked and at her mother and said, "Ya llego la hora que tanto esperabamos". Even though Guadalupe just gave birth to Vicente. He was Guadalupe's youngest. Guadalupe was very anxious to assist her mother with the birth of her first grandchild.

They got up from their chairs and walked very fast to Digna's room. Digna was young and healthy; however, she was very nervous because this was going to be her first born. She asked for her husband, but he was at a awake of one of their neighbors that had died on that day.

Mama Dolores, a licensed midwife, had delivered lots of children; but this child was different because it was going to be her great grandchild.

Both females prepared the room to welcome the baby. Digna wasn't afraid because she knew that Guadalupe and Dolores were ready. Both had the experience and were on duty 24/7 to help in the community before the doctor could make any house call.

Guadalupe sat next to Digna and while holding her hand, she kept telling her stories about all nine babies she had given birth and her last one was just two months old.

With stories and plenty of loving care, it only took Digna about two hours to give birth to a gorgeous baby girl.

Mama Dolores was tired but couldn't resist holding her great granddaughter. The baby was cleaned and placed next to her "Mamí".

Digna couldn't believe that this beautiful little creature was her daughter. Her husband came running into the room and started to cry when he saw his wife and their daughter.

The following day, a doctor came to check mother and child. They were in excellent condition. The newborn weighed 8 pounds and was 19 inches long. The doctor jotted down the exact time, date and birth of the baby.

He made sure that he had all the necessary information to be documented on the birth certificate...

Digna and Juan decided to name the baby Norma because at that time a very popular soap opera "Norma" that was heard on the radio throughout Puerto Rico. The middle name "Iris" because those eyes glowed with such beauty just as a rainbow after rain.

The baby was welcomed by nine aunts and uncles. So, I, Norma Iris was the luckiest baby.

The parents have been living with their since they got married. Now with the newborn, they must think about getting their own place.

When the grandmother heard that they were planning on moving, she began to cry. She wanted to add an extra room to her house because she was getting so use to me.

Every morning, my grandmother used to take care of her youngest son and her granddaughter. Everyone had their chores in that big happy family.

Many years ago, family was very important. They all worked together so that each member could make in life. Never forget from where you came from.

STORY 52

Do you believe in Angels?

It was a cool Autumn day when Carmen saw a little girl all by herself in the school yard. She was very sad. There were many students playing, however, everyone just passed by her and never stopped to ask her why she was there alone. She was dressed in a worn black coat, bro-ken shoes and very dirty. This girl just sat and watched the children play.

She never spoke to anyone. Many students were playing ball around her. Sometimes they would bump into her, but they kept on with their game.

The following day, Carmen decided to go to the school yard before entering the school. She was very curious about that little girl because Carmen didn't see her inside the school the previous day.

Carmen walked very fast towards the school yard. She didn't want her teacher or classmates to see her. Carmen was very surprised to see the little girl in the same spot as the day before.

As Carmen was walking, she thought to herself that this it isn't a place for a young child. Carmen was in the 6th grade almost 11 years old. The young kids were supposed to be in the school yard with their teachers and some parents.

When Carmen got closer, she could see the back of her dress. It was disturbingly shaped. Carmen figured that was the reason the other kids just passed by and made no effort to speak to her. Deformities are a low blow to our society and heaven forbid if you make a step to help someone who is different.

The little girl lowered her eyes slightly when Carmen approached her. She got so close to her by this time that she could see her shape. She was badly deformed. Carmen smiled to let her know it was OK; Carmen told her that she was there to help, and to talk.

Carmen sat down beside her and opened with a simple, "Hello"; the little girl acted in shocked and mumbled a "hi"; after a long stare.

Carmen smiled and she shyly smiled back. They talked until it was time to go to class. The school yard was completely empty. Carmen asked her why she was so sad. She looked at me with a sad face said, "Because I'm different"; I immediately I said, "That you are!" and smiled. The little girl acted even sadder. Then Carmen and said, "I know." "You remind me of an angel, sweet and innocent."

She looked at Carmen and then slowly got to her feet and said, "Really?" "Yes, you're like a little Guardian Angel sent to watch over me" She reply in a sweet tone of voice, yes, and smiled.

With that she opened the back of her black coat and allowed her wings to spread. She then said "I am. I'm your Guardian Angel," It was a beautiful sight to see her with a twinkle in her eyes.

Carmen was speechless — sure I was seeing things." She said, "For once you thought of someone other than yourself. My job here is done;"

Carmen got to her feet and said, "how come no one stopped to talk to you?" She looked at her, and said, "You were the only one that could see me," and then she was gone.

After that incident in the school yard, Carmen started to feel so different. She began to change the minute she walked into her classroom.

Carmen thought that she was going crazy.

You see, it was testing day. Carmen was given a very hard test. She just moved from Puerto Rico. According to everyone, all the teachers, she wasn't smart enough because she didn't speak any English.

A couple of weeks went by. The test results indicated that Carmen had a very high score. She passed the test in flying colors. Carmen proved to her teacher that she was very smart.

Carmen was transferred to a gifted school where she was treated very well indeed....

STORY 53

Imagination

Children have much vivid imagination to forget about bad experiences at home or in school....

The following study will indicate how I managed to forget about my environment by just imagining things...

I was only ten when I first saw him. I remember that switch from one situation around my surrounding to the other. I used to have imaginary friends and it worked fine for a while....

I used to make believe that I will get help from God. Why did I think like that? Well, to begin with, when I had an assignment, I did it with no problem.

I remember that day so clearly. It was right after school started on September 1959, my first week in school in New York....

Many people came to see the apartment on the second floor, but they said that it was too small for their family.

On that autumn day of 1959, I just knew that the man that took the apartment was going to be my friend. He wasn't too tall, and his hair was white and long. He also had a close-cropped white beard. By the way, the lady next door smiled when she saw him. I guessed he must have reminded her of someone from yesteryears. He was carrying a box; it was marked "early birds" on its side.

There were some moving men helping him. He kept very busy all day long. Some neighbors wanted to know what he did for a living, but no one even dared to ask him.

Two weeks went by and as it did, I watched the new tenant very closely. I'd hear him in his apartment listening to music, TV, and talking. I never got close enough to hear what was said in his living room, but we shared a wall between our kitchens.

One day, mom caught my sister and me with a glass against my ear. I put the glass very close on the wall trying to hear the conversation next door. Boy; did we get into trouble for that!

We were grounded for three days. That was the punishment for ease-dropping, as mom called it. My sister didn't want to play detective with me anymore. She didn't want any part of my games. My brothers were too small to know about the game.

So, I was on my own....

The next day, I ran into my new neighbor after my three days of punishment. He was coming in as I was going out. I was hurrying and just as I jumped from the second step of the stairs. He came in the front door, and we crashed. He fell backwards but as he did, he caught me and saved me from falling.

The door slammed into his back, and I heard him grunt from it hitting him. I just knew I'd be in more trouble, so as soon as he let me go, I started apologizing like crazy.

He stood there for a minute, then raised his hand chuckling. I thought he was going to hit me! Instead, he said, whoa, slow down young lady... it's not a problem. I would have done the same thing if I were your age. Then... he started laughing. "In fact" he said, "I have done it in my younger days". I asked him, are you going to tell on me? My mom will kill me if you do. He smiled and said, No, it's our secret, you don't tell, I won't tell.

He told me that his name was Mr. Reilly. I found it strange that he didn't tell me his first name. It didn't matter. I always use last names with people not related to me....

After a couple of days, Mr. Reilly offered me a job; he paid me to take out his trash. He would sit it outside his door every other morning, and I would take it on my way out to school. He paid me five dollars a week. My parents thought it was too much, but he insisted. I thought to myself that Mr. Reilly was a cool guy.

He was a little overweight and older than my parents......

I was so curious about Mr. Reilly. He always had some visitors, which I never saw coming or leaving. Some of them only stayed for maybe an hour. I was just guessing. This Mr. Nice Guy may be a spy.

I was also very puzzled by the end of October because I didn't know what Mr. Reilly did as far as work. I began to guess again. He was maybe a secret agent or something. He didn't work hours like my father or Mr. Alvarez in apartment 2B.

I noticed he was home when I got home from school, and he was there when I left in the morning. Sometimes he was gone for two or three days, but he still paid me the five dollars even if I only took his trash out once that week.

One day, I overheard him talking to someone inside his place. It appeared he was upset about something. I heard the other man say that it wasn't his fault. He also stated that it would be ready on time. I could tell he was nervous, and then they came out.

They stopped in the hall in front of Mr. Reilly apartment. They closed the door as they left. I heard Mr. Reilly say something about being disappointed, and they left the building.

I tried to figure out what the whole deal meant, but it was over my head. The visitor was small like me. I think they call people like that midget. He was dressed funny; in clothes no one wore in my neighborhood.

After that incident, I started pretending I was a secret agent, and it was my job to spy on the other spies especially the one who lived next door.

Things went back to normal after Mr. Reilly settled down. Since he didn't visit anyone that lived in our building, it was kind of boring spying on him. I knew better than to try listening again through the wall. If I got caught again by my mom, I would be grounded forever.

One afternoon, it dawned on me that I have never seen the inside Mr. Reilly's apartment. I told my sister to take a walk with me. Adelin, so shy said, "No. I don't want to get in trouble." She claimed that Christmas was around the corner, and she wanted nice presents.

I still was determined to see Mr. Reilly's apartment. I thought I would ask him to help me with my homework. I went to his door, and as I was about to knock, I heard, come in young lady, it's open. I don't know how he knew that it was me, but I did as he said.

As I walked in, he was sitting at a desk. I noticed it was only one of three pieces of furniture in the room. He had a TV, a couch, a desk and a chair. On the desk there were letters, lots and lots of letters. I couldn't see who they were from. Mr. Reilly had gotten up from the desk and met me before I could get close enough to see. He smiled at me and said, "So; you need help with your homework, do you?"

Surprised, I asked... how do you know? He again smiled; his eyes seem to sparkle as he did. It made me feel like everything was okay; it made me forget he knew beforehand.

Why aren't you out riding your bike he asked? I don't have a bike, I answered. The next thing I knew, and I was leaving his place with my homework and completed.

When I returned to my apartment, I looked at the clock over the TV; one and a half hours had passed, and all I remembered was we had done my homework. That's when I knew Mr. Reilly was someone special.

In mid-November, there was a big argument between Mr. and Mrs. Rentas up in apartment 3A. It started out kind of easy with only a word. Then it got louder until finally everyone in the building heard it. My parents told me I wasn't allowed to go upstairs. I wanted to go and see them fight, but my mother said if I put one foot on those stairs, I would be grounded for a month. So, I just stood at the stairway and listened.

Then, everything got very quiet, and I heard..."It isn't nice to find pleasure in another's misery." I turned around and looking at me with the happiest smile was Mr. Reilly. He said, " excuse me," and then he stepped passed me and went upstairs.

A few minutes later, I heard a door close. Then, Mr. Reilly came down smiling more than before. He went to his apartment not saying a word. Mr. and Mrs. Rentas had stopped fighting. There was no yelling or fighting. All that I could hear was the normal sounds of pipes rattling, people walking, and other normal sounds of a three-story brick apartment building.

Two days before Thanksgiving, my parents sent my sister and me to Mr. Reilly's apartment. They wanted to invite him to our Thanksgiving's dinner. They said they didn't know if he had plans. My parents thought that it would be nice to have him. It would also be the neighborly thing to do.

So, we went next door…

We knocked and stood waiting for him to say come in. We waited and a few minutes went by, and we knocked again. Still there was no answer. We decided to try the door and to my surprise it was unlocked. As we pushed it open, we said," Mr. Reilly? Are you here?" When he didn't answer, we opened the door more and stepped in-side.

By this time, my sister was so scared that she just wanted to leave. I told her that I must look around. As I did, I noticed everything seemed the same from the last time I was there. The only difference was that there weren't any letters on the desk. My sister couldn't take it anymore and left me alone….

I was concentrating on my investigation. I saw now that there is a roll of paper with names laying there. I was just about to reach for it when I heard, "It's not polite to invite ones self-inside another's home!" I jumped about two feet then turned around. There, smiling as always was Mr. Reilly, eyes twinkling.

Well young lady: "Do you have a message for me?" I just stood there, embarrassed. "Well?" He said. I stared at him a moment then remembered why I had gone to his apartment; oh yeah, I started talking. My parents wanted me to invite you to our house for Thanksgiving's dinner. Mr. Reilly's smile widened and he replied, tell your parents that I would be happy to join your family on that special holiday. He also asked me if he needed to bring anything. It was my turn to smile; only your appetite I replied.

Thanksgiving Day

Mom brushed off her apron as she went to answer the door. I was busy mashing potatoes, and my sister was setting the table when we heard the knock. "Am I too early?" I heard Mr. Reilly say after Mom opened the door. "Goodness No!" You're just in time, my father replied with joy. The boys were playing, and I was finishing mashing potatoes.

As I walked into the living room, I felt very happy. My brothers and my parents were talking to Mr. Reilly. Then Mr. Reilly said, "Oh... I almost forgot" Mr. Reilly handed dad a paper bag with something inside.

My father pulled out what looked like a bottle of wine, and stated, now Mr. Reilly, you didn't have to do this. I guess I kind of frowned because Mr. Reilly smiled at me and said to my father, it isn't wine, its Sparkling cider, these young children are too young to drink. Also, I don't indulge myself. We walked to the table where Mom asked my sister and me to help bring the remaining items from the kitchen.

The boys were happy to sit next to Mr. Reilly. My father sat head of the table and my mom beside him. My sister and I were sitting side by side.

Our Thanksgiving dinner wasn't anything special; Mom had baked a small turkey which she bought on special. We had mashed potatoes, rice, pageant peas, green salad, stuffing and cranberry sauce. . For dessert Mom had made a pumpkin pie topped with cool whip.

After dinner, Mr. Reilly helped clean up and then he offered to wash the dishes. My first thought was alright! No dishes for me tonight, but as usual, I was wrong.

Mom told Mr. Reilly guest don't do dishes in our home, "do they my dear daughter?" Knowing what was next; I said no, and I went to the kitchen with my sister and started the water. My parents and Mr. Reilly talked for a while then I heard him say, you must let me supply Christmas dinner and with that he left.

December came and with it, all the songs, commercials, and billboards. My dad was working two jobs by now. The money was just to pay the rent and bills. My parents had enough money to get us a present and a tree. I already knew we wouldn't have much, but we were used to it. Christmas was never my favorite time of the year because I saw how it bothered my parents. They didn't feel comfortable in New York as they did in Puerto Rico. Money was very tight.

During the next few days, I saw Mr. Reilly often. He was either coming or going to his apartment. On the first Friday of the month, he had pinned an envelope to his trash, it just said "READ THIS".

Inside was a note that read, I'm sure you'll need this before Christmas, consider it an advance pay for the month. Attached was a twenty-dollar bill. The note was written in red ink. After that I rarely saw Mr. Reilly.

I saw the midgets several times during the next two weeks, but Mr. Reilly only once.

A couple of days before Christmas, Mr. Reilly was on his way out, with a big suit bag like those used when traveling. I asked him what was in it, he looked at me and with a sly smile, replied, "Why, my Santa suit of course!" then he started chuckling. I just thought he was being a wise guy and smiled back. He continued walking down the hall humming jingle bells as he did.

Two days before Christmas, I saw Mr. and Mrs. Rentas carrying groceries into the building. They never looked happier. Mrs. Rentas whispered softly to her husband as they walked. All the neighbors heard Mrs. Rentas when they told them that her husband had stopped drinking. He was even working and helping around the house.

On Christmas Eve, my father sent me to ask Mr. Reilly if he wanted to join us for some "coquito" and "arroz con dulce".

I knocked and knocked, but he didn't answer. I put my ear to the door and listened but heard nothing. I went back and told my parents that he wasn't home.

When I returned to our apartment, Mr. and Mrs. Rentas stopped by, then, Mr. Rodriguez and the Smith family showed up.

Next thing we knew, there were several people at our tiny apartment talking, and drinking "coquito". Mr. Rodriguez took out a guitar and started playing "parranda" songs, slowly, everybody started singing.

I couldn't help but wish Mr. Reilly was here too. It was almost mid-night when everyone left. My parents and I picked up the glasses and took them to the kitchen. Mom told us to leave everything in the sink. All the dishes will be cleaned in the morning. I filled the sink with dish washing detergent. I placed the glasses and small dishes in the sink. I went back into the living room with my father.

My sister and boys have been sleeping for a couple of hours by now. They went to sleep early so that Christmas morning would get here faster.

Our tree was only about two feet tall, but it was beautiful. We all helped with the decoration. My father let each one of us put the tinsel and decoration while he did the lights.

We stood still in the living room looking at the tree; there were only seven presents under it. Each of us had one gift from my parents.

I got one for Mr. Reilly. I looked up at my parents and they were smiling at me. They knew that I was thinking about Puerto Rico, but still, love filled the room...

On Christmas morning, I woke up hearing my parent's saying "Oh my goodness!" I quickly rushed into the living room and couldn't believe my eyes. The tree we had only the night before had grown. It was an easy six feet tall, fully decorated and sparkling like it was covered with stars. Underneath it there were presents lots and lots of presents.

In the dining room, the table was filled with food, ham, turkey and dressing. There were all kinds of food. Even Christmas cookies. My parents were amazed. Where did it all come from, they whispered.

We looked at each other and, at the same time said, "What happened?" I started to reach for one of the many gifts when I saw a note tied to a branch of the tree. I pulled it off and looked at it; all that was written on it was, "To the Pagán family". I handed it to Mom and waited as she opened it.

I watched as she silently read the note inside. Tears welled up in her eyes and started rolling down her face. Mom, what is it I asked? She looked at me and smiled, she handed me the note and I read, Merry Christmas. It was signed with S. Nicholas. Who is this person I asked? My Parents smiled again and said, the answer is found with the gifts. Each gift was signed your friend, S. Nicholas.

Who is S. Nicholas I again asked? My father reached down, picked up a gift wrapped in shiny red wrapping paper, here, he said, to me.

I looked at my sister and maybe this one will answer your question.

There wasn't a name tag on it. She quickly ripped it open, and inside she found Barbie doll. My sister longed for that doll for years. In the box was a note, it said, "It isn't polite to question a gift origin", Love; Mr. Reilly. You may know me better as Saint Nicholas or Santa for short.

That was one great Christmas morning, even though we were far away from Puerto Rico.

This story, my friends, was just a dream…

STORY 54

The Process of Life

Lots of people don't want to face the fact that they are getting older. Getting old is just a process and should be appreciated.

Every year we celebrate birthdays. A birthday is the process of aging. So many wastes or damage this process by not taking care of their health. When you are eating and exercising properly, you are taking care of the process of life.

Aging is a natural process of life. It begins the moment we are born. Strangely enough, most of us live under the illusion that we and our loved ones will never become old.

When old age arrives, we are often unprepared. The natural order becomes reversed. The young help to care for the old. Those who need to be taken care of for the first time have a hard time accepting that they need help. This condition is a product of our culture that does everything it can to conceal the loss of youth.

Confronting this reality is the beginning of a healthy relationship to life, aging and death.

STORY 55

Living with Dementia

The quiet after the storm: It's raining in Ponce and it's quiet now. The water trickles down the spout and drops are still splattering from the eves. It's soothing. I slept well, better than any night during the last past weeks. A warm glow, an inner peace fills me. I'm content and very happy. I have decided to move with my parents......

I had a strange effect of knowing that my mom had Alzheimer. I didn't fully understand what the doctor was telling me, but after the first shock of the news there was a moment of sadness and fear. Then I felt a sudden wave of peace and serenity when I started getting a lot of information about the sickness.

Dealing with this disease alone wasn't easy. My dad is also very sick with diabetes, heart problems arthritis and many other medical issues that come with age. He was there in the same household but wasn't much help. I have siblings that I believe didn't care.

Many times, I called my sister, and she didn't say anything about coming to Puerto Rico to give me a hand. I had a full-time job, and it wasn't easy reporting to work with a smile I was an instructor in the National Guard and I always did my job and reported on time.

There were many times that I came home from work and found my dad on the floor. My mom was crying because she didn't know what was going on. They were all day without eating even though I have left lunch in the fridge.

After that incident, I decided to retire from the job I really enjoyed doing. It was a sad decision, but my parents always were first on my list.

The early signs that something was wrong with my mother were subtle.

"She was getting angry a lot. She would go to her neighbor's house without telling me." She also got lost walking down familiar streets.

Her first thoughts after being diagnosed were to just sit and do nothing. "Lying there like vegetables", but the darkness didn't last.

"You can either just roll over or let it come or begin living your life because I am not dead," she told me in the living room.

My whole life changed after I moved with my parents. I made sure I was at her side when she went to see her doctor. He would give me a list of specialists. They were all very helpful. We became a team. Her primary doctor was the best. He told me one day that if other care takers followed orders from their physician, their love ones will be in better conditions.

Ironically, there are advantages to Alzheimer's. My mother became more focused on what was important to her. She stayed in contact with everybody she loved.

At first, she was afraid of what her friends might say. I was always there with a little humor, and they responded with their continued support.

She still had many ups and downs, which she didn't admit. This dis-ease never stopped me from taking mom shopping or dancing.

In fact, in her good days, she was making plans for the coming holidays or events. I gave a monthly journal to her doctor, Dr. Elvin Pacheco Segarra. He was happy with some of the progress she was making.

Unfortunately, I want to point out, the incidence of Alzheimer's in-creases with age. About half the people that reach 80 can expect to get it. Statistics from the Alzheimer's Association confirm this fact.

"This catastrophe could be averted – with more research...

There's an answer out there."

For now, I emphasize the value of early diagnosis. It makes all the difference to be prepared and plan the rest of anyone's life.

Knowing what she was up against, I had the time to prepare; mentally, physically, emotionally and spiritually for what was going to happen.

As soon as she started her medication, the anger stopped. As for brain function, relative to the world, she was still in the normal range, because I started monitoring her behavior.

Mom exercised her mind by playing dominos with my dad and me.

She exercised her body by doing Zumba.

My mother, the mother of three, a grandma of four and great-grandmother, still did her chores. She didn't get lost anymore.

She would tell me, "It's strange, but being diagnosed with Alzheimer's has made a profound difference in me for the better!

She would question me "I'm going to die? And then gave me an an-swer. So, what!" I am ready……

She confided, "When I was younger, I was always waiting for or reaching for different goals in life, instead of living in the moment".

She used to tell me that I was the reason for her being alive. I kept her on her toes. There was never a dull moment…

My dear mother died on December 16, 2013, at the age of 83. I miss mom and sometimes I feel as if she is still with me. I smile and keep on doing my daily routine……

I am presently retired and enjoying life. My dad still lives with me. All his ailments are controlled. We go for walks, and I keep him eating healthy. At 87, my dad looks great!

STORY 56

My Sister and Best Friend

What can I say about my dear sister Adelin which I love with all my heart…?

Well, like any normal family, we grew up surrounded by lovable parents. My sister is younger than me. We shared everything.

As we got older, we got even closer. We used to talk about boys and friends in general. When it came time to choose a high school, my sister went to the school I went, Prospect Heights H.S.

I used to give her a lot of advice and she did listen. She was a sweet and gentle child. I was the opposite. I guess I was the mother hen to all my siblings.

I recalled one time when a girl came to our block in Brooklyn. She was calling my sister. My parents weren't home. Adelin went downstairs and this girl way older than us wanted to fight. I ran so fast from our apartment to meet this girl.

This young lady came with another girl claiming that Adelin was going out with her cousin's boyfriend. I told them to mind their own business. It wasn't my sister fault that the so call boyfriend didn't want her cousin anymore.

Well, guess what? The girls came toward my sister to hit her. That is when I got so angry that I turned into a lunatic on top of one of the girls. It happened to be the oldest one. I warned her not to get close to Adelin. She didn't listen.

In the meantime, the girls around the block came to join me. I told them that I can take care of the situation, but to stand by just in case I needed help.

Adelin just stood there crying. I took a stick and was hitting both girls. The two girls couldn't fight back. I beat them badly. They were on the ground for a while. I stopped fighting and they ran without a word.

When the fight was over, we went to the corner store for some ice-cream. The owner gave us free milkshakes because he knew those girls were trouble. The whole block congratulated me, and the two losers went to Bonds Street with their clothes ripped and messed up hair......

There were a lot of situations where I had to help Adelin. I was always there.... Things were no different as adults....

In the following you will see how close we are that is scary....

I used to think that my sister was part of a Central plan made by God....

It is easy to say that a person has a serious advantage in life if they come from a loving and supportive family. Many people still succeed even though they come from less-than-ideal family situations. By having our basic needs and knowing that our parents loved us, it made it better to cope with all the challenges of day-to-day living. It was much easier to face any obstacle as we grew older.

Adelin and I were always coming up with different ideas to help around the house. My mom didn't know how to handle simple every day problem. She used to tell us to wait for our father to come home. We got tired of that answer; therefore, we made our own decisions without telling her.

This was no coincidence. I truly believe that God organized us into families so that we can grow up in happiness and safety. Sometimes I think that we learned to love each other selflessly. It was the key to true joy.

Our neighbors were not surprised when we have graduated from high school with honors and went on to college. My sister, brothers and I had a dream. That dream came true. It was to finish our education and be ready for the future.

Our family always came first. Perhaps we were one of the lucky ones who were raised in a happy and secure household with two loving parents.

Likely, as adults, we wanted the same happy environment for our family. Now a day, living peacefully in a family isn't easy. For us, family values were number one. Those values, taught by our parents, strengthen our family.

Many people who have lived through disasters never say, "All I could think about during the earthquake was my bank account." They always say, "All I could think about was family." It shouldn't require a disaster for us to know that this is the truth.

When we were growing up, we made a pledge. I reminded my siblings that we were a team. No one would even dare to bother us because we were there for each other.

We made believe that were actors in some sort of play. I told them to think of the parts we had or will play, in our family r ole. We looked at all the responsibilities that went along with each one of us. We all put a lot of efforts in put into strengthening our family.

I am saying this because we moved to New York and my parents weren't ready to raise us there. Things were very complicated in the new environment. In Puerto Rico, my parents had it all.

We were always helping our parents by keeping a peaceful home. We never complained about anything. My sister and two brothers helped me by putting each other's need first. We never bother to ask for new clothes or toys. All four us learned how to recycle at a very young age. We never got discouraged.

No matter how hard things were, we tried to keep our home almost perfect.

I remember one Christmas day that we told our parents that we were happy by just getting hats and gloves as gifts. I promised my siblings that I will save every penny to buy what we really wanted without letting our parents know.

Guess what? We did fine. Since we were so good in school, we all put together a business. I told dad that we needed a typewriter to do our school work. I started typing term papers. My brother Papo did the cover. Julio did some writing and Adelin put all the papers together. We made a couple of dollars weekly. We had so much money that we bought leather coats and nice outfits. Sometimes my dad would borrow from us. He had to pay back with interest of course.

As we got older, the boys drifted apart, but Adelin and I remained close....

When I got married, my sister was the one that gave me the money needed for the reception. We both paid for the whole event. We even bought my mother's her dress, shoes and accessories. We paid for the rental of my father's tux.

A couple of years later, my sister was getting marry. Once again, we both paid for everything. We never bother our parents with our problems of monetary expenses. My dad just paid the necessary bills for the house. If my mom needed anything, my sister and me were there to buy it. My mother never asked for much. We spoiled her all the time. My father was happy because he didn't spend anything on her.

Even after we got married, we took care of our parents. They moved to Puerto Rico, and we mailed them packages and money....

STORY 57

The Retirement Home in Paradise

A hundred dead and dying flowers occupied the shelves in Alma's garage. Many sunlit mornings push past her window and beam in hot amber bars against her curling wallpaper.

They coax her to the nursery, where she meticulously searches for the most colorful, healthy-looking plants. There were Petunias and violets, each blessed with the delightful promise of continual budding.

They would jerk and twist in their crates in the back of the car, waiting for their debut to new soil.

Alma's son decided her future, so the foliage will now sit for a bone-dry day on the shelf.

Cathy makes her tea at six o'clock each morning. She has never been to England and hates her "first generation American" title. She speaks with an English accent acquired from her parents, dead and gone, reads etiquette books from cover to cover, writes on fancy stationery to old acquaintances who seldom return a word.

Cathy's house seeps lace, buckles under the weight of flashy chandeliers, drowns in inherited China used once a year when her brother and his family visit for Thanksgiving. He does not speak with an English accent.

Judy pours God onto the road every morning with rice flower and colored spices in the hopes of dispelling negative vehicular energy.

She powers washes the house once a month; she prays; she reads all the important books and follows their words humbly and blindly.

Judy sleeps in a bed with her boyfriend who never kisses her and three spiders who kiss her often. "And I'll take this," she says, handing the clerk a small wind chime. She picks up peacemakers wherever she finds them: incense, candles, lavender bath balm, a book of inspirational quotations compiled by Roger M. Baldwin, Ph.D. Judy keeps a modest home, whose roof shelters a wild daughter, a growing son, her boyfriend, and herself.

The wind never blows too much around her house. Judy spends most of her time as a counselor at the retirement community. She works at the quilt store. Sometimes she makes quilts inspired by the work of Picasso, whose art she greatly admires. Judy believes above all things in happiness derived from the simplest of pleasures: the song of a sewing machine, brightly patterned fabrics, Mr. Fuzzy the cat, the perfect color of thread.

Judy takes art classes too. It helps her see the colors brighter. The staff of the general believes her to be positively imbalanced. Judy's daughter is moving to New Jersey. She says. It's up north, west of some cattle ranching town that no one's ever heard of, she says.

Now Judy moves all her quilting things into her daughter's old room, but she forgets one thimble, which sits in the corner, occasionally illuminated by the headlights of her son's truck as he returns from another lost rodeo, or sometimes by the moon.

A visiting singer would have thought that the weekly carolers were the highlight of Alma's week, but nobody knew for sure.

Judy would be the speaker at her a retirement home. She will be working with students from her old high school. Toward the beginning of their visits to the Paradise Retirement Home, she would ask only once who is willing to help her. No one gave her an answer…

Judy was forced to ask again. The second time through, the students only want to sing. They would only sing the first, third, and last verse. To the singers, the shortened version always sounded funny and cheap, and maybe it sounded funny to Alma and Judy too.

Maybe that was the taste in her mouth on the rainy night that she didn't wheel out into the entryway to hear the singers. The singers didn't know that she felt hung up by the dwarfed version brought toyou by Alzheimer's, by old age or maybe just by wanting to hear the whole song.

In fact, when the wailing ambulance pulled out into the rain, they didn't even know it was Alma. Alma died in her sleep. Now Judy has no one to express her crazy way of thinking.

STORY 58

The Fact of Life

"Your hands are like icicles on the horizon," John said and took a sip of coffee. Mary nodded blankly at him, barely registering the observations that tilted his tongue and flavored his mouth.

"Do you see how you are shaking?" he asked, not taking his eyes off her. He started ordering dinner. John fumbled down distractedly on the table. He found his plate and devoured a fry in the half-reflective way that dressed all his actions.

To this, she murmured a vague, "Mmhmm..." It was enough of a reply to fill the empty space he controlled over the table, but still enough to be noncommittal and inattentive.

Mary reached through the maze of their cups and plates to spear a French-fry from his plate. She shifted her weight. The chair rocked under her, threatening her already uncertain balance and attempted grace in one blow. Mary shifted the feet of the chair, hoping to find some sort of balance, but again the seat rocked under her, still precarious.

"Look at the angles to her face," John went on, working his words around mouthfuls. His eyes never wavered in their stiff critical stare of wonderment and interest. "There's just something about her that screams vulnerability."

"Hmm." Mary swallowed the hot, gritty remains of her tea. Her cup clunked as it hit the table, jolting the settled objects, but his attention never strayed from the Raphael-wonder.

Mary picked up her croissant, then lowered it back to her plate seeing the tanned lines of her knuckles holding her fingers in place. She turned her palm up and followed the trained lines that traced her destiny.

"You really have to wonder about people like that," John continued in the silence. "How they think, how they feel, how they see the world. Don't you ever just wish you could go up and introduce yourself to a stranger and learn their entire life story?"

Mary repossessed her croissant and took a voice-saving mouthful, nodding her head disjointedly in case he possessed the consciousness to glance at her tongue-trapped tangle on the other side of the table. She sneakily slid her feet out of her shoes and flexed her toes in their freedom under the tablecloth-tiered table.

Mary had so much pain in her bones. Her thoughts drowned in the haze of mid-stride wonderment, but not before the emptiness and pain of dismissal.

"I guess it's time to go," John said finally, still not moving his unblinking eyes or shifting his stranger-struck body.

Mary mumbled affirmative and followed through with her purse. Her purse was very full. It knocked against her hand in the fruitful search for cash. Dumping the entire contents out for the finding and usage of a pen, she crumpled up her eyebrows, figuring the total into halves.

"Mind getting this one for me?" John asked, raising himself up to gather his belongings before heading out the door. Still his attention wandered over to the daisy, blooming at the opposite table. "This was fun. Let's get together again sometime soon, OK?"

She fell back in her seat, drowning in the whirlpool of inattention. Establishing their funds, she turned to see herself in the shadowy glass window reflection and saw herself slipping away from reality....

STORY 59

The Lonely Old Maid

Emely suspects she has only had one true affair and that is with her dogs. All those before having been stingy attempts to get to her money...

Emely sits everyday watching her synthetic roses. There is a crack running the length of the ceramic pot that marks their station on the brick step.

She sits observing their activity, isolates herself from the solemn sermon their blushing heads deliver, ducking in the wind. She is always waiting for something to happen.

Emely has lost or perceives she has lost. She sees death everywhere. The looks for death on the horizon is what she fears. She has lost the ability to make things occur.

How useful youth was in the day-to-day creation of happenings. Now, she has displaced the seasons, and the pleasant stretch of nothingness, a featureless backdrop, assimilates itself to her emotionless face, as she welcomes the weather.

She lives in very comfortable house that her father left her. The house located in a small town in Montana. Its strong walls and fine structure are the envy of the town. People want to buy her property, but she always says no...

Emely used to live in New York where life was on the fast lane mode. Here in the other hand, winter dominates every day of the week.

The other day, Emely, enquired around town about the land next to her home. She wanted to know whether anyone currently resided there. They were concerned about her, but no answer was given.

Her accent was obvious that she came from the city that never sleeps…

She spoke in disturbed sometimes but very secure. Her language of dinner parties and familial get-togethers were always in her conversations.

Even though she was a German descent, she had no trace or tone of being German.

She walked self-consciously, away from them, shielding herself from their accusatory recognition, feeling as an outsider, a fugitive. As though wearing the flag of her inheritance on her lapel.

Her father died when she was twenty and that is how she got that property…

Emely never visited her father or cared for him. She was all he had. Her mother moved with Emely to New York when was only six. This man was very strict. He did what he thought was best. He didn't know he was being abusive. He didn't know any better.

Emely doesn't receive visitors warmly. All prospective suitors dispatched by well-wishing relatives invariably retire back to their distant homes after an evening of her company.

Unsettled and discouraged, for she has created that for herself a feminine magic that cannot be penetrated by mere mortal man.

Emely appears in their perception abrupt, evasive, and preoccupied. She concentrates on cultivating a solid, scarlet heart to beat a constant rhythm against the world of the dying.

She is keeping death out in the physical sense, assimilating herself to the prospect of solitary eternity and forming no attachments. Emely refuses to be attached to an abusive relationship.

Sometimes she feels an inexplicable longing for the anonymity of the city she once knew. She politely declines moving back to New York. Emely is preferring to spend her days in the soft sunlight, arranging the weary roses.

She attempts to sweep away the misguided bugs with a few hesitant gestures of the hand. Soon blue saline solutions will wave a salutation to such foreign guests. Her light fingers graze the frayed edges of their heads; the bloody inks are particularly exciting in the sunlight.

When the thought of blood transpires, the dizzying swell of the heart's diastole and systole rises in her chest, a pressing undulation. So perhaps it comes as no conscious surprise when, upon waving the pruning shears in order to trim the petals of their half-eaten siblings, she clips her finger instead of a stem, loosening a sizeable flap of skin over a current of blood.

Emely resists the urge to suck the wound, but stares at her finger, suddenly regarding it as one does an unfamiliar object; a digit not attached to herself. How exquisite a ruby red the blood appears to be, and how warm against the skin.

It is amazing how, upon mutilation, a body part becomes something external to the person to which it belongs, merely a treasured belonging. She stares at the finger for so long that it ceases to be a finger, in the same way as a word fails to register in the consciousness as legitimate when it has been repeatedly vocalized.

Perhaps there is a separate self that exists beyond the body of physical composites. She puts down the sheers and rearranges the flowers, marveling over her secret discovery.

Oh, dear God. Please help me. Now is but a moment passing. When does the future become the present and the present become the past? When do the living become the dying, and the dead become the forgotten? The inhuman become the commemorated for the death that cleans the slate. Where does the tongue become the throat, and the voice become the word? The heart cease to be the person, but something bigger altogether?

Emely was found dead withing her flowers. No one came to her wake. No one never inquire about the lonely old maid from New York....

STORY 60

In Arms

The helicopter flew into our forests two days ago, chopping the air like a large dragonfly with gauze wings splayed, plastered in metal and broken.

Everyone heard it at dawn, and Jimmy wiped the dew wet inside his ears so that he could hear it again, chopping the air through our trees. The men jumped up, and so did he, hush hushing the fear and surprise. Jimmy forgot to breathe.

They found it today, sunning itself, its shadow short in the high hours of noon, waiting…

By the time Jimmy got to it, running, yelling, victory in his ears, the men had already gotten to the pilot. He sagged over the side of the rusted door with a small red hole on one side of his head and a large splash of black death yawning on the other. His army uniform scattered in green shaded shreds. A bullet can take away a lot with it; it comes in like a thief and leaves like a drunkard.

Jimmy climbed on the top of the metal creature, beating its green head with his fists, thinking it would crush in like a tin cup, victory in his ears. But no, the enemy would be stronger.

Jimmy hurt his hand. There was blood on metal oozing, he did not care. He had wrestled a beast and put it to its death. He broke his red glass bangle.

Jimmy used to wake up with the taste of his dreams in his mouth. They say that if you are in perfect silence, you can hear air beating inside your ears.

He could hear his voice beating in his mind even if he was dead. Jimmy lost himself to him without knowing, and one day he panicked; he could not find himself. Jimmy could not remember what he used to be like before. But then he did not care.

He was in himself, he was in his home, his soul. Jimmy could have heard him even if he was dead.

STORY 61

First Love

Carol was just thirteen years old when she fell in love with a boy four or five years older than her. It was the most joyous feeling Margo has experienced. She still cannot get over it, as they say when a woman falls in love, she can never fall in love again. Although she was a teenager, she still has vivid memories of that boy and how she felt for him.

Margo was a smart, bubbly and cute teenager, who enjoyed life and was living life to the fullest, when suddenly her life changed because of him.

Margo had set her eyes on him the first time when he had come to the colony park. He was chatting with his friends. Margo found him so handsome, his curly, dark brown hair and large dark brown eyes!

She was stunned! Though now when she looks back, she laughs it off as mere infatuation, but she doesn't know why she felt an instant connection with him.

When she looked into his eyes, her heart fluttered, and she used to feel so nervous and excited at the same time.

You won't believe it, but Margo never spoke to him, but still she felt a strong connection to him. Ricky was so handsome and so good looking, that whenever Margo used to look at him, she could not stop herself from staring.

He hardly bothered to even turn around and look at her. For Ricky was insignificant as she was much younger than him, therefore, he hardly even tried to take any interest in Margo.

Each day when Margo used to go to the park, she used to fix her hair differently. She used to wear her best dresses to look nice for him.

Her never noticed her....

Margo was so mad at him for not paying attention to her games. Sometimes she stood by the window, so that she could see Ricky playing in the park. She would spot him in a second. The rest of the times she would just sadly retreat to her studies or did some other work.

As days passed things remained the same when slowly and gradually, he started noticing that she stares at him all the time.

Once she remembers that she was standing in the neighborhood Bakery, and he suddenly Ricky walked in with his friends. Margo turned around and as usual started staring at him. Margo was in shocked. She noticed Ricky staring at her!

There was admiration and tender love in them! She then left the Bakery feeling very shy and still now she cannot forget that look of his eyes in the Bakery.

This boy was very tall and fair and had the loveliest hair and a very smart moustache and whenever she looked at him, her knees got very weak.

One afternoon Margo was returning home from school. She saw Ricky sitting on his bike waiting for his friends. He saw her coming and when Margo passed him, he did not do anything. When she went a little further, she heard some noise behind her. She looked at him, he smiled at her.

Margo was too shocked to respond in any way. She turned around and went to her house. She did not know what to do, but she was fascinated by his first smile.

The following day, Ricky was in front of her building waiting for her. Margo couldn't believe it. He was all smiles. This time he had a car. They didn't say a word to each other. She just got in his car and they drove away.

Ricky didn't take Margo to school. He took her a small apartment where he lives. Margo was still in shocked that she was in his apartment. Without a word, they began to undress....

Ricky was an experienced man with women of all ages. Margo, a sweet 13 years old in experienced kid. She was simply following his gestures. Margo had no idea of how serious this situation was leading to.

They were together for almost eight hours. He kissed her very softly at first. Then, he showed her some different position and every time, there was penetration. Margo felt lots of pain. This was the first time she had sexual intercourse. She thought that this was normal.

When Ricky got tired of his new bait, he motioned her to get dress. He took her home after eight hours. They had nothing to eat. There were just two body having sexual contact...

Margo still couldn't believe what just happened. Her body was all sore. She went straight to her room and felt asleep.

Everything was so sudden that she was lost for words as to what should her next step may be, but fate had other plans for her .

Just imagine her bad luck, that when she could think of having a serious relationship with Ricky. Her father informed that they were moving...

All Margo could think was of Ricky. He has finally acknowledged her presence. He has smiled at her and even had sex. Now, she had to leave the city for good!

Her father was transferred to another town, and she had to leave the very next day! Margo had to travel all alone, as her father had arranged for school admissions in that town.

I could have had a beautiful relationship with this Ricky. He never knew that she was only 13 years old and pregnant with his child....

Margo didn't know till now whether it was love.

First love is like a fresh blooming flower in the morning sunlight, it is like the first most memorable fragrance you might have smelt in your entire life!

Anyway, those are ways of God no one can question them, but again Margo wants to repeat that was her first love, and she will never forget him...

STORY 62

Just A Brief Romance

It was one of those days, when it rains unceasingly, and Tina must hurry up to catch the bus to go to work. Her hair looked untidy as she tried to pull up the hood of her raincoat over her head.

Water dripped from her hair. Suddenly her phone rang. She looked a bit alarmed as she was expecting some colleague of hers to call. It was not one of them.

It was her cousin calling her.

Her name was Denise. She was twenty- six, tall, dark with a warm smile and sensitive eyes which looked eternally joyful. All Tina's siblings and her were married.

They had arranged marriages and were living comfortably so now it was Denise turn to get married. She was working as a receptionist in a hotel located near the Airport.

"Tina, I got married"

"Who is the lucky guy?"

"His name is Kevin. He is a driver by profession. He drives his Uncle's car who happens to be my Boss".

Her joyful voice made her shudder. She could no longer keep track of what she was saying. A driver by profession, my cousin had committed a mistake. What more could she say when there were so many young men with lucrative pay packages who were interested in her. She had chosen a taxi driver over them.

"Where are you staying?"

"In my in-law's place"

"Take care"

Denise ended their conversation abruptly. There were pains of despair cutting in her heart.

Denise was a girl extravagant taste. She wore jeans which cost two thousand dollars. Her father happened to be a director in college, who had spent all his money on his dear daughter's education.

He was a man of strict principles. Other than that, he took special pride in the fact that he was a "Boricua".

Tina really did not know how her uncle would be able to tolerate his daughter's discreet behavior. The incident or accident as he would call it would ruin them all....

Two hours later after reaching her job, Tina called his Aunt. She was crying over her daughter's betrayal.

Never had her Aunt suspected anything existing between Denise and her new husband Ricardo...

Denise was trusted always by her parents. My Uncle would never understand his wife. The old generation has pride. They wanted to control their children's lives....

STORY 63

The Departure

It was drizzling outside. Arnaldo drove the car through the occasional mist, climbing the winding roads up the high ranges. Debbie did not say anything. They knew it was their last journey together. The last time he would be taking her to her job.

Arnaldo remembered all the moments they had together from the moment he first met her. How happy they both were together!

The wedding spoiled their relationship. Debbie belonged to a different religion. Arnaldo regret not marrying a Jew.

Debbie was catholic and still, she wanted to marry Arnaldo…

Arnaldo remember that his parents denied their greedy love and desire to be together.

Arnaldo's rage and grief reflected on the speedometer of the car.

"Please, go slow", Debbie said at last.

When Arnaldo had a sideways glance, he saw her digging in her bag.

"Can you please pull over?", Debbie asked.

She looked sick. Arnaldo stopped the car under a cherry blossom tree which stood by the roadside, shedding flowers all over the place, bathing the ground under it in blood red. He looked at her.

"Why did you want me to stop?"

She took out a bottle of imported perfume from her bag. Her favorite brand.

"You may take this. Please don't forget me, I beg."

I could see her eyes welling up. I didn't know what to say. I felt my heart drowning in icy water.

"No,". I said, "I can't take this dear. This fragrance will remind me of you every day. I can't have that pain all days with you have gone forever from my life".

Her eyes started to spill even before I finished my words. That was the first time I ever saw her crying since I met her. I couldn't hold back my tears either which found their way down silently. I took her hand in mine.

"Please don't cry, darling".

My words were broken. I held her hand tight, like I never ever wanted to let her go. Arnaldo kissed the back of her palm. His tears kissed her even before his lips could do. The drizzle and the fog that remained on the windshields curtained them from the rest of the world.

A few hours later Arnaldo was back at the same place, alone, after dropping Debbie off at her job. Leaving her forever.

STORY 64

Deceiving Love

How do one start off? Beverly and Joe had no idea. Countless emotions were filling their inside. They were too young to understand adulthood.

Everything was guiding them to sex.... Should we have sex? This was the question that was always on Joe's mine.

The first time Joe laid eyes on Beverly was on this very day a year ago. Joe was walking slowly towards Beverly.

Joe was nervous and speechless. He didn't know how to ask a girl out. How could he ever ask Beverly to be his girl? She was popular in school. He was just a bore.

The first eye contact... He still remembers, it seemed like everything stopped for a while.

All he could see was that fascinating smile that blew away his mind. Beverly slowly trapped him.

She wanted Joe to believe he was the first.

This beautiful, elegant girl standing in front of him was his girlfriend! He still couldn't believe it.

The first time when her soft lips touched his, he felt love for the first time in his life.

Their lips seemed to be working in their own magical way dancing along with their tongue.

The way Beverly kissed him made him forget everything around him. It was definitely the feeling of love that she was pouring within him.

Then her touch on his bare skin, it felt as if she was making a sculpture on his body. She started using her magical fingers roaming all over him. Wow! He was in heaven with this goddess.

The way her lips felt, was something he could never forget. She made him feel like he was the only one. She wants to savor him forever.

Joe felt a tingling sensation inside his belly that was craving for her. When her fingers touched him, he couldn't help but let out a moan.

"You didn't just fill me within you, but you also devoured my soul, our souls met that day my lovely Beverly." That is what Joe was going to tell Beverly when they meet at a nearby restaurant.

Beverly, in the other hand, had an unforgettable speech that will blow Joe's mind. He was going to find out the truth about his goddess….

STORY 65

The Rain Child

The house is full of grief....

Rachael twisting an escaping strand of her straightened hair in her finger. She bit her lower lip to stop herself from getting emotional.

Outside, as she hears thunder, a sudden smile of secrecy escapes her pressed lips.

Abandoning her family in time of their need, she took one step back. Rachael started listening to the sound of her bangles as they gently clink against one another.

She took step and then turning around, she ran out of the main door.

Her long, curly hair is brushing softly against her back as she breaks into a sprint. Her lips slightly apart with the struggle of breathing. She was hoisting her ankle length skirt up. Rachael continues running until she reaches the far end of her back yard.

Around her, mango trees were swaying with the wind, waving to the lightning in the sky. She stood still, closing her eyes. Her head turned towards the clouds.

Rachael's fingers had let her Tulip red skirt fall beautifully over her legs as her arms slowly start moving upwards.

A warning thunder resounds in the sky, nature's call, and as if on cue, a drop of rain falls on her forehead. Within seconds, other plops on her nose till eventually, the drops cover her face.

Rachael smiles: loving every minute of the beauty with her eyes closed and then, she began spinning. She doesn't know how she looks but if her dad were standing next to her right now, he would have said that she looked like a rose amidst the greenness of nature.

Her father is her most favorite person in the entire world.

He always says that when If I'm happy, he's happy.

But I haven't told him yet that I'm only happy when he's around. Now, it may be too late…

"Darling," He'd say on a random day, as we both sat in our lawn, lazing around and taking in the beauty of the sunshine. "Have I ever told you the story about you and the rain?"

Rachael giggles and say, "Yes! But I want to hear it again."

He'd chuckle at her excitement and start off with the story she over a hundred times in my life.

"You were only 10 months old!" He told her, with stars in his eyes, every time he repeated that story. "A miracle baby.

One day, we had left the main door ajar, and you heard the rain pouring outside and crawled out." His face would turn into dismay. "It was a good fifteen minutes before your mother, and I found you. God, the horror in my heart! Would you believe, just when I was ready to call the cops, I saw you from out the window, sitting near the mango trees, giggling in the rain? I never left the door open again!"

At this memory, he fondly laughed. "My rain child."

STORY 66

Nothing Matters

"Small town guys"-the phrase really hurts Wilma when she realized that she is being "unintentionally" not like for being fancy.......

Sometimes Wilma feels doomed, why she is not among those who were born in metro cities, why she is not given the privileges to see the smog less sky, mornings of noise less chirping, simple people, milk tea in stained and small glasses, our small happiness and so on.......

Now it is a very hard task to describe her town. It is a casual small town. You may come across this type of random cities while you travel by train. It is so insignificant that you can't even remember its name after some time... So, it is better not to take its name....... Just for the sake of randomness, her city is nameless...

Exclusively this term can define your dream. They are insane in the sense, even you can't think in a dream about our dreams; we are that much productive in making our dreams.... Do you want an example? have a look'....

1. This is a kind of out-of-box dream... I wanted to use the word "fucking" many times in speaking to achieve metropolitan Polishness to like me.

2. Using pretentious words in conversation.... Like "procrastination", "entrepreneurship" which is famous one in my college, "narcissism" ...etc.......

3. Listening to English music, ridiculously imitating your gesture when you listen to those craps, this is my point of view or even trying to mug up the lyrics.......

See, this English is playing a great roll in our dreams, they are very crucial ingredient of our dream. This language, in fact, ease the way to win a debate; more pretentious words in conversation will help you to prove her wrong at any point of conversation, we fear "pretentious" words...

"Demotivating" mojito:

Wilma believes that she is the first person to use "demotivating" as an adjective before mojito.

Before coming to this big city, she did not know about what the hell is "mojito"???is it "mojito" or "mozito"???and how can it have a variety called "virgin"??

Then one day she got disappointed when she discovered -it is nothing but tap ice water with some essence of lemon and costing $5.00 a glass.

It is too high!! But the matter that saddened her the most is she was corrected by one of her linguistic-genius friends that it is – "Mojito" and everyone with her burst into laughter.

After that incident Wilma stopped buying mojito. My first and last mojito was shocking....

You know one thing, guys??? These "mojito massacre" and the other things you did with Wilma was just a toughening process for her.

She absorbed all your so-called 'critique'. It is like a piece of activated charcoal in polluted water......

But sadistic pleasure comes at that moment when she realizes that you are in the same longitude, same latitude and same level of dignity.

Vilma knows that it is useless to tell you not to bully anyone. One more thing Wilma is not criticizing all the metro-kids, but some of them are insensible in their own way of "criticizing" . Now you may be thinking when Wilma repeats to her friends.... Who am I? that 'I' is as random as the name of her town? That 'I' never mattered ...

STORY 67

The Sacrifice

Usually, parents are the one who sacrifice everything for the sake of their children.

But there are some children who sacrificed their passion and dreams for the sake of their parents due to some reasons such as financial, family, and health.

This is a story of a boy who sacrificed his dreams and passion at very early age.

Like others, he also had the dream of becoming a sportsman.

One day while practicing for athletics, he got a serious knee injury, which buried his dream of becoming a good athlete.

As the injury was severe, he was advised to not to play sports anymore, Then his parents consoled him to quit sports so that there would be no health problems in future. The young boy sacrificed his sportsman dream for the sake of his health, thereafter, he never played any of the sport but his dream was still alive.

Another incident that he sacrificed his dream of going abroad for higher studies as that time his father had suffered severe heart stroke.

At that time his father was heavily suffocated and told his son to call ambulance, boy called the ambulance and rushed him to hospital.

Finally, they reached hospital and treatment was started and all going fine. Then after a while doctor came said "Your father is safe, and you brought him on time otherwise things would be different". These words shocked the boy, which led him in a dilemma that if he goes abroad, who will take care of his parents? He dropped off his dream and stayed with his parents.

Also, he sacrificed his love life and freedom because his parents were badly affected by his sister's marriage which was a love and arrange marriage.

Even though it was love marriage there were quarrels in his sister's mothers-in-law house. There were quarrels in his house also and his parents were mentally disturbed for almost 5-6 years.

For these reasons he sacrificed his freedom and love life and was unable to relocate to other locations for higher studies, job purpose etc., As he must take care of his parents.

By God's grace, after this much of sacrifices now I am experiencing a little bit of happiness as my parents are good now, they are retired and living happily.

For the happiness of his parents, Michael had sacrificed all his dreams, career, passion, etc.

If you don't experience sadness, you will not be able to enjoy happiness. Sad and happy both are complementary words.

Parents never tell us to "leave your career and be with us", but at some point, they think about us and feel that "our children are not with us". Try to postpone your work or sacrifice your time to spend with your parents.

Mother can show her love to her children limitless; father cannot show his love to children but, in universe father is only person who loves the entire family and sacrifices everything for his family.

Respect your parents and love them from bottom of your heart. They are not going to live forever.

STORY 68

The Interview.

It was the early 2010. A good year to start a business. Many of Ramona's friends are over 30 years old and still single....

Ramona was unemployed and was eager to start her own company. She decided to be a matchmaker. Like all single and beautiful women, Ramona was very popular.

It was around August, when Ramona decided to create "Cupid Enterprise". People were always asking her about dating in her hometown, therefore, she took advantage of that opportunity.

The local newspaper did a full section on her with a huge photo. Later that month, she received an email from some radio program inviting her to a show. The show was about young entrepreneur.

Ramona was going to be interviewed on the radio! She didn't listen to any station, and she had no idea who he was going to interview her.

She told her family and they all said, "Go for it! It could be fun!"

She finally met the person that was going to do the interview. His name is Joey. He informed her that their meeting will be the following week. It was going to be an on-air interview...

I remember very clear the day I showed up for the interview. Joe was sitting at his desk looking very professional. I was dressed to kill. I had a beautiful navy-blue suit, black shoes and the cutest purse. My hair was pulled back. My makeup was very simple, however, I looked great.

Joey took one look at Ramona and was stunned. The interview went very well. Since it was a live interview, people started calling left and right. It was a very productive interview for both Joey and Ramona.

After the interview, they decided to go for a couple of drinks. They were talking like a couple of old friends.

Let me tell you that weeks turned into months. Her mother told her that they looked so cute together. Ramona admitted that she enjoyed his company. Also, let me remind you, that Joey worked at a local radio station, and Ramona own dating agency. They were well known throughout the whole city…

Guess what? They were engaged a year later…

Joey and Ramona have been married for twelve years. They have four wonderful children.

"Ramona would have missed out on a lot in life if she would had skipped that interview!"

STORY 69

The Wrong Number

Helen was a freshman at Boston University when something strange happened to her....

She was texting her friend Olga. For some reason, instead of sending her text to Olga, the phone sent it to a random New York number. It was a man on the other side. He texted her back asking who she was....

When they figured out the strange phenomenon, Arthur asked Helen if she wanted to be his friend.

Arthur decided to go to Boston. He has friend there and it will some sort of mini vacation. Arthur told Helen that he wasn't a mental patient. He has master's degree in biology and that he really wants to finish his education in medical school. Helen was a freshman, however, she had one goal and that was to become a mechanical engineer.

They finally met in Boston as planned. Arthur and Helen hit it off from the minute they met.

After seven years of dating and going back and forth from Boston to New York, they got engage. They are both professionals and are planning a June wedding....

STORY 70

The Coffee House

It was at a coffee house when it happened....

The place was packed as usual. Diana stood online and started looking around. She was just looking when she saw the most gorgeous man a few people ahead of her.

They made eye contact a couple times. Diana couldn't believe that this nice-looking guy was looking at her. Helen's heart was beating out of her chest!

Dave ordered; Helen waited her turn. She got her own cup of coffee. She walked over to the table where the cream and sugars are kept. He came over to fix up his coffee. He picked up the sugar bowl and asked me, "Do you take sugar?" To her surprise, he promptly dropped the bowl right at her feet! It covered both of their shoes!

They both cracked up. They decided to get a table together....

STORY 71

The lot

The dead car that gave Wilma her boring status a relationship for life…

Wilma was about to turn 30, therefore, she decided to do something 'fun' every day for the last month of her twenties. She ended up doing a lot of stupid meet-up things, including Cards Against Humanity tournament at a pub.

Everyone there was told to make sure their cars weren't parked in a certain lot.

Of course, Wilma's was in that lot, but when she went out to move it. Her car was dead. She had to call for a tow truck. The minute she met the tow Pete, the truck driver, was paralyze. She took one look at him, and something clicked in her.

They ended up spending the next two hours in the truck, just talking, laughing, and flirting HARD.

He dropped her off at her home. Wilma gave him her number. She had just enough time to text her sister. Wilma wanted to tell her sister about how thankful she was that her car broke down.

They have been dating for about a year. Wilma claims that Pete is the love of her life!"

STORY 72

Dog meets Dog

Brenda and her husband Freddie met walking dogs…

It was a sunny summer day before Brenda's summer college class began. She was walking her roommate's dog. Brenda had no makeup on. She had not washed her hair in three days. She was just thinking how she really needed to look human. Brenda wanted to look good for her classmate or while sitting on the grass waiting for the dog to potty.

Suddenly, she heard someone say hello… When she looked up, she saw a good-looking guy with a Golden Retriever.

They talked for a couple of minutes while their dogs smelled each other's butts. and we each went back to our apartments. Soon, we began to secretly anticipate each other's schedules so that we could take our dogs out at the same time and be able to talk.

After running into each other several times, he finally asked me out on a date. Now, a couple of years down the road, we have been blissfully married for five months!"

STORY 73

Love

Love Is not just a four-letter word... Love isn't always the answer. It doesn't always conquer that emptiness in your life. Yet, many lack a clear understanding of what love is.

Some people idolize it as the answer to everything. The be-all and end-all solution to their problems. As a result, our relationships with the person we care suffer.

Therefore, love is not enough...

An unrealistic understanding of the concept of love can cause us quite some trouble. What happens when we overestimate the power of love? It can be seen all around us. When we think that love is everything we need, it's likely that our relationships lack existential ingredients.

Love alone cannot compensate a negligence of existential concepts such as patience, compromise and mutual respect.

If, on the other hand, we understand that love really is not always enough, we also understand that maintaining a relationship takes effort. When we realize that love alone cannot solve every problem, we are more willing to confront the underlying issues firsthand. We do not simply expect that love solves all our problems. It doesn't do that at all. All it does is cloud our perception about the situation. Before you realize it, relationships that are solely based upon love start to fall apart.

It's entirely possible that we fall in love with someone we're not compatible. In the best case, we fall in love with someone who's just too different from us. This person might have other dreams and ambitions about life.

In the worst scenario, we fall for some truly dysfunctional characters that are abusive, manipulative or narcissistic in nature. These are most likely to people that do not treat us with the same respect we treat them.

For this reason, when evaluating a partner's compatibility, heart and mind must work together. It might feel great if you have fallen head over heels in love. But guess what, having butterflies in your stomach is simply not enough.

When it comes to your compatibility, you will also have to consider the plain facts. The way that person treats you. How their dreams are comparable to your own wishes. How your partner treats others.

Love does not overcome relationship problems

So, we've fallen head over heels in love. We get to know that another person and we begin to get a more realistic picture of them. We start to realize that our partner is just another human being with faults, problems and weaknesses. In most cases, this is a very natural process. In fact, this might be the necessary requirement to truly accept the significant other for who they are.

In some cases, however, this process is not so healthy. This is the case when we think that our love for the other person will solve relationship problems. We think love with help us to find a way to work things out. And we wholeheartedly believe that our boundless love will aid us to overcome the differences.

However, nothing changes. None of your relationship problems are solved. None of the negative or abusive behaviors of your partner cease the only thing that love changes is the way we feel about relationship problems. It won't solve them, but it does make us feel better about them. There's a big difference between solving a problem and deluding oneself into accepting it.

Remember that the word love is not just letters put together.

That word is easily spoken, and misused.

We like to hear it because it makes us feel good. It creates lots of comfort. Especially when it comes from the person you care. When hearing that word for the first time, one can be truly misled.

It is the case with all words, they are the unmanifested expressions of ideas and concepts. Only the actions can make them real.

It takes a lot more than just words to truly love someone. Some people say they love us, but they do not act upon their words. Their actions do not coincide with their words.

The word love is not going to fix you at all.

Always keep in mind that love does not automatically restart a new life as soon as someone tells you that she or he love you. The mistakes committed in the past will not be undone. The pain about unresolved issues will not fade.

Ultimately, love is not going to fix you. Just because you love someone does not mean you become a better person. Being loved by someone else will also not make you a better person.

It is certainly true that a relationship can help someone to start living up. The situation is not solved. It might even get worse as days go by.

We also must keep in mind that sooner or later all the exhilarating and overjoyed feelings of the early stages will make room for something new. Before you notice it, reality will stop, and it will take hold. That's the point when you realize that you are still the same person that you were before.

Love inspires us to be better that is true. It will help you to strive for our growth as a person. Eventually, love alone cannot effect that change. Love is not enough to live your true potential. You alone have it in your hands to be more than you are today.

Sometimes you think that love justify sacrificing yourself. That is so wrong.

Love requires compromise. Even more so, it takes sacrifices to maintain a healthy relationship. That is the wonderful thing about love. It makes us care for the needs of another person. After all, we want our partner to feel just as great as we do. For this reason, we are willing to give up something that is our own to share it with someone else.

Sacrificing your own needs, wishes and desires is a natural part of any relationship. In fact, if such a harmony between giving and taking cannot be established, the relationship is bound to fail.

Nevertheless, love should not be taken as justification for sacrifices. It should not be the cause for you to sacrifice your dreams and ambitions just for the sake of another person.

If you must give up everything that you stand for, your dignity and individuality, then it might be a one-sided relationship. If you must sacrifice yourself just to be with someone, it had better raise a red flag.

Do not think that love is always peaches and cream…

Love isn't just bright sunshine. It isn't just pure heaven and happiness. Love is more than that. It is frustration, it is forgiveness. Love is your ability to accept another person passionately. It gives you strength to stand on this person's side even when a storm sweeps across their life, destroying everything.

True love is when you stick together during the ugly moments of life just as much as you did during the enjoyable times.

Love isn't always enough. It's not going to replace hard work, dedication and mutual respect. It is the very structure of a relationship. Love is the start of something beautiful. Yet, the foundation of a relationship requires much more than just love. It needs to be molded and shaped. It will have to stand the trial of fire, water and air. Only if two people are willing to accept that love is not enough, a long-lasting and healthy relationship can be established.

I want you to always remember that it's very important not to let love consume you. It shouldn't be our most important priority life. It shouldn't be allowed to serve as justification for sacrifice.

STORY 74

The Creativity

Bryant is a make-up artist who frequently holds makeup artistry classes at the local community college. Usually, most of his students are middle-aged housewives who want to fine-tune their makeup skills.

One morning, Bryant held a class that would be attended by men as well. Only one man showed up, Roy.

Roy was a gentleman in his best years with a seemingly unlimited interest in makeup artistry. He was strong with the idea to learn as much as he possibly could. Roy wouldn't stop until he was satisfied with the result of his work.

Conceivably, Roy was the number one subject of conversation when the other women were alone. Rumors quickly started to spread. Was Roy perhaps a transvestite? Why else would he attend such a class?

The community college was in a conservative rural area, which is why the other participants were quite doubtful of the man's intentions.

Throughout the lessons, Roy carefully listened and wrote everything he learned...

When the classes were slowly coming to an end, the outer attendees simply could not hide their curiosity any longer. They finally asked Roy why he was so interested in makeup artistry, he gave the most inspiring beautiful reply: He said, "You know, my beloved wife partially lost her eyesight because of diabetes. She's no longer able to apply her makeup. I think she's beautiful, even more so without makeup. She knows this and I tell her every day, but the thing is this, she simply feels not comfortable leaving the house without make-up.

Leah never went outside without wearing any makeup-up. Seeing the love of my life like this makes me sad. So, I decided to take this course to surprise her! I do not only want to learn how to apply her makeup; I want her to wear the most beautiful make-up, so her inner beauty also shines on the outside."

Everyone got up from their sits and began to clap their hands. They thought that this guy was special. Roy was attending class to help his wife. They also felt ashamed because they thought so many ugly things about this wonderful individual.

STORY 75

The Farewell Notes

Miguel was diagnosed with lung cancer. He had only six weeks left to live. It was a shocking diagnosis. Miguel decided to use the time he had left to make all the necessary arrangements for his wife Lourdes. They had been married for 40 years. They had four awesome children all grownup.

He began cashing out his pension. Miguel used the money to pay off their house.

He then arranged a trip for his wife Lourdes and the rest of the family to Spain. A journey that it was a must. He had promised the whole family that they will visit Spain someday....

When they went to visit a specific church in Spain. The priest was waiting for them. It was in this church that Lourdes' parents had married more than 60 years ago.

On that day, Miguel and Lourdes renewed their wedding vows and had the most beautiful day of their lives. Lourdes cried during the whole ceremony. The tears were real joy does not sorrow.

After the ceremony the had the whole village over for brunch....

Many months have gone by since their return from Spain...

Miguel died exactly six weeks after he was diagnosed with cancer. After his death, Lourdes discovered that he hid hundreds of notes around the entire house, shortly after they arrived from Spain.

Throughout the course of many months after Miguel's death, Lourdes found one note after another. The notes are beautiful and very personal declarations. Those notes were meant to encourage Lourdes cope during this difficult time.

Miguel also reminded his wife in these notes to fully enjoy every aspect of life. He wanted Lourdes to sell his car and to move on with her life.

It was the most heartwarming farewell gift one could ever imagine.

STORY 76

Love letters from an Enchanted Island

In 1970, Ramon Rivera moved from Puerto Rico to New York City. The migration wasn't easy for the young man. He became terribly homesick. He missed his hometown and the company of his friends.

In order to distract himself, Ramon began searching for a potential pen friend from his homeland. He found a woman called Alicia Castro from Puerto Rico. She was interested in establishing correspondence with him.

The two slowly got to know each other, with one letter after another.

A year later, the two had fallen in love with each other, without having ever met. The young coupe many plans to meet, however, Alicia was her parents' caretaker. She was an only child. Her father had cancer and was continuously going to different doctors appoints. Her mother was in the same boat.

Alicia didn't have the heart to leave her parents in a nursing home. She told Ramon that if he didn't want to wait for her to be free her commitment with her parents, she will understand.

Ramon was a caring man. He tried to go to the Puerto Rico but couldn't travel. Every day he had an emergency at work. He was a Director at a hospital.

It took seven years for Alicia and Ramon to meet. They met for the first time, at St. Patrick Cathedral.

Guess what? Their first meeting was the day before their wedding. The two got married and had eight children...

STORY 77

Happy Ending

Ray and Anne were the life of the party. Ever since they got married, right after college, they moved into the biggest house in upstate New York. Their friends were all upper class.

Both Ray and Anne were hard workers. Both had a law degree. Anne adored her husband. Ray couldn't face any new adventure without Anne. They were meant for each other since grammar school.

One summer evening, the young couple were invited to a cookout way up in the mountains. Ray knew his way up the Catskills, but as they were heading for the party, it began to rain. It got very dark too soon. Ray was an excellent driver, however, the curbs on that road were endless. The heavy rains didn't help the situation.

There were a couple of cars heading for the party. Trees began to fall that many of the guests began to return home way before the celebration began. Those people were driving too fast without thinking of the other drivers. That is when Ray and Anne crashed....

Ray and Anne had a very bad accident. They both were hurt. however, Anne was worse than Ray. She fell went into a deep coma.

Month after month there were no change in Anne status. Ray never stopped visiting his wife at the hospital.

Almost everyone, including the doctors, had given up hope. Ray remained faithful to Anne. He always prayed that she would one day recover.

Every time Ray visited Ann, he started talking to her. He always was recounting all the beautiful moments they spend with each other.

One day, Ray decided to showed show Anne the video of their wedding day. She slowly began moving her hand. She whispered his name and began gaining consciousness.

Several weeks after she had woken up, the doctor told Ray that Anne was recovering very well.

The minute Anne is fully recovered she will be sent home.

When the couple left the hospital, she told Ray that she heard his voice while she was in a coma. It was his voice and loving care helped her to return to consciousness.

STORY 78

Simply Pure Love

After the Twin Tower attacked, on September 11, 2001, all branches in the military were deployed. Many of those young soldiers didn't have any idea what it meant to serve in foreign soil.

Every week the Army or any other branch sent troops to Iraq and places like Afghanistan.

After ten years, the activation of Americans is still going strong....

In 2011, bomb disposal expert, James Adams, was severely injured after the explosion of an improvised bomb in Afghanistan. The explosion took all his limbs. It really changed the life of the 20-year-old United States soldier forever...

While recovering from the injuries in a military hospital, Adams was confronted with the painful realization that his limbs had gone. He also had to face the fact that he would be dependent on assistance for the rest of his life.

It was an incredibly difficult situation not only for him, but also his family and especially his longtime girlfriend Linda.

Instead of giving him up, Linda became James' assistance in his recovery. She helped him recover and took care of him during his incredibly challenging time.

Linda played an important part in James' quick recovery. She never went away from his side and helped him greatly.

When he learned to walk again with his new prosthetic limbs, she was there for him.

After James had recovered, he proposed to his beloved girlfriend. They had a beautiful June wedding in 2005.

This is really a beautiful ending of an incredibly inspiring love story. This also shows that nothing can ever stand in-between two people who really love each other.

STORY 79

Declaration

When Vicky saw Mariano, an Italian tennis player, during a contest on TV. She immediately became interested in Mariano. Vicky was so determined to meet the tennis player. Vicky kept asking the TV commentators for Mariano's agenda, phone number, email, etc.

Vicky never gave up. She bothered everyone on the TV program until they finally gave in. Once she had his email address, she contacted him. They both agreed to meet.

When they saw each other, it was magic. It was love at first sight. They began dating. The many phone calls and family gatherings, led to engagement. Mariano was so impressed by Vickey that he could hold his feelings. They got married six months later.

The young tennis player moved to the United States permanent. He applied for the U. S. citizenship. He was so in love with Vicky that he promised her that he would, one day bring her an Olympic medal.

Mariano was determined to live up to his promise, but things happened differently....

One beautiful summer evening the young couple decided to go for a drive. Everything was very romantic. Mariano and Vicky have been married for two years and their love for each other have grown stronger every day.

On that romantic summer evening, other people wanted to enjoy a night ride. Mariano was shocked when this guy came driving out of nowhere. That driver hit them so hard that their car was a total lost. His beautiful wife Vicky was hurt badly.

Vicky and Mariano were taken to the nearest hospital. The doctors and nurses work on Vicky all night long…

The following day, Mariano was release from the hospital. Vicky was still in a coma. She never woke up. Vicky was pronounced dead three hours after Mariano was sent home…

It was an unbelievable tragedy. Mariano never forgot the promise he had made Vicky. He remembered what he had pledged to his beautiful wife. It was an agreement that kept him going through his difficult time.

He was obsessed on becoming the best tennis player in the world. Mariano very determined that he was finally selected to become part of the United States Olympic team.

During the competition, Mariano was faced with incredibly challenging competitors. He had three match attempts but failed in two.

Seeing his chances of ever reaching the platform declining. He put everything he had left into the third and final attempt.

As luck would have it, he managed to play two games, which won him an Olympic gold medal.

When he was awarded the medal, it was broadcasted to millions of viewers all around the world. Mariano simply couldn't help himself. He broke out into tears while holding a picture of his wife Vicky.

STORY 80

The Most Horrible News

It was April 2, 1990. This was the day Vivian's life changed completely. On this day, she found out she had Leukemia.

The first day of Vivian junior year of high school. She had Chemistry first and second period. All she could think when I walked into the lab was how she was going to stay awake?

As she walked in, she saw professor standing by the door. The professor walked over to her.

"Name?" She asked with an annoyed tone.

"Vivian." She said.

"Do you have a last name?"

"Romano."

"My name is Vivian Romano." Vivian stated.

It took the professor a moment to check the list and check off her name. She then told her, "See the girl with the blonde hair? That's your lab partner for the rest of the year. No substitutions or swaps."

"Alrighty." Vivian said and sulked off to meet her lab partner for the rest of the year, no substitutions or swaps. She sat down next to her new lab partner.

"Hi, I guess you're my lab partner for the rest of the year, no substitutions or swaps." She said with a smile.

"Hi. My name is Vivian."

She smiled. "Well, my name's Emma. I moved here from New Orleans a few weeks ago. I come from a public school in New Orleans, and I have no clue if I'm going to be able to keep up."

"Well Emma, if you ever need help you know where to find me." We both smiled and began to listen to the lecture.

When Mrs. Brooks finally let us loose with the Brunson burners and extremely dangerous chemicals it was chaos. The table next to us managed to melt the glass beaker spilling all the contents onto the table leaving a small cat sized hole in the lab table. The table behind us exploded the contents of their beaker everywhere burning multiple innocent bystanders. We weren't doing too well ourselves.

Emma had beautiful long blonde hair and she forgot to tie it back before we started. About five minutes into our experiment, I looked over and her hair was sizzling and smoking. The smell of her burning hair was overwhelming.

"Emma." I said.

"What?!" She cried. We were both becoming flustered with the assignment.

"Emma!"

"What! Vivian?"

"Your hair!"

"My hair? Oh God." She sprayed her hair down with the water that was sitting on our lab table for events such as this.

"Miss Kramer, I see that you did not follow one of my rules. Do you know what the penalty is for not following my rules?"

"Yes, Mrs. Brooks." Emma said. People all around Emma and Vivian began to giggle.

"And what would that be?" She asked Emma a cruel smile beginning to form on her face.

"I am banned from the lab for the rest of the semester."

Vivian couldn't let Emma fail.

"Mrs. Brooks, I distracted Emma and she forgot to pull her hair back." Vivian told Mrs. Brooks.

"Alright, detention for a month, Mondays, Wednesdays, and Fridays. I will be seeing you after school today to start your detentions." She told Vivian.

"Yes, Mrs. Brooks."

"Oh, Emma, next time, I will kick you out of my class." She scolded Emma and returned to the front of the room.

When Mrs. Brook's back was turned Emma whispered to me. "You didn't need to do that. It was all my fault. I'm lucky I didn't lose all my hair. It's a good thing that this happened. I've been meaning to get my hair cut short for such a long time. This was the extra push I needed."

She told me in a rush of words. I had a hard time following her.

"Well, I am glad you are not angry at me." Said Vivian

The bell rang a half an hour later and they packed up...

Both girls walked to their lockers. They got their books for their next class.

They couldn't believe that they could have so much homework the first day of school. It was crazy...

Vivian and Emma slowly walked back to their lockers. They dumped what they needed to bring home into their backpacks.

There was no need to hurry. Both girls weren't going anywhere important, just home.

"I just wanted to thank you again for covering for me in chem. class today. Before you go report to detention, I owe you big time." Emma said.

The next morning, Vivian couldn't get to chemistry class quick enough. Emma walked in ten minutes later with her hair pulled back into a low ponytail with a ribbon. It was almost like she was mocking Mrs. Brooks.

Emma sat down next to Vivian, her non-substitutable or swappable lab partner. Vivian and Emma were happy to be lab partners.

"I see you remembered to tie your hair back." Vivian said, half laughing.

"Yes, I did." She smiled.

"Your hair looks nice today." Vivian told her.

"Thank you, Vivian." She said to me and began to work on our newest lab assignment.

Three broken beakers and two hours later they had successfully completed the experiment and lab papers...

Mrs. Brooks came around to their table and looked impressed. She passed by without saying a word. Emma and Vivian hi fived when she was over criticizing some other kid's experiment, but not theirs.

This little ritual of chemistry class went on for months...

After Vivian finished her detentions, they began studying at the library. Emma felt blessed because she found a true friend in this new school.

They girls went to Halloween parties, they even celebrated Thanksgiving together. Life was good.

Now, Christmas vacation began, and the two girls were happy shopping at the mall.

They spent their time going to different activities. The outdoor ice rink, and also, they went to museums in their town. Both girls had so much in common.

One time, the went to a party, and guest what? They met a pair of twins!

Now, four of them have more things in common. It is so incredible that life have been great for the happy couples. They couldn't believe what was happening.

Springtime was approaching. They were getting ready for spring break.

April first came and went without a problem...

The following day Vivian got to the chemistry class. Emma was not in her seat. Vivian began to worry. Even her Emma's boyfriend was worried. He couldn't reach her whole entire day.

After school the two young man, Jeff and Jerry, stopped by Emma's house. They rang the bell.

Emma answered the door and told them to come in. She took them up to her room and told them to sit down. They did what she said. She did not look like she wanted to be disobeyed.

"Vivian, Jeff and Jerry, I went to the doctor today." She told them, sitting down next to her.

"And?" Vivian asked trying to prompt her.

"They found something strange in my blood work. Something not good.

They say that I have Acute Lymphoblastic Leukemia. They need to do more blood work but-" I cut her off.

"You have cancer?" they all asked once.

Emma began to cry. "Yes, I have cancer." She said as a matter of fact.

"You have cancer?" Vivian said again.

"Yes, Vivian I have cancer. There is nothing I can do about it but accept the fact that I have cancer and start an extremely aggressive chemo. regimen and hope it works."

"Are you going to lose your hair?" Jerry asked her.

"Yeah. I guess I'm going to get that short haircut that I've been wanting." She laughed.

"Are you going to live?" asked Jeff.

Emma's friend couldn't understand that such a young girl could be dying due to cancer.

"They say I will since I caught it so soon. There is an 85% survival rate."

"There is still 15%."

"I know. I'm going to kick that 15% in the butt and make it wish it never thought of saying I was going to die."

"Are you afraid?"

"I'm very scared. Are you afraid?"

"I think I'm even more scared than you."

'Stay positive'. That was the last time Vivian saw Emma smile...

That summer her cancer took a turn for the worse. The doctors could not seem to get her into remission. She laid weakly in her hospital bed covered up to her neck in blankets. She was a weak and tired version of the Emma they met so many months ago.

Emma spent her summer vacation in the hospital... She never returned to school.

It was September second. Vivian had just come back from eating in the cafeteria at the hospital. She sat down next to Emma. She looked up at Vivian and smiled.

Her smile was weak but still beautiful. She whispered to me, "Thanks for being my best friend." The monitors went dead. Emma was gone...

STORY 81

Getting Dumped

Sharon stared silently at his picture. Laughter surrounded her as she remembered that she was in public…

Her focus returned to the picture and her heart clenched some more. Squeezing her eyes shut, Sharon locked her phone. She was trying to ignore the ache in her chest–right where the heart was ought to be.

Sharon couldn't get upset in front of her friends. She couldn't show them that she was heartbroken and miserable. She needed to put up a good face to save her dignity.

Sharon smiled and laughed. Everyone around her smiled and laughed too. The only difference? Sharon was certain that she was the only one who was faking it.

It had been a month since her fight with Leroy. A month of anger and resentment. A month of hope that maybe, maybe Leroy would text her. Maybe, he realized that he missed her, and would drop everything and just call her. That was all Sharon wanted from him. A call, a text something that showed her that he still cared. That she meant something to him.

It wasn't long before Sharon was dropped home by her friend. She knew something was wrong. She could feel it. She didn't question Sharon as she dropped her off. She just smiled.

Once inside her room, Sharon let out a huge sigh and slumped back onto my bed. Her phone rang, signaling that she had a text.

With a smile, Sharon opened it, hoping that it would be Leroy. It wasn't. It was Gregory.

Gregory and Sharon had become close since last month. As much as she hated to admit it, Gregory was her rebound. He kept her sane, plus he helped her get through with it.

A familiar pain set in as she returned to the earlier picture. Leroy's hand was over another girl's shoulder, their heads touching. She mentally destroyed their love for each other. He hated taking pictures and now he is all over Facebook with his new love.

Sharon scrolled down, reading the caption as her heart tightened some more.

Sharon's teeth clenched as she found her throat hooked. She had known that scum for five years and never once did regard her as his sweetheart. Letting out an annoyed sigh, Sharon angrily double tapped the post before locking her phone.

Sharon rolled to her side. There were angry tears running down her face. Maybe that was all she needed. A motivation or even a force telling her how their friendship just wasn't going to work out.

Maybe this was the end. Sharon will just have to learn to live with it.

STORY 82

The Jogging Partner

Their daily jog together was always special. At least that is what Mildred like to think of their jog. It's not like they run as partners…

It is hard to remember the days when Mildred and Mark did not run together. She would jog right behind him. Mildred was always trying to keep up with him. It would have been so easy to say hi the first time. But with each passing day. It has gotten harder and harder, and now impossible.

They had occasional looks back and forth, but those were probably coincidences. Of course, Mildred always looked at him. As for the times his glance met hers. Perhaps something else called his gaze. She was way too shy to budge from her routine to approach confirmed rejection. Why can't he just make the move? Mildred knows, that's a funny one. Look at him and then look at her…

Mildred doesn't turn red from exercising. She does blush when she is nervous or embarrassed. Her cover story would be that her redness is from my heavy-duty workouts. After all, she is at the gym. She is struggling to keep up with herself. Her mind is going very fast.

Even he has weaknesses. It's not like she thinks he's perfect or anything. How could he be perfect with shoes that smell like that? He comes close to perfection. His feet come close to her as he lifts them on the treadmill.

It's hard for her to hold back a little smile. She can't get away from it this time. It draws her closer. The occasional silent connection she has with him.

Mildred tries to look cute in her gym clothes, but it's hard. The mirror tells her that she looks fat and ugly. Those are the only things the mirror ever tells her.

Mildred leaves the gym and can't stop thinking about him. Still, she hopes he feels the same. She had left a note in his bag which was next to treadmill which she introduces herself and left her phone number.

Mike never returned to the gym or even called her....

STORY 83

The Smooth Talker

This might sound like every other love story, and it may be.

Her name is Maureen Brown, which she is always been quite happy with that name.

Now, I suppose it's only polite to tell you a bit about Maureen before I jump into her story. She is five feet, 5 inches, has brown hair that comes to her shoulders. She is not talented in any special way. These are her basic facts.

His name was Andrew Rivers, and he was perfectly wonderful in every way. When he first came to Maureen's school, in twelfth grade, he was a bit weird and didn't fit in right away. He was into music and played the drums and the guitar. He wasn't good at either. What he was good at was singing, and when he did, you wanted to cry and laugh and sing along with him all at once.

Her name was Maureen Brown and his was Andrew Rivers. They loved each other...

About two months into their last year of high school, Andrew asked Maureen out. She was surprised since they never had conversation together. She had hardly ever talked to him. Maureen didn't have a boyfriend, and she didn't know how to say no.

It may help you to know that at her school there were couples that were simply together for the name, and some that were together only to have a date for dances, for kissing and other things.

When Andrew asked Maureen out, she had no idea what his intentions were. Maureen didn't like having no idea. She, by no means, was a hostile person.

Andrew was starting to feel offended after Maureen had said that she would date him, he hadn't said another word to her. She went up to him and they had a talk about the whole situation.

Maureen: "Hey, Andrew."
Andrew: "Hey."
Maureen: "So …"
Andrew: annoyingly, said nothing
Maureen: "You asked me out."
Andrew: nothing again
Maureen: "Why?"
Andrew: "Why did I ask you out?"
Maureen: "Right."
Andrew: "I felt like it."
Maureen: very irritated, answered "You felt like it?"
Andrew: "That is what I said, isn't it?"
Maureen: angry… "I'm sorry. I'm not. I didn't realize you were such a jerk, and I don't want to go out with you anymore."
Andrew: "Are you dumping me?"
Maureen: "What do you think?"
Andrew: "Why?"
Maureen: "I feel like it."
Andrew: smiling… "Do you like Italian food?"
Maureen: "I hate it."
Andrew: "You've never had it."
Me: "How do you know?"
Andrew: laughing… "I'm good at reading people."
Maureen: "Well, obviously you suck, because I've had Italian food a million times and I hated it every time."
Andrew: "Would you like to go out with me tonight?"
Maureen: "You're asking me on a date?"
Andrew: "Yes."
Maureen: "Read my answer."
Andrew: "Wonderful! I'll see you tonight. Be ready by six."

Maureen hated this strange boy who she really knows him. They had only really spoken twice. He made her angry. The only problem was that she couldn't figure out if she liked that or not.

That night at six sharp, Andrew showed up at her doorstep. Her parents have never been met any of her boyfriends.

He walked right into the living room where her parents sat watching the baseball game.

When he came back out, Maureen asked, "What'd you say?"

"I told them I'd have you back by eight."

They didn't talk much on the car ride. He had a CD playing that sounded kind of like Bob Marley, but I'd never heard the song before.

It wasn't until they got to the restaurant that she realized she didn't know where they were going. A small sign stood in front of the building, but the name was too far away for her to be able to read it.

What she could read was the sign beneath where the name should be, and it said, "The best Italian cuisine for miles."

"Italian, huh?"

He smirked.

They walked inside and it was only then that she realized exactly how small the building was. There were little tables in the center of the room, about five of them, and a couch against one wall for sitting while you waited.

They were the only customers. A sign read "PLEASE SEAT YOURSELF," but they guess because of the lack of business, a waiter came over to seat them. He tried to show them to a table, but Andrew said, "Oh, no, thank you. We'll be sitting here."

There were many other dates, all very unusual. Maureen was used to dances and movies, but with Andrew she got sunsets and local concerts.

Once he took her to a bingo night that his aunt was hosting. Oddly enough, that was the night they first kissed.

Maureen remembers so clearly the day of graduation, the day she realized that Andrew and she wouldn't always be together.

After they threw their hats and got their diplomas, he found her.

"End of high school, huh?" he said.

"Yeah."

"What do you want to do, Maureen?"

"With my life?"

"Sure."

"Be with you."

He didn't smile like she wanted him to.

"Don't you want to go to college?"

I sighed. "Want to, or have to?"

Now he smiled. "You choose."

"I should go to college."

There was a long pause before Maureen said, "Andrew, what about you?"

"What about me?"

"What are you going to do?"

"I don't know. Do what I do best, I guess. Play my music."

"Oh. Yeah. That's cool. See you later?"

"When would I see you?" asked Andrew.

"Bye, Maureen."

"Bye."

Thinking back, Maureen wishes she had said something better than bye. She wishes she had told him that she loved him more than words could describe.

Also, that when he sang to her, she felt like she was all that mattered in the world. She wanted to tell him that if he had just asked, she wouldn't have gone to college. She would have played his music with him.

Maureen is sitting in front of her computer. She is searching at "people finder." She wants to call him and hear his voice, but she was afraid. She is afraid that he won't be her same Andrew.

She got a glass of cold water and sat on her couch. She pictures herself having one last conversation with him.

Maureen: "Hey, Andrew."

Andrew: "Hey, Maureen."

Maureen: "Why are you wearing a tie?"

Andrew: "Why shouldn't I be?"

Maureen: "I don't know."
Andrew: "I have a job."
Maureen: "Good."
Andrew: "I'm a lawyer, Maureen."
Maureen: "That's great."
Andrew: "You don't sound like that's great."
Maureen: "Don't I?"
Andrew: "I live in an apartment in the city. I talk on the phone with other businesspeople."
Maureen: "I'm proud of you."
Andrew: "I have a diploma hanging up on the wall in my office. My office." …
Maureen: "Do you still play music, Andrew?"
Andrew: "Music."
He looks at her as if he doesn't remember the word.
Andrew: "No, I don't play my music anymore."
Maureen: "Oh."
Maureen: "I loved you, Andrew."
Andrew: "Loved? Past tense?"
Maureen: "I think so."
Andrew: "I love you."
Maureen: "Why'd you ask me out?"
Andrew: "I thought you were beautiful and smart, and I loved how shiny your dark brown hair was. I liked how you weren't too loud, and you didn't wear low-cut shirts like most other girls."
Maureen: "I wish you'd said, 'Because I felt like it.'"
Andrew: "Sorry."
Maureen: "Me too."
Andrew: "I have to be going."
Maureen: "Yeah."
Maureen: "Wait!"
Andrew: "Yes?"
Maureen: "I'd never had Italian food before."

STORY 84

My Best Friend

Who do you consider your best friend?

It is very simple. A best friend is the one that calls you and makes sure that you are doing well.

When I was working, I had lots of friends. I went to numerous parties. I had no problem driving in the snow, in the dark, or in a bright sunny day.

Now, I cannot do favors, drive people around and so on. I have problems with my vision, and I only drive short distances and in the early morning hours.

On some occasions, I start driving and must stop or return home. The sun is very bright, or the sky starts turning gray. My condition is bad. My doctor told me to start making plans. I never give up. I went to see my optometrist and received new eye drops. I can see much better these past few days. I won't be going for another eye operation.

During those bad days, is when you know who your true friends are.

Well, now that I am retired and can only say that I still have one friend that is always there for me. His name is Paul Chique.

We know each other for more than twenty years…

Paul calls me every morning to make sure that I am going to the gym or ready to do my chores. He lives very far from me. That is the rea-son he calls….

At the present time, Paul is taking care of his mother. She is not do-ing well. I am there if she needs me, but I cannot go to her side all the time. I am also taking care of my father. So, both Paul and I have our hands full.

Let me tell you why I enjoy Paul's company. We both have the same interest in music, art and movies. He is an artist and had done a lot of the jewelry I own.

Sometimes we go to the beach, and he starts drawing something. I just look at him and begin writing. It is so funny because sometimes I wrote about the same thing, he just drew....

When it comes to cooking, he is the best. I just tell him to come over and we will invent something in the kitchen. He makes great egg rolls and Chinese rice.

The other day he came to the rescues...

My uncle Kike was in the hospital. Kike was the one I used to call when I needed a driver. He was always there for me. I feel so bad because I cannot help him. It has been raining for almost three days straight; therefore, I cannot drive....

On that morning, when I needed help, Paul came to my house. He helped with my housework, prepared breakfast for my dad while I fed the dogs. We took my car for inspection and went to visit my uncle at the hospital. This visit was awful because this is when the doctors and nurses asked us if we wanted to pull the plug.

My dear uncle has been on life support for a month. The situation is critical because it happens right after Hurricane Maria. Electricity is very poor.

In my town, Ponce, we still didn't any electrical power...

When the doctors came to see my uncle, I was there with Paul and the rest of the family. The hospital staff just shook their heads and unplugged my uncle, Jose Enrique Pagan Rodriguez.

I stayed there almost all night, however, his wife, Migdalia, told us to take her home. She didn't want to see him go. I went to my uncle for a couple of minutes and thank him for everything he for me. I also told him that it was alright to leave. I was happy not sad to leave the hospital.

We drove in darkness to my uncle's house. I told Migdalia that we will see later....

When I got home about 2 am; I got a phone call from my cousin Miggie. She told me my uncle just died.

Kike, that was the nickname we called him, was well known in Ponce. He helped everyone in need. The nurses and even some doctors knew him for his good service around town....

Paul always makes my day. When I am sad, he would start singing. I just laugh because sometimes he sounds awful...

You know today we took an IQ test. We both scored 160!!!! I know we are smart because we do stuff that normal people have problems doing.

Everyone keeps telling us that we should get marry. My answer is always no. The minute two people start living under the same roof, the fun is gone.

There is never dull moment when we are together. I know that if we get marry, we will stop being the best friends.

Paul knows that I am here for him, and I know that he is always there for me. Thank you for being my best friend.

STORY 85

Making Friends

In the following, I am going to narrate a story that happened to me as I was growing up. This will explain why I am happy the way I am now. It will also explain that it isn't easy finding or friends.

There was a time when I had a lot of friends. I wasn't a bit shy. I was popular, or I thought I was. I always had someone to share my secrets. All through high school, though, I didn't slip in and out of friendships. Why because I was in the honor roll. I helped my so call friends with their schoolwork.

When it came time to go to college, I was quite nervous. I was going to be rooming with someone I didn't know. I was going to live in a town about 800 miles away from home. There wouldn't be a single person I knew there. I had no idea how I was going to make friends in this new environment.

The first week of classes, something happened. It changed my life forever. In my English class, I was asked to talk a little about my life. I told everyone where I came from. I spoke about the place I called home. I express myself very well. If I was nervous, it didn't show. I shared a lot of information.

As always, there was a final question for each student. It was always the same: "What is your goal for this class?" Now, most of the students said it was to get a good grade, pass the class or something similar, but for some reason, I said something entirely different. I said that my goal was to make just one good friend.

While most of the students sat in silence, one student came to me and held out his hand. He then introduced himself. He asked me if I would be his friend. The whole room was silent. All eyes focused on us, and the hand extended just in front of me. I smiled and stretched my hand out to take his and a friendship was formed. It was a friendship that lasted all through college. It was a friendship that turned into a romance. It was a friendship that brought two people together forever....

During that time, I was happy yes, however, one thing really messes everything up. There was a war, and my best friend was drafted. He was killed in Vietnam, and I never had a chance to tell him thank you for all the good and bad times we shared together.

Many years went by, and I never forgot my friend. I met someone else, and we got married. We got a divorced because of so many differences in our lives....

After I graduated from college, I started working in a law firm. I made friends right away; however, there was one girl that I do prefer to keep her name anonymous. We became extremely close, but soon I figured out unfortunately, that we weren't as close as I thought we were....

Before our friendship ended, she came over to my house frequently. We spent a lot of quality time together. We always talk about men we found attractive. We also talked about our friendship.

Everything was great. We got along just fine we had what I thought was a strong bond. We enjoyed each other's company. We had fun together.

Then one day, everything changed. She came over after work. I was putting together a presentation assigned by our supervisor. I was happy to see my friend because the following day we were going to present our project to the whole staff. This presentation was important because that meant that we will be promoted to the next level.

As were exchanging information, I received a call from my sister. I took the call and went to another room to talk. I was gone for about half hour. When I came back, I noticed my "friend" was gone. I was very confused. I did not expect that. I remember thinking to myself.

"She could have at least said I am leaving or just goodbye." When I was ready to go to bed, I noticed that my presentation was gone.

That night I couldn't sleep. I remember turning on my bed… Just thinking to myself… "She could have stolen my presentation. She's my "friend" right? Or was she?"

The following day I went to work. The whole office was congratulating my friend for the outstanding presentation. My supervisor was angry at me because I showed up late and wasn't there to be part of the presentation. I didn't say anything. I simply left the room.

I went looking for my friend. I confronted her about my presentation. I told her that I have worked very hard on my own and she got the credit. Our boss thinks that you did it all alone.

She told me "I'm your friend. I would never do that to you. Unfortunately, I took her word. The following day, my supervisor went to her office and to my surprise, she returned with the presentation. She showed me the whole presentation and even the changes were there that I personally had made. My friend forgot to edit the work and half of the presentation had my name on it….

I was in shock! I just did not know what to say. It then later struck me that it happened. I felt lost and confused, hurt, used, and betrayed. I thought I could trust my so call friend.

I do not regret meeting her because it showed me that even the people you care about will betray you.

I learned a lesson that helped me a lot in the future. I learned that you could have acquaintances, but those could never be real friends.

STORY 86

Vicente Pagan Rodriguez

My dear uncle
9 November 1948–27 February 2015

My uncle and I grew up together. We were always playing and getting in trouble.

When we were just on primary grades, I was always defending him, why? Because my uncle was a sweetheart. He never did any harm. The kids in our class used to bother us because he was dark, and I was light complexion. My response was always the same. I used to reply to those fools that I was born in the daytime and my uncle at night.

The teasing got so bad that I used to fight with a stick or just plain punches. My uncle didn't want to fight.

One day as we were walking down the street of New York City. A white-haired old man was begging for money. My uncle, Vincent, gave him a quarter.

Noticing my surprised look and he said: "That poor unfortunate reminds me of a story which I will tell you, the memory of which continually pursues me.

My uncle and I were always telling stories. We were the story tellers of the class....

Uncle began his story:

"My family, which came originally from Ponce PR, was not rich. We just managed to make ends meet. My father worked hard, came home late from the National Guard, and earned very little. I had two sisters and seven brothers.

"My mother suffered a good deal from our reduced circumstances. She often had harsh words for my father, indirect and clever reproaches. The poor man then made a gesture which used to distress me. He would pass his open hand over his forehead, as if to wipe away perspiration which did not exist. He would answer nothing. I felt his helpless suffering. We economized on everything, and never would accept an invitation to dinner, so as not to have to return the courtesy.

All our provisions were bought at bargain sales. My sisters made their own dresses. My brothers shared their clothing, and I had old worn-out rags.

The price of food was very high. Meat and fish were only eaten on Sundays. Our meals usually consisted of rice and beans, prepared with every kind of sauce invented by my mother.

She kept telling us that the food was healthy and nutritious, but I should have preferred a change.

"I used to go through terrible scenes on account of lost buttons and torn pants."

"Every Sunday, we were dressed in our best, we would take our walk along the breakwater. My father, in his Army uniform. He would offer his arm to my mother, and they would walk very proud with all nine of us. My sisters, who were always first, would walk ahead of us.

My sisters marched arm in arm. They were of marriageable age and had to be displayed. I walked on the left of my mother and my father on her right. I remember the arrogant air of my poor parents in those Sunday walks, their stern expression, their stiff walk.

They moved slowly, with a serious expression, their body's straight, and their legs stiff, as if something of extreme importance depended upon their appearance.

"Every Sunday, when a ship was returning from unknown and distant countries, my father would always say the same words:

"'What a surprise it would be your grandfather were on that one! Eh?'

My Vicente went on with his story:

"My grandfather, my dad's father, was the only hope for the family.

I had heard about him since childhood, and it looked to me that I should recognize him immediately, knowing as much about him as I did. I knew every detail of his life up to the day of his departure to New York, although this period of his life was spoken of only in hushed tones.

"It seems that he had led a bad life he had wasted his money, which action, in a poor family, is one of the greatest crimes. With rich people a man who amuses himself is generally called a sport.

Among needy families, a boy who forces his parents to break into the capital becomes a good for nothing rascal. This distinction is just, although the action is the same, for consequences alone determine the seriousness of the act.

Well, Grandpa Juan had visibly reduced the inheritance on which my father had counted on. Then, he moved to New York.

Once there, my grandpa began to sell something or other. Soon he wrote that he was making a little money and that he was going to be able to help my father.

This letter caused a profound excitement in the family. My grandpa, who up to that time, had not been worth anything suddenly became a good man, a kind-hearted fellow, true and honest like the rest of the family.

One captain of a ship told us that grandpa had rented a large shop and was doing well...

Two years later a second letter came, saying: 'My dear Julio, I am writing to tell you not to worry about my health, which is excellent. Business is good. I leave tomorrow for a long trip to South America. I may be away for several years without sending you any news. If I shouldn't write, don't worry. When my fortune is made, I shall return to Puerto Rico. I hope that it will not be too long and that we will all live happily together . . ..'

This letter became the gospel of the family. It was read all the time. It was shown to the whole town.

For ten years nothing was heard from Grandpa Juan; but as time went on my father's hope grew, and my mother often said:

"'When grandpa gets here, our position will be different. There is one who knew how to get along!'

So, every Sunday, while watching the big ships approaching from the horizon, pouring out a stream of smoke, my father would repeat his eternal question:

"'What a surprise it would be if your grandpa were on that one! Eh?'

"We almost expected to see him waving his handkerchief and crying:

"'Hey! Julio!'

"Thousands of schemes had been planned on the strength of this expected return; we were even to buy a little house with my grandpa's money–a little place in the country near Ponce.

In fact, I wouldn't swear that my father had not already begun negotiations.

The elder of my sisters was then eighteen, the other one sixteen. They were not yet married, and that was a great grief to everyone.

At last, a suitor presented himself for the younger one. He was a clerk, not rich, but honorable. I have always been morally certain that grandpa's letter, which was shown to him one evening, had swept away the young man's hesitation and decided to marry my younger sister.

He was accepted eagerly, and it was decided that after the wedding the whole family should take a trip to New York.

My sister's wedding was very simple. Only immediate family attended the celebration. My father told everyone that once we return from New York, we shall have the biggest wedding celebration ever....

New York is the ideal trip for poor people. It is not far; one crosses a strip of sea in a ship and lands on foreign soil, as this little island is a Commonwealth of the U.S. Thus, as a Puerto Rican, with a ten hours' sail, can observe the neighboring people at home and study their customs.

This trip to New York completely captivated our ideas. It was our sole anticipation and the constant thought of our minds.

At last, we left. I see it as plainly as if it had happened yesterday. The boat was getting up steam; my father, puzzled, was supervising the loading of our three pieces of baggage.

My mother, nervous, had taken the arm of my unmarried sister, who looked lost since the marriage of my other sister. She was acting like the last chicken in the farm.

Behind us came the bride and groom, who really wanted to be alone. My older brothers were just playing around. They didn't care what was going on.

The whistle sounded. We got on board, and the vessel, leaving the breakwater, forged ahead through a sea as flat as a marble table. We watched the coast disappear in the distance, happy and proud, like all who do not travel much.

My father was swelling out his chest in the breeze, beneath his sport jacket that was washed that morning. He spread around him that odor of detergent which always made me recognize Sunday.

Unexpectedly, he noticed two elegantly dressed ladies to whom two gentlemen were offering oysters. An old, ragged sailor was opening them with his knife and passing them to the gentlemen, who would then offer them to the ladies.

They ate them in a dainty manner, holding the shell on a fine handkerchief and advancing their mouths a little in order not to spot their dresses. Then they would drink the liquid with a rapid little motion and throw the shell overboard.

My father was probably pleased with this delicate manner of eating oysters on a moving ship. He considers red it good form, refined, and, going up to my mother and sisters, he asked:

"'Would you like some oysters?"

My mother hesitated on account of the expense, but my two sisters immediately accepted. My mother said in a provoked manner:

"I am afraid that they will hurt my stomach. Offer the children some, but not too much, it would make them sick." Then, turning toward me, she added:

"As for Vicente, he doesn't need any. Boys shouldn't be spoiled.'"

I remained next to my mother, finding this discrimination unjust. I watched my father as he arrogantly conducted my two sisters and his son-in-law toward the ragged old sailor.

The two ladies had just left, and my father showed my sisters how to eat them without spilling the liquid. He even tried to give them an example, and seized an oyster. He attempted to imitate the ladies, and immediately spilled all the liquid over his sport jacket. I heard my mother mumble:

"He would do far better to keep quiet."

Abruptly, my father appeared to be worried; he retreated a few steps, stared at his family gathered around the old shell opener, and quickly came toward us. He looked very pale, with a peculiar look. In a low voice he said to my mother:

"'It's extraordinary how that man opening the oysters looks like my father Juan."

"Surprised, my mother asked:

"Who? Your father?"

My father continued:

"Why yes, my father. If I did not know that he was well off in New York, I should think it was him."

Confused, my mother hesitated:

"'You are crazy! If you know that it is not him, why do you say such silly things?"

But my father insisted:

"'Go on over and see for yourself Lupe! I would rather have you see with your own eyes." She got up from her chair and walked to her daughters...."

In the meantime, I was also watching the man. He was old, dirty, wrinkled, and did not lift his eyes from his work.

My mother returned and I noticed that she was trembling. She ex-claimed quickly:

"I believe that it is him. Why don't you ask the captain? But be very careful that we don't have this mam on our hands again!"

My father walked away, but I followed him. I became strangely moved.

The captain, a tall, thin man, with blond whiskers, was walking along the bridge with an important air as if he were commanding a presidential ship.

My father addressed him ceremoniously, and questioned him about his profession, adding many compliments:

"'What might be the importance of going to New York? What did it produce? What was the population? The customs? The nature of the trip?" etc., etc.

"You have there an old, the shell opener, who seems quite interesting. Do you know anything about him?"

The captain, whom this conversation began to bore him, answered dryly:

"He is some old Puerto Rican who I found last year in New York. I brought him back home. It seems that he has some relatives in Ponce, but that he doesn't wish to return to them. He claims that he owes them money. His name is Juan, Juan Pagan or Torres or something like that. He told me that he was once rich, but as you can see, that is what's left of him now."

My father turned ashy pale. He became speechless. He was so ashamed of this man. My father's face showed lots of sorrow…

After a few minutes, he turned to the captain and said:

"Ah! Ah! Very well, very well. I'm not in the least surprised. Thank you very much, captain."

"He went away, and the amazed sailor watched him disappear. He re-turned to my mother very upset that she said to him:

"'Sit down; someone will notice that something is wrong.'

"He sat down on a bench and paused:

"'It's him! It's him!'

"Then he asked:

"'What are we going to do?'

"She answered quickly:

"'We must get the children out of the way. Since Vicente knows everything, he can go and get them. We must take good care that our son- in-law. He doesn't have any ideas of what is going on".

"My father looked absolutely confused. He murmured:

"'What a tragedy!'

"Unexpectedly growing furious, my mother exclaimed:

'I always thought that thief would never do anything, and that he would never drop down on us again! As if one could expect anything from a Pagan!'

"My father passed his hand over his forehead, as he always did when his wife reproached him. She added:

"'Give Vicente some money so that he can pay for the oysters. All that it needed to cap the climax would be to be recognized by that beggar. That would be very pleasant! Let's go to the other end of the boat and take care that man doesn't come near us!'

"They gave me five dollars and walked away.

"Amazed, my sisters were waiting for our father.

I told them that mama got a sudden attack of seasickness. I went to see the shell opener and asked him:

"'How much do we owe you, sir?'

"I wanted to laugh he was my grandpa! He answered:

"'Two dollars and fifty cents.'

"I held out my five dollars and he returned the change. I looked at his hand; it was a poor, wrinkled, sailor's hand, and then I looked at his face, an unhappy old face. I said to myself:

"'That is my grandpa, my dad's father, my grandpa!'

"I gave him a ten-cent tip. He thanked me:

"'God bless you, my young man!'

"He spoke like a poor man receiving a donation. I couldn't help thinking that he must have begged over there! My sisters and brothers looked at me, surprised at my generosity.

When I returned the two dollars to my father, my mother asked me in surprise:

"'Was there two dollars and fifty cents worth? That is impossible.'

"I answered in a firm voice

"'I gave him a tip.'

"My mother started staring at me, she exclaimed:

"'You must be crazy! Giving a tip to that man, to that bum".

"She stopped at a look from my father, who was pointing at his son-in- law. Then everybody was silent.

"Before us, on the distant horizon, a purple shadow gave the im-pression that something was rising out of the sea. It was New York.

"As we approached the breakwater a violent desire held me once more to see my grandpa Juan, to be near him, to say to him something consoling, something tender.

Since no one was eating any more oysters, the old man had disappeared, having probably gone below to a dirty room which was his home."

My uncle and I made up so many stories that our English teacher told us that we should write them. It was easy for my uncle and me to be so talented. I believe that we got that from our ancestors. I miss my uncle a lot….

As I sit here writing, memories of the many parties and my own prom came to mind. My uncle Vicente took me to my prom and a lot of other parties. Since we were only two months apart, we had the same friends.

We were the life of the parties….

STORY 87

The Parachutes

Some of our stories were not all made up. The following were real situations that happened to my uncle and me.

These are very amusing:

My father and grandfather came from drill one Sunday afternoon. They brought home small parachutes. Vicente called me right away. He kept telling me that one was for me and another one for him. Keep in mind, that we were just six years old....

As we were climbing the balcony, my grandfather ran towards us. He hugged us and didn't get angry. My grandfather was angry at my dad. He yelled at him because he took those parachutes.

Those small parachutes were used to drop food and supply from the planes to the fields. He reminded my father that all supplies were to be used during drill and not to take anything home....

When my uncle Vicente and I were in grammar school, we were al-ways doing our homework together. It got to a point that we couldn't work alone. We couldn't keep quiet either. So, the teacher kept us apart. She also called my parents and told them about the situation. I was transferred to another school, and he dropped out of school.

He started working in a factory. The pay was very low. I kept telling him that he was too smart to work there.

During the early 70's, my uncle was drafted. He decided to join the Army. Right after basic and advance training, he was sent to Germany.

I forgot to mention that my uncle got his H.S. diploma and used his G.I. bill to further his education. I was so proud of him. Many didn't believe in him. They only said that he was no good, but I knew better.

Let me remind you that when he returned to New York from Germany, he worked in the Police Department. He did an outstanding job there as a Motor Vehicle Operator. He then decided transfer to Transit Department for City of New York.

He was an outstanding soldier and city worker until he was diagnosed with cancer.

My uncle never gave up. He went to the best doctors....

He was a cancer survivor for almost sixteen years....

R.I.P. my dear uncle. You will never be forgotten.

STORY 88

Liduvina Perez Echevarria

The emotional impact of a person living with cancer
Liduvina first reaction…
She told us about her visit to the doctor…
Liduvina began her story like this: "There is a fear that goes through you when you are told you have cancer. It is so hard at the beginning to think about anything but your sickness. It is the first thing you think about every morning. I want people living with cancer to know it does get better. Talking about it helps you deal with all the new emotions you are feeling. You must follow your doctor's orders. Remember, it is normal to get upset."

When Liduvina was told she had cancer, she thought her life was over. This was about ten years ago. She started thinking about her family. The sad part was that she only concentrated on how her family was going to take it. She didn't think twice to take care of her sick mother.

Once she told me that she was feeling great. Sometimes she missed her appointments just to be with her mom. Her mother died in April 2014.

Liduvina kept talking about her sickness….
The bad thing about cancer is that it affects not only you, but also your family. You may feel scared, uncertain, or angry about the un-wanted changes cancer will bring to your life. Sometimes you may feel numb or confused. You may also have trouble listening to, or remembering what people tell you during this time. This is

especially true when your doctor first tells you that you have cancer. It's not uncommon for anyone to shut down mentally once they hear the word "cancer."

There is nothing fair about cancer and no one deserves it. A cancer diagnosis is hard to take and having cancer is not easy. When you find out you have cancer, your personal beliefs and experiences help you figure out what it means to you and how you will handle it.

As you face your own mortality and cope with the many demands of cancer, you may look more closely at your religious beliefs, your personal and family values, and what's most important in your life. Accepting the diagnosis and figuring out what cancer will mean in your life is challenging.

After you are diagnosed with this horrible sickness, you may feel shocked, disbelief, fear, anxiety, guilt, sadness, grief, depression, anger, and more. Each person may have some or all these feelings, and each will handle them in a different way.

Your first reaction might be shocking. No one is ever ready to hear that they have cancer. It is normal for people with cancer to wonder why it happened to them or to think life has treated them unfairly. You may not even believe the diagnosis, especially if you don't feel sick.

One might feel afraid. Some people fear cancer itself, while others may be afraid of the cancer treatments. They even wonder how they'll get through those treatments.

You know what is so strange; Liduvina stated that she was feeling guilty. She asked herself many times if she could have noticed her symptoms earlier or wonders what may have caused the cancer. She was always wondering if she was exposed to something at home that led to cancer. Sometimes she worried that other members of her family will get cancer, too.

At this time, we do not know what causes most cancers, but a few are known to be hereditary. This means that it is passed from a parent to a child. If one family member develops it, others in the family may have a higher risk of getting it. This can cause even more concerns for the person newly diagnosed with that deadly disease.

Liduvina was feeling hopeless and very sad most of the time. She used to tell me what would happen to July. I told her many times that I would try to take him to Ponce if he wishes to do so…

She recently told me that it's hard to feel positive and upbeat, especially if the future is uncertain. Just thinking about treatment and the time it will take out of your life can seem like too much to handle. Feelings of sadness or uncertainty may be made worse by your past experiences with cancer.

Sometimes she was very negative. She didn't want to talk to anyone. She told me on one occasion that she could see and feel her body changing. She was trying to make everyone happy. She also began to develop ways to cope with the new, unwanted changes in her life.

It took some time for her to become aware of those losses and changes. It helped her to share her grief with us. There was always someone near her. She sometimes was willing to talk and confide with her mental health professionals. Her feelings needed care too, just like your physical body needs care.

Liduvina was a very wise lady. She was always telling us how she was day by day. She kept on with more advice and her feeling….

She told me that occasionally one might feel angry while other people may not outwardly express their anger and frustration.

Liduvina kept telling me the many strange things about this cancer. That sometimes you may direct your anger toward family members, friends, or health care professionals. It was usually not done on purpose. The cancer patient is only trying to escape their feelings. She also told that it was hard to let people know that she wasn't angry with anyone. It wasn't her fault. She just needed someone to listen.

On March 2015, I went to her house for a visit. She made a feast for Paul, his mom and me. I bought the dessert. Tio July was so happy to see us. As always, he was making jokes. Liduvina started telling us about her cancer. Paul's mom told her that she was going into surgery the following week.

She told Liduvina about her breast cancer. Both ladies, whom I love dearly, kept talking about the situation. I just stood there with no word coming out of my mouth. It was so sad listening to them.

Suddenly, I changed their conversation. We started taking photos of each other. I am glad I did that because now I can share those happy moments.

We finished our photo shoot hour. Liduvina made her famous coffee which I named many years ago, chuchu coffee.

We ended the day with a group hug. It was getting late; therefore, we decided to leave. I stayed in Mayaguez because I was helping Paul with his mother.

Dolores, Paul's mother, went into surgery the following week. I stayed with her after the operation. Also, I made sure she did her follow up checkup.

In May 2015, Liduvina came to visit me in Ponce. She was looking great! Junior, her son, came to see her for mother's day. Liduvina told me that she was going in June to New York. They were going for a couple of celebrations with the family over there. She kept telling me to join her. I told her that I couldn't leave my father alone....

Liduvina stayed in New York until September 2015....

Things were not the same after her returned to Puerto Rico. She started getting very sick. Her weigh kept dropping.

When I went to see her, I couldn't believe my eyes. She was wasting into nothing. I started talking to her about my childhood. I thank her for always being there for me. There are so many happy memories I shared with her.

I recall one cold winter day in New York. I was operated on my leg. Liduvina called me the night before. She asked me if I needed anything. She was going to see me the next day. My parents were living in Puerto Rico. I really didn't have anyone to bring me anything. My sister was working; she took off to be with me.

Well, I told Liduvina what I wanted was some of her famous coffee and to bring me some rice, beans and beef stew.

The operation was a success. Liduvina came to see me with my cousin Wanda. They brought the food, and I ate the whole thing.

When the nurse came to check on me, she told me that I was going to be on a liquid diet for one day. I told her that I wasn't hungry. The nurse reported everything to the doctor. When the doctor came to see me, he was worried because I didn't want to eat. He told me that if I didn't eat, I was going to stay a couple of days in the hospital. I informed him that I needed to rest and that I would eat everything during dinner.

I was released the following day....

When I was about 6 yrs. old, Liduvina used to take care of my uncle Villen and me. We became her shadow. She just got married with my uncle Julio. She was left in Puerto Rico alone, because my uncle was in the service.

Liduvina took Villen and me everywhere. We went to the river and the beach. Her parents used to live in Guayanila, PR. Their house was right next to the beach. It was so beautiful around that area. There was always something to do because Liduvina had a very large family. There were kids all over the place. We had a lot of family outing in Guayanilla and in Ponce. I do miss those days.

Liduvina's parents were very sweet. Don Angel, Liduvina's father, was always waiting for us every Sunday morning. He used to tell me not to play with the chickens because that was going to be our lunch. His wife, Doña Luz, used to twist those chickens' neck and within minutes, the chickens were in the pot.

While living in New York, we spent many holidays with Liduvina and the rest of the family. They had three kids, Junior, Sandra and Wanda. Wanda died in January 1981 and Sandra in August 2020.

Liduvina suffered a lot when Wanda died. The whole family was suffering during that time. Wanda was truly a wonderful daughter, cousin, friend etc. She was always happy. Heaven received a cute and adorable angel.

When Liduvina returned to Puerto Rico in September 2015, the doctor told her that she only had a couple of weeks to live. It was devastating seeing her getting worst day after day.

My sister came to see her just before Christmas. Liduvina got so happy when she saw us. We sat next to her and talk for hours. Liduvina didn't want us to leave, but we had to.

I went to see her couple of times after Christmas. My uncle called me on April 29, 2016. He told me that it was time. Liduvina had just a couple of hours. I called one of my cousins and we all went to Isabela that very same day.

Liduvina couldn't talk, but she was aware of everyone around her.

There were a lot of people in her bedroom. She kept crying that her body was hurting. It was impossible not to cry. I left the room so that no one could see my tears. When everyone went to the dining room to eat, I was alone with her and my uncle.

At this point, I had flashbacks of my dying mother. I didn't see my uncle. I saw my father sitting there holding my mother's hand. I had to hold my tears because I didn't want my uncle to notice my sad face. I started making jokes. I asked Liduvina who was her honey bun. She replied very softly, July. I also asked her, who is the love of her life, she replied once again, July. I told Liduvina that she can leave because July would be taken care of by the whole family.

I didn't want to leave my uncle, but I couldn't stay either. My father was in Ponce, and I must make sure that he ate and took his medication.

Every day my aunt Lucy called me to tell me about Liduvina. My aunt Lucy was going home, and my other aunt Lolin stayed. My family really came very close during those days.

By May 2, 2016, aunt Lolin returned to PR with my aunt Norma. They stayed endless nights without any sleep taking care of Liduvina…

On May 7, 2016, my aunt Norma called. She just said that Liduvina died at about 7:20 a.m. I got the call at 7:25 a.m.

Even though I knew that day was going to come, I wasn't ready. One is never ready to accept any death in the family.

You know, Liduvina had two funerals. We had a wake in Guayanilla on May 10, 2016. My uncle July was happy because we were there to give him moral support. He told all his friends that we were his family.

The following day, Liduvina body was place on a horse and buggy. We went the beach where she used to spend her happy moments. There were plenty of people.

As we approached the seaport, many boats started blowing their horns. We got off the car and stood beside my aunt Lucy. All the sudden, my body started to shake. I started moving my arms and feet. I didn't want anyone to notice what was going on with me. Then, I was feeling better. We walked to the car speechless.

The Liduvina was then taken to Isabela for another viewing. She was buried in Isabela on 12 May 2016.

Rest in peace my dear Liduvina.

STORY 89

My kids have paws

You know, people ask me, when I first meet them, if I have any children. My answer is always the same. Yes, I have three children. The only difference from yours is that my children are four legged and have paws.

If you want to cause a commotion in a place where animal and human behavior is studied, all you must do is claim that your dog loves you.

Disbelievers, opponents, and even some passionate supporters will pour out into the halls to argue that statement.

Among the doubters you will find the veterinarian Fred Metzger, of Pennsylvania State University. He claims that dogs probably don't feel love in the typical way humans do.

Dogs make investments in human beings because it works for them. They have something to gain from putting so-called emotions out there.

Metzger believes that dogs "love" us only if we continue to reward their behaviors with treats and attention. For most dog owners, however, there is little doubt that dogs can truly love people.

I want you to read the following story about a dog named Rocky and his owner Rita. They were from the Finger Lakes region of New York State, near Rochester.

Rocky was 65-pound Boxer, classically colored with a chestnut brown coat and a white blaze on his chest.

At the time of this story, Rocky was three years old. Rita was 11 yrs. old. Rocky had been given to Rita when he was ten weeks old. She immediately bonded with him. She used to pet him and fed him. Rita taught Rocky many basic commands. She even let him sleep on her bed.

Whenever she was not in school, the two were always together and within touching distance. The whole family would often fondly refer to the pair as "R and R." Rita was a very shy girl; therefore, as the dog grew, he gave her a sense of security.

When Rocky was next to her, she felt confident enough to meet new people. Rita wasn't afraid to go to unfamiliar places when Rocky was around. Rocky took on the roles, not only of a friend, but also of defender. Also, when encountering strangers, he would often deliberately stand in front of Rita, as a sort of protective barrier. He seemed to be without fear.

Once, Rita was going shopping. She was about to enter a store when there were two large men dressed in biker outfits already ahead of her. They burst out of the door, yelling at the shopkeeper and nearly knocking Rita over. Rocky rushed forward putting himself between the frightened girl and the two threatening men. He braced himself and gave a low rumbling growl that carried such menace that the two men backed off.

Rocky always gave Rita full protection. There was, however, one weakness in Rocky's armor. It was a fear of water that was so life threatening that it was almost pathological. Boxers are not strong swimmers in any event and are often shy of the water.

Rocky's fears began since his puppyhood. At the age of seven weeks, he was sold to a family with an adolescent child. The boy had emotional problems and acted as if the attention given to the new puppy somehow meant that he was less important.

The boy, in a jealous rage, put the puppy in a pillowcase, knotted the top and threw it into a lake. Fortunately, the boy's father saw the incident and managed to retrieve the terrified puppy before it drowned. The father reprimanded the boy and returned to the house.

The next day, the horrified father saw his son standing waist deep in the lake trying to drown the struggling puppy by holding him under water. This time Rocky was rescued and returned to the breeder for his own safety.

All those early traumas made water the only thing that Rocky truly feared. When he came close to a body of water, he would try to pull back and seemed emotionally distressed.

Every time Rita would go swimming, he would pace along the shore trembling and whimpering. He would watch her intently and would not relax until she returned to dry land.

One late afternoon, Rita's mother took R and R to an upscale shopping area. It was located along the edge of a lake. It featured a short wooden boardwalk which was built along the shore over a sharp embankment that was 20 or 30 feet above the surface of the water.

Rita started walking along the boardwalk. She was enjoying the sounds of water. It was then that a boy on a bicycle skidded on the damp wooden surface, hitting Rita.

She was hit at an angle which propelled her through an open section of the guard rail. She let out a shriek of pain and fear. She hurled outward and down, hitting the water face down. She was floating there and unmoving. Rita's mother was at the entrance of a store a hundred feet or so away. She rushed to the railing shouting for help. Rocky was already there, looking at the water, trembling in fear. He was making sounds that seemed to be a combination of barks, whimpers, and yelps all rolled into one.

We can never know what went through that dog's mind as he stood looking at the water. The water was the one thing that truly terrified him and that had nearly taken his life twice.

Now, here was a frightening body of water that seemed about to harm his little mistress. Whatever he was thinking, his love for Rita seemed to overpower his fear. He leapt out through the same open space in the rail and plunged into the water...

One can thank the genetic programming that allowed the dog to swim without any prior practice. He immediately went to Rita and grabbed her by a shoulder strap on her dress. This caused her to roll over so that her face was out of the water. Rita gagged and coughed. Despite her dazed state she reached out and managed to cinch her hand in Rocky's collar. All this was happening while the dog struggled to swim toward the shore. Fortunately, the water was calm.

They were not far from shore; therefore, Rocky quickly reached a depth where his feet were on solid ground. He dragged Rita until her head was completely out of the water. He then stood beside her, licking her face, while he continued to tremble and whine. It would be several minutes before human rescuers would make it down the steep rocky embankment.

This incident stated that if it has not been for Rocky, they surely would have arrived too late. Rita and her family believe that it was only the big dog's love of the little girl that caused him to take what he must have considered a life-threatening action. This certainly casts doubt on Dr. Metzger's theory that dogs don't love us but act only out of self-interest. Why should Rocky behave in a way that he certainly felt would risk his life? Surely, if he was evaluating the costs and benefits of his actions then he would have known that, even in Rita's absence, the rest of the family would be around to feed him and take care of needs.

Marc Berkoff, a behavioral biologist at the University of Colorado, has a different interpretation. He stated that dogs are social animals. All social animals need emotions as means of communication.

For example, you need to know when to back off if another animal is growling. More importantly, however, emotions keep the social group together and motivate individuals to protect and support each other.

Berkoff concluded that strong emotion is one of the foundations of social behavior. It is also the basis of the connection between individuals in any social group, whether it is a pack, a family or just a couple in love.

Recent research has even identified some of the chemicals associated with feelings of love in humans. These include hormones such as oxytocin, which seems to help people form emotional bonds with each other.

One of the triggers that cause oxytocin to be released is gentle physical touching, such as stroking. Dogs also produce oxytocin, and one of our common ways of interacting with dogs is to gently pet them. This an action that probably releases this hormone associated with bonding. If dogs as social animals have an evolutionary need for close emotional ties, they have the chemical mechanisms associated with loving; it makes sense to assume that they are capable of loving, as we are.

Rocky's fear of the water was absolute, and never did abate. He continued to avoid it for the rest of his life. No one ever saw him so much as place a foot in the lake again. No one, at least not Rita or her family, ever doubted his love for her. He lived long enough to see an event occur which would not have happened had he not cared for her as much as he did.

When Rita graduated from high school, she posed for a photo in her cap and gown. Beside her, sat a now much older Boxer. The smiling girl had an arm around the dog, and her hand was cinched in his collar, as it was the day that Rocky clearly showed her just how much he loved her.

I told you this story because I do believe dogs can love a human being.

I always had dogs. When I was a kid, at one time, we had a dog, a cat and a bird. The dog belonged to me. The cat was just there. He had no official owner. My sister owned the bird. We were taught at an early age to love animals....

At the present time, I have three dogs. They are Blackie, Titi and Pica. Those dogs follow me everywhere. There is never a dull moment in my house. I taught them to dance. Whenever they hear music, they run towards me. They know when I am happy because of the music I play.

I call them my little angels. Why are they my little angels? Well, when my mom was alive, they took care of her. They knew when my mom wasn't doing well. I know they miss her because sometimes I call her name and they look around for her.

Now, I live with my dad and the three dogs. My father has so many ailments that I don't know where to begin my second story.

Let me tell you one scenario where the dogs saved my father's life...

Before I retired, I used to get up a 5:00 am. I used to prepare my parents breakfast and their lunch.

On one day, I noticed that my dad wasn't well. I couldn't depend on my mom because she had Alzheimer.

Before I left for work, I asked my dad if he was feeling better. He said that he was fine.

I reported to work, however, my mind wasn't there. I was thinking about my parents. I conducted my 8:00 class and then I was on my break.

I tried calling home and there was no answer. I waited a couple of minutes and to my surprise, my neighbor was calling me. She told me that the dogs were barking for a long time. She began calling my parents and there was no answer. The dogs were making very strange sounds. I thank her. I went home.

When I got home, I found my mother crying on top of my father. He had fallen and was unconscious. The dogs stopped barking; however, they were making strange sounds. I went to the kitchen and prepared a malt for my dad. I gave it to him. My dad had no idea what had happened. I told him that his sugar level dropped, and he was unconscious.

My dogs saved my father's life....

There were many incidents involving my parents and my dogs...

Since my mom's death, I must make sure my dad is well taken care. The dogs are always on the alert. If my father falls, they will go and get me. It is strange, but I do depend on my four-legged kids. Train your dogs and they will be you friends for the rest of their life.

STORY 90

My Nephews

A person can learn a lot from books, but many things can only be learned the hard way. What do I mean by this? Well, one can learn by living, suffering or even enjoying life. I am sitting here thinking about my family. There were many lessons learned. We were so close, and we always took care of each other.

One evening, at approximately, 7 p.m., I was in my room in Ponce. The weather was pleasant; however, it was too quiet. Suddenly, my dogs began to bark. I got worried. I thought that maybe they saw someone trying to break in. If they kept barking, I would have to go downstairs. I was trying to get up from my bed, but I went down. I thought of the many lessons I've learned in life would end up at the bottom of rubbish or something.

I only could tell you that everything in the room started shaking. I couldn't move at all. A heavy-duty magnetic field was pulling me toward the ground. This weird sensation lasted a couple of minutes. I thought that it was the end of the world. I turned the T.V. on and to my surprise there was a news flash of an earthquake that just hit Puerto Rico. I went to check on my dogs and they were still shivering.

They came into the house, and I calmed them down. I let them stay on the sofa until morning. I then decided to write what had happened so that my nephews could read it after I am gone. I hope they'll find it useful.

I'm writing this today, April 24, 2016, so that you, Ray and Rebustino, can get an idea that life is too short to waste. There are many reasons why I started writing about the earth shocking event. I feared the earthquake might really destroy me.

All the lessons I've learned in life would have disappear with me. By writing this, I hope to pass on the few of my memories to you and the rest of my family.

The most important message that I want to bring across is that most things you worry about will not bother you the next day. A year later you will not even be able to remember them if you try.

As you got older, you did not worry about what grades you got in high school or college. You are not even worrying about the games you lost when you were in the little leagues. You won't worry about what other people thought about you. Most of the things you worry about now will never happen.

Life will still go on no matter what. Please learn to enjoy every day and try to enjoy it as if it is your last. It has taken me a long time to understand this, and I wish I had understood it sooner.

Happiness is not a destination but a journey. You will never be smart enough, or rich enough. Whatever it is you want, there is always something better. Enjoy the journey of learning, working, and living. If you enjoy the journey, you'll probably achieve a lot more than if you focused on goals.

If you do decide you want to be "successful", I can give you the formula for success. There are only three things you need to do:

First, decide exactly what it is you want.

Second, determine the price you will have to pay.

Third, and this is the hardest and most important part, pay the price.

Material things don't make you happy, but memories will always stay with you. Whatever it is that you buy, you will soon get used to it. It will make you happy for a short while, but it will not make you happy forever. I can't even remember most of the toys I've had in my life, but I still think of my times with your mother, my brothers and your grandparents. Life then was full of happiness. I remember walking with your mother to school and how happy we were. I also remember hugging your Grandma when I came home from school. Those memories will never go away.

Your family is the most important thing you have in life. Friends, boyfriends, girlfriends and co-workers come and go, but the only thing that you can always count on is your family. If you find a friend who is always there for you, you're extremely lucky. They exist, but they're very rare.

Rebustino, one day, you will have your own family. Ray, you have yours. You guys must love them and look after them. You will understand in the future that just as your grandmother and father died, your mother will die as well. Strive to be good sons.

Don't be surprise if one day, you will be like your parents. Your parents were not perfect, and you will not be either, but you can be loving and good.

Never stop learning, and always be ready to teach yourself things you don't know. The only things you will remember are things you care about. No one can teach you everything you need to know. You will also forget most of what you study, and that is fine.

Remember to always stay curious, and you'll be surprised how much you can learn. Let me tell you something that when people speak of intelligence, what they generally mean is curiosity. All great discoveries start with a question. Children are born curious, and school can beat it out of you. Never stop asking questions.

Ray and Rebustino, you're never too old to learn. I want you two to promise me that you are never going to live someone else's life. Find your gifts and the things that give you pleasure, develop those gifts, and pursue them. Do what makes you happy and be great at it. You have skills and gifts that no one will ever have or see again.

I think that's very important when you learn how to cope in life. Once you learn how, you'll want to change it and make it better.

It is up to you do decide whether you will be strong or not. Many people suffer great tragedies and live full and happy lives. Remember the people you love. Accept those terrible things that may hap-pen. Try to live as if each day is your last with those you love. There is nothing else you can do.

Currently, I want to thank you both for letting me be part of your lives. You both gave me a chance to be not only your aunt, but also your second mother. Sometimes I laugh at the things we did together. I always looked forward to each of your birthdays, little leagues games, school plays, graduations and much more.

I remember very clearly those summer days in Massapequa. We used to be at the pool very early. You guys were taking swimming lessons. I was very impressed when within days you both learned how to swim.

I was always present at every birthday party. Your mother and I would pick up a theme to decorate the basement or park. As always, I was the clown. I believe I had more fun than the kids....

There were other funny occasions that I remember clearly. Rebustino and I went to see lots of movies. After each show, we would go to a restaurant. Rebustino was the perfect gentleman. While eating, we would chat about the movie.

We went to see the Titanic, The Mask, and The Flintstone just to name a few. I really enjoyed every moment spent with you two.

Sometimes your parents would go out and I stayed babysitting. We played with your Nintendo, electronic bowling machine and even Yahtzee.

I hope you still remember those happy times, because I will never forget them....

STORY 91

The Language Center, Fort Allen Juana Diaz PR

Before I begin writing about my work at the Language Center, I will narrate a few facts of this wonderful institution.

The Puerto Rico National Guard Language Center was established in 1976. It has performed its mission of providing English language training to Non-prior service Warriors, Airmen, military families, and Puerto Rico National Guard citizen Warriors.

It was originally founded as the English Technical Language School. This school was located at Camp Santiago Training Site in Salinas, Puerto Rico. It has been functioning as a State-operated educational program within the Puerto Rico Army National Guard for over 40 yrs.

It aimed at reducing the number of trainees returning from Basic Training. The problem was that if the new applicants didn't go to the Language Center, they would be returning from the United States due to lack of proficiency in the English language.

The Defense Language Institute English Language Center at Lackland, Air Force Base, in Texas approved the Puerto Rico National Guard Language Center as a non-resident English Language Training Pro-gram in 1979.

It wasn't until 1984 that the National Guard Bureau approved federal funding to operate the Language Center.

The following year, in May 1985, the Language Center relocated to its present site at Fort Allen, Juana Diaz, and PR.

The Language Center has a very important vision. The vision is that it must be an accredited, prestigious institution. The school would facilitate language acquisition and military skills. I know it can be done because all instructors are fully qualified. It is also aiming in the transformation, readiness and retention of Warriors and Airmen for America's Army and Joint Forces.

The PUERTO RICO NATIONAL GUARD LANGUAGE CENTER conducts an intensive full-time ENGLISH LANGUAGE TRAINING program consisting of seven hours daily of English instruction, five days a week.

In addition, students are normally assigned two hours of homework/study hall daily. The AMERI-CAN LANGUAGE COURSE curriculum consists of a combination of classroom learning and individual language laboratory instruction. They also receive military classes.

The students don't go home on weekends; therefore, they are speak-ing English 24/7. Family members are allowed to come for visits on Sunday afternoons. During some holidays, students pack their belonging and head home.

When I began teaching at the Language Center, what I like best was the discipline. Every day I looked forward on going into a classroom where students are there to learn.

All instructors at the Language Center are well qualified. They all have a secondary level or adult education certifications. Our academic background is from B.A. or master's degree.

It didn't matter what level of teaching I received, I was always ready. It was challenging teaching a slow student. Some didn't like to study. They came in with a bad attitude; however, after an hour of teaching them, they changed. They were even willing to participate in a conversation.

At beginning of a new lesson, I introduced the swim or sink method of learning. They were impressed. The following hour they were ready with no negative attitude. I used to start the morning with a famous quotation or idiom. They learned those crazy idioms.

Sometimes, I even took a chance of talking about Ebonics. They wanted more......

As every English teacher knows, Ebonics are not taught in the classroom. I taught it because that is the only way students will learn the difference between an idiomatic expression and Ebonics.

Idiomatic expression is mastering the language. Ebonics should be taught to show that it is only street language.

I taught some of my classes through music. A slow student or even an advanced student enjoyed them. Why, because music is the universal language....

After lunch, the students were usually sleepy; therefore, I took them out of the classroom to show them sounds associating them with our environment.

There were many funny and sad situations in the classroom. I treated each situation with kindness. The students knew that no one was supposed to make fun of the other.

The saddest day for me was retiring from the Language Center. The staff is part of my extended family. The students were my children because I took them with no English whatsoever to a fully bilingual individual.

The staff at the Language Center is part of me. I consider them my extended family.

Mr. Eliu Rivera and Myrna Rolon were always there to give me a helping hand when I was going to introduce a new lesson. I learned a lot from them when I went to work there. They had a unique way of teaching. Some students used to tell me that I taught just like Mr. Rivera. Others stated that I even had corny jokes like Ms. Rolon.

Let me also mention Ms. Awilda Quinones, Ms. Nitza Santiago, Mr. Julio Gonzalez, Ms. Gladys Sanchez and Mr. Luis Rivera. They always had kind words for me.

I want to thank my supervisor, Ms. Noris Rodriguez. She was always there when my mom was in the hospital.

When mom died Noris and all the instructors were at my side on that sad day.

My buddies, Iris Quijano and Saul Ortiz went to the cemetery and stayed with me even after my mom was buried.

The military side was also very helpful. They made sure that the warriors treated the instructors with respect.

My thanks to the Puerto Rico National Guard for giving me the opportunity to teach at the Language Center.

THE HISTORY OF SHORT STORIES

With the rise of the realistic novel, the short story evolved in a parallel tradition. Its first distinctive examples may be seen in the tales of E. T. A. Hoffmann. The character of the form developed particularly with authors known for their short fiction, by choice.

They wrote nothing else or by critical regard. It acknowledged the focus and craft required in a short form.

An example is Jorge Luis Borges, who won American fame with "The Garden of Forking Paths". This was published in the August 1948 Ellery Queen's Mystery Magazine.

Facts about Jorge Luis Borges
Jorge Luis Borges died at 86 years old
Born: August 24, 1899
Died: June 14, 1986
Birthplace: Buenos Aires, Argentina
Best known as: Author of the short story collection "Ficciones"

GLOSSARY

Autobiography – a detailed description or account of the storyteller's own life.

Biography – a detailed description or account of someone's life.

Captivity narrative – a story in which the protagonist is captured and describes their experience with the culture of their captors.

Epic – a very long narrative poem, often written about a hero or heroine and their exploits.

Epic poem – a lengthy story of heroic exploits in the form of a poem.

Fable – a didactic story, often using animal characters who behave like people.

Fantasy – a story about characters that may not be realistic and about events that could not really happen.

Folk tale – an old story which has been passed down orally and which reveals the customs of a culture.

Historical fiction – stories which take place in real historical settings, and which often feature real historical figures and events, but which center around fictional characters and/or events.

Legend – a story that is based on fact but often includes exaggerations about the hero.

Memoir – like an autobiography, except that memoir generally deal with specific events in the life of the author.

Myth – an ancient story often meant to explain the mysteries of life or nature.

News – information on current events which is presented by print, broadcast, Internet, or word of mouth to a third party or mass audience.

Nonlinear narrative – a story whose plot does not conform to conventional chronology, causality, and/or perspective.

Novel – a long, written narrative, normally in prose, which describes fictional characters and events, usually in the form of a sequential story.

Novella – a written, fictional, prose narrative normally longer than a short story but shorter than a novel.

Parable – a succinct, didactic story, in prose or verse, which illustrates one or more instructive lessons or principles.

Play – a story that is told mostly through dialogue and is meant to be performed on stage.

Quest narrative – a story in which the characters must achieve a goal. This includes some illness narratives.

Realistic fiction – stories which portray fictional characters, settings, and events that could exist in real life.

Short story – a brief story that usually focuses on one character and one event.

Tall tale – a humorous story that tells about impossible happenings, exaggerating the hero's accomplishments.

Genre–A literary genre is a category of literary composition. Genres may be determined by literary technique, tone, content, or even (as in the case of fiction) length. The distinctions between genres and categories are flexible and loosely defined, often with subgroups.

The most general genres in literature are, in loose chronological order, epic, tragedy, comedy, and creative nonfiction. They can all be in the form of prose or poetry. Additionally, a genre such as satire, allegory or pastoral might appear in any of the above, not only as a subgenre (see below), but as a mixture of genres. Finally, they are defined by the general cultural movement of the historical period in which they were composed.

Genre should not be confused with age categories, by which literature may be classified as either adult, young adult, or children. They also must not be confused with format, such as graphic novel or picture book.

Action fiction Adventure Comic Crime Docufiction Epistolary Erotic Fiction Fantasy Gothic Historical Horror Magic realism

A BAFFLING SHORT STORIES COLLECTION

Mystery Nautical Paranoid Philosophical Picaresque Political Psychological Romance Saga Satire Science Speculative Superhero Thriller Urban Western List of writing genres

Narration- "Narrator" redirects here. For other uses, see Narrator (disambiguation).

Narration is the use of a written or spoken commentary to convey a story to an audience. Narration encompasses a set of techniques through which the creator of the story presents their story, including:

Narrative point of view: the perspective or type of personal or non-personal "lens" through which a story is communicated

Narrative voice: the formal or type presentational form through which a story is communicated

Narrative time: the grammatical placement of the story's timeframe in the past, the present, or the future.

A narrator is a personal character or a non-personal voice that the creator, the author of the story, develops to deliver information to the audience, particularly about the plot.

In the case of most written narrative's novels, short stories, poems, etc., the narrator typically functions to convey the story in its entirety. The narrator may be a voice devised by the author as an anonymous, non-personal, or stand-alone entity; as the author as a character; or as some other fictional or non-fictional character appearing and participating within their own story. The narrator is considered participant if he/she is a character within the story, and non-participant if he/she is an implied character or an omniscient or semi-omniscient being or voice that merely relates the story to the audience without being involved in the actual events. Some stories have multiple narrators to illustrate the storylines of various characters at the same, similar, or different times, thus allowing a more complex, non-singular point of view.

Narration encompasses not only who tells the story, but also how the story is told for example, by using stream of consciousness or unreliable narration. In traditional literary narratives such as novels, short stories, and memoirs, narration is a required story element; in other types of chiefly non-literary narratives, such as plays, television shows, video games, and films, narration is merely optional.

REFERENCES

1. Browns, Julie, ed. (1997). Ethnicity and the American Short Story. New York: Garland.
2. Goyet, Florence (2014). The Classic Short Story, 1870-1925: Theory of a Genre. Cambridge U.K.: Open Book Publishers.
3. Gelfant, Blanche; Lawrence Graver, eds. (2000). The Columbia Companion to the Twentieth-Century American Short Story. Columbia University Press.
4. Hart, James; Phillip Leininger, eds. (1995). Oxford Companion to American Literature. Oxford University Press.
5. Ibáñez, José R; José Francisco Fernández; Carmen M. Bretones, eds. (2007). , Contemporary Debates on the Short Story. Bern: Lang.
6. Iftekharrudin, Farhat; Joseph Boyden; Joseph Longo; Mary Rohrberger, eds. (2003). Postmodern Approaches to the Short Story. Westport, CN: Praeger.
7. Kennedy, Gerald J., ed. (2011). Modern American Short Story Sequences: Composite Fictions and Fictive Communities. Cambridge: Cambridge University Press.
8. Empirical Poetics, and Culture in the Short Story. Baltimore, MD: Johns Hopkins University Press.
9. Magill, Frank, ed. (1997). Short Story Writers. Pasadena, California: Salem Press.
10. Patea, Viorica, ed. (2012). Short Story Theories: A Twenty-First-Century Perspective. Amsterdam: Rodopi.

11. Scofield, Martin, ed. (2006). The Cambridge Introduction to the American Short Story. Cambridge: Cambridge University Press.
12. Watson, Noelle, ed. (1994). Reference Guide to Short Fiction. Detroit: St. James Press.
13. Winther, Per; Jakob Lothe; Hans H. Skei, eds. (2004). The Art of Brevity: Excursions in Short Fiction Theory and Analysis. Columbia, SC: University of South Carolina Press.

ABOUT THE AUTHOR

Norma Iris Pagan Morales was born in Ponce, Puerto Rico. She comes from a very lovable family. Her parents, Juan Jose Pagan Rodriguez and Digna Morales Figueroa, now deceased, always helped her with her projects as a writer and teaching career. Norma had four siblings, Adelin Milagros Pagan Morales, Juan Jose Pagan Morales and Julio Manuel Pagan Morales. Julio Manuel Pagan Morales died on September 19, 1998. He was also known for his writing / composer skills.

Norma did all her academic studies in New York City, Puerto Rico and Canada. She worked in the City of New York Police Department. As an Educator, she worked in New York City Bd. of Education as an English Teacher, in Puerto Rico Bd. of Education as an English teacher and in the Puerto Rico Army National.

She has teaching certifications for English as a Second Language and Teaching English as a Foreign Language.

She has published four books: Proud of My Puerto Rican Bequest, Porque Soy Boricua? Poemas del Alama and Art in Written Form.

CPSIA information can be obtained
at www.ICGtesting.com
Printed in the USA
BVHW040923280822
645587BV00015B/45